Jayne Ann Krentz is the critically-acclaimed creator of the Arcane Society world, Dark Legacy series and Rainshadow series. She also writes as **Amanda Quick** and **Jayne Castle**. Jayne has written more than fifty *New York Times* bestsellers under various pseudonyms and lives in the Pacific Northwest.

The historical novels she writes as Amanda Quick all feature her customary irresistible mix of passion and mystery, and also have a strong psychic/paranormal twist.

Visit her online:
www.jayneannkrentz.com
www.facebook.com/JayneAnnKrentz
@JayneAnnKrentz

WHEN
SHE
DREAMS

AMANDA
QUICK

PIATKUS

PIATKUS

First published in the US in 2022 by Berkley,
an imprint of Penguin Random House LLC
First published in Great Britain in 2022 by Piatkus

1 3 5 7 9 10 8 6 4 2

A CIP catalogue record for this book
is available from the British Library.

ISBN 978-0-349-43228-1

Printed and bound in Great Britain by
Clays Ltd, Elcograf S.p.A.

Papers used by Piatkus are from well-managed forests
and other responsible sources.

Piatkus
An imprint of
Little, Brown Book Group
Carmelite House
50 Victoria Embankment
London EC4Y 0DZ

An Hachette UK Company
www.hachette.co.uk

www.littlebrown.co.uk

For Frank, as always, with love

WHEN
SHE
DREAMS

Chapter 1

You poisoned me."

The words tumbled out in a slurred mumble, not the scream of rage Maggie Lodge intended. The drug had plunged her into a waking nightmare. The office of Dr. Emerson Oxlade, Dream Analyst, was starting to revolve. Bits and pieces of the walls and ceiling were becoming transparent.

"Calm yourself, Miss Smith." Oxlade spoke in stern, authoritative tones. "Remember, you have extremely delicate nerves and are therefore inclined toward hysteria. It is why you came to me for therapy. I am attempting to help you."

Oxlade knew her as Miss Smith because she had booked the consultation under that name. It was her long-standing habit to use a false identity when she made appointments with experts in the field of dream analysis. She had initiated the practice after she had been released from Sweet Creek Manor Psychiatric Hospital, and it had served her well. The proof of its effectiveness was that she had not resided in another asylum since leaving Sweet Creek.

"I did not come here for therapy," she said. "I distinctly told the receptionist that I was booking a consultation. There is nothing wrong with my nerves. I am not hysterical, damn it. I'm furious."

But she knew she probably sounded as if she were on the edge of hysteria. She should have heeded the warning she got last week when she walked into the office for the first time. The space was drenched in invisible shadows.

She had told herself the bad energy had been left behind by some of the troubled people who had come to Oxlade for help with their nightmares. Now she wondered how much of the dark stuff had been laid down by Oxlade himself.

It wasn't the first time she had wandered into a pool of energy that was so murky it was impossible to distinguish the source. But if she made it a rule not to go into any space that reeked of other people's nightmares, she would become housebound. Her sensitivity had already done enough damage to her personal life. She would not allow it to turn her into an agoraphobe.

"I assure you that you have not been poisoned," Oxlade huffed. "My enhancer has some side effects, but most people find them enjoyable, even exhilarating, provided they have someone to guide them through the experience. That is why I am here. I will show you how to make the most of your talent for lucid dreaming. Together we will achieve great things."

"Bastard."

"I gave you a very light dose this first time. I've never used it on anyone with your powerful dream talent. Didn't want to overdo it. In a few minutes you will be deep in a waking dreamstate. The enhancer has hypnotic effects. It will cause you to become extremely suggestible. That will allow me to take control of your experience."

"Stop it," she said, trying to fight off the terrifying sensation that her mind was starting to separate from her body. "You *drugged* me, you fraud. You're no better than the others."

Screaming for help would have to wait. She had to focus on overcoming the visions, and at the moment she could not do two things at the same time. Her priorities were clear: Escape first. Scream later. The inevitable nightmares would no doubt follow, but she could handle bad dreams. She was an expert.

She gazed up at the disappearing ceiling, groping for a strategy.

"Do not fight the effects," Oxlade said. "It will make the process more difficult. Remain calm."

"Shut up."

"You will learn to embrace my enhancer, Miss Smith. I will guide you."

He was still speaking in the clinical manner of a doctor who knows what is best for a patient, but now she detected a disturbing element infused into the words. Lust. Not the sexual kind. Some sort of sick desire.

Should have picked up on that unpleasant little quirk sooner, she thought.

But the first consultation had seemed to go well in spite of the energy in the office. Oxlade was the latest in the long line of doctors, therapists, quacks, and con artists she had encountered in the past few years, but he was the one with the most respected reputation. He wrote papers for scientific and medical journals. He gave guest lectures at distinguished academic institutions.

After the first consultation, Oxlade had been eager to have her book a series of appointments with him. Now she knew why he had been so enthusiastic. He was obsessed with her—not with her as a woman but with her talent for lucid dreaming.

It was not the first time she had found herself in such a situation, but none of the other so-called experts had attempted to drug her. Oxlade had slipped past her usually sharp defenses.

The walls and floor were almost invisible now. Oxlade's desk and the bookshelves crammed with weighty volumes and academic journals drifted around her in midair.

"Just another few minutes, Miss Smith, and we will be ready to begin our journey through your astonishing dreams," Oxlade said.

She realized she could hear him but she could no longer see him. That was not good. Cautiously she turned her head on the cushion, searching for her tormentor.

Oxlade floated into view. He was ensconced in his big leather chair, tailored trousers artfully hitched up over his crossed knees, pipe wedged in the corner of his mouth, notebook at the ready. The gold signet ring on his little finger sparked ominously. Behind the lenses of his spectacles his pale eyes glittered with a sheen of unwholesome excitement. *The eyes of a reptile*.

His head began to change shape. It grew longer, snakelike. His pipe was now a thin, forked tongue.

She knew she was letting the hallucinations gain control. She could not allow that to happen. This was a nightmare. She knew how to handle bad dreams.

You need a plan.

She had to move if she wanted to escape, but the revolving room was disorienting. It affected her sense of balance. Nothing seemed solid or substantial, not even the couch she reclined on.

The couch.

Getting off the couch was clearly a crucial first step. Thinking logically wasn't her strong suit at the moment, but she was suddenly very certain she could not get out of the office if she did not get off the damned couch.

The room was badly warped. Everything was wrong, but she knew how it was supposed to look. *Oxlade tossed you into the deep end of a dream*.

She pulled hard on her self-control, forcing the hallucinations to recede. The furniture settled back on the floor. The walls and ceiling grew solid. She took a deep breath and struggled to a sitting position.

Oxlade was annoyed. He leaned forward, his viper eyes glinting. "Lie down, Miss Smith. You will get dizzy if you try to stand."

With another fierce effort of will she succeeded in swinging her legs over the side of the couch. She was profoundly grateful she had worn trousers to the appointment. Not that the choice of attire was simply a stroke of good luck. Countless hours spent in the offices of dream analysts, psychiatrists, and therapists had taught her there was usually a couch involved. She had also discovered that some practitioners were not above trying to seduce their clients on said couches. It was easier to deal with such situations when one was wearing trousers.

When the soles of her T-strap sandals hit the floor she planted her hands on the cushion on either side of her hips and pushed herself to her feet.

For a few seconds she wavered, terrified she would lose her balance.

Oxlade dropped his notebook, jerked the pipe out of his mouth, and shot to his feet. "Miss Smith, I insist you sit down immediately."

She ignored him to focus on the door. Getting through it was step two in the plan.

She tried to walk toward the door and discovered she could not move because Oxlade had grabbed her arm.

"Take your hand off me," she said. It was gratifying to discover she was no longer slurring her words. Her voice sounded stronger, too. She was gaining control over the waking nightmare.

Oxlade tightened his grip. His eyes glittered. "You can't leave. Don't you understand? Everything depends on you."

She tried to pull free and lunge for the door.

Oxlade yanked her back. "You can't walk out on me, you silly woman. I need you."

She swept out her free hand and grabbed the nearest heavy object, a glass ashtray. She swung it awkwardly at Oxlade's head. He yelped, released her arm, and scrambled backward, barely escaping the blow.

"You must calm down, Miss Smith," Oxlade gasped. "You are suffering a fit of hysteria."

She started toward the door again, but halfway across the room she remembered her handbag. She could not leave it behind. Not only was there a little money inside, but there was some identification in her real name.

She changed course and swiped the bag off the console. When she realized Oxlade had not made another grab for her arm, she glanced back over her shoulder. She was just in time to see him reach into a desk tray and seize a syringe. He rushed toward her.

"You leave me no choice," he said. "I must sedate you. Don't worry; I will make sure you get the help you need."

The chilling words came straight from the heart of some of her worst nightmares, the ones that harkened back to her time at Sweet Creek Manor. Another wave of panic washed over her. It would take her a few precious seconds to get the door open. She did not have those few seconds.

Oxlade closed the space between them. He held the syringe as though it were a stiletto.

"I'm sorry to have to do this, Miss Smith, but it's for your own good."

More words from a nightmare.

She dropped the handbag and picked up the large ceramic vase sitting on the console. Filled with water and an impressive bouquet, it was almost too heavy to lift, but desperation gave her strength. She used both hands to heave it at Oxlade.

He tried to dodge, but it was too late. The vase struck him in the middle of the chest. He grunted, dropped the syringe, and staggered backward. Water and flowers cascaded over him, soaking his elegantly tailored suit, shirt, and tie.

The back of his knee came up against the edge of the couch. He collapsed onto the cushions.

"You are hysterical," he gasped. "You don't know what you are doing, what we could achieve together. I forbid you to leave this room."

She seized the strap of her purse, got the door open, and stumbled into the small waiting area.

The flinty-eyed receptionist was on her feet, transfixed with shock.

A middle-aged woman sat, frozen, in the waiting room, a copy of *Reader's Digest* clutched in her gloved hands.

Maggie heard the door of the inner office slam shut behind her. Afraid Oxlade was pursuing her, she spun around—and nearly lost her balance.

Relief flooded through her when she saw that Oxlade had sealed himself inside his office. There was an audible click when he locked the door.

She took a deep breath, slung the strap of the handbag over one shoulder, and opened the door of the small waiting room. She was about to rush out into the hall, but she paused long enough to look back at the stunned woman holding the magazine.

"Take my advice," Maggie said. "Find another dream therapist."

She did not wait for a response. She escaped into the hall, slamming the door behind her. Bracing one palm against the wall to steady herself, she made her way cautiously toward the stairs.

She wondered if the frozen woman would take her advice. Doubtful. People rarely took good advice. She was an excellent example of that particular character flaw. She had lost count of the number of times she had told herself to give up on the search for a dream analyst who could help her learn how to gain better control, yet here she was, fleeing another disastrous encounter.

Emerson Oxlade could have stepped straight out of a horror film— *Doctor X*, perhaps, or *Mad Love* with Peter Lorre.

Fortunately, he didn't know her real name.

Chapter 2

Adelina Beach
Five months later . . .

Maggie did her best to ignore the coatrack, but that proved impossible. It loomed in the corner of the office of Sage Investigations, casting an invisible shadow over the cramped, sparsely furnished room. A fedora dangled on one brass hook. A well-worn trench coat was draped over another.

Neither the hat nor the coat was the source of the bad energy in the room. No question about it—the coatrack was the problem. It did not belong in the office. It was wrong.

She told herself the coatrack was none of her business and tried to focus on the reason she was sitting in the office of a private investigator—the third one that day—at ten thirty in the morning.

"Someone is attempting to blackmail my employer," she said. "I want you to find the individual and put a stop to the extortion threat."

Sam Sage leaned forward and folded his arms on the desk. He was not what she had expected. He certainly looked the part. He had the resolute and rather intimidating features and the cold, nothing-can-surprise-me eyes of a man who has shed whatever illusions he might once have had about the world, but there was more to Sam Sage. She was not sure how much more, but the realization that there were hidden depths was vaguely reassuring. She needed a detective who could be counted on to keep secrets.

In spite of his stony, seen-it-all aura, she got the impression she had caught him off guard. It was as if he had expected someone else to walk into his office but she had appeared instead. Now he was trying to decide what to do with her.

Then again, maybe he was simply surprised to have a client. The expensive fedora and the hand-tailored suit, white shirt, and striped tie suggested he had once been successful, but the shabby office made it obvious he was no longer prospering. Sage Investigations was on the second floor of a modest two-story business building. A café and a news-stand were on the street level. On the way down the hall she had passed the doors of a secretarial firm and a small-time bookkeeping business.

The used furnishings reflected the man. Somewhere along the line all the cushioning and decorative elements had been stripped away, leaving just the essentials—a scarred wooden desk, the squeaky chair behind the desk, a couple of client chairs, and a dented metal file cabinet.

There was a telephone, a brass desk lamp with a green glass shade, a calendar from the Adelina Beach Garage & Service Station, and a tray for pens and paper clips. Everything seemed to fit into the room—everything except the coatrack. It shouldn't be in the office, but a man had to have a place to hang his hat and coat, so she supposed it qualified as an essential item of office furniture.

Sage had been reading the morning edition of the *Adelina Beach Courier*, the heels of his leather shoes stacked on the corner of the desk, when she opened the door a short time ago. He had immediately risen to his feet and shrugged into the suit coat. The paper was now neatly folded on one side of the desk.

"How much is the blackmailer demanding, Miss Lodge?" he asked.

"One thousand dollars."

Sam's brows rose. "The extortionist is not a small-time operator."

"The note claims it will be the one and only demand, but I'm sure you're aware that once an extortion demand is met there is always another and another."

"I've heard that."

She ignored the wry sarcasm. She had read enough Dashiell Hammett to know that private investigators were supposed to talk that way. It went with the cynical, world-weary air.

"Every advice columnist gets crank letters, but this one is different," she continued.

"You're an advice columnist?"

"I work for one."

She pulled the envelope out of her handbag and put it on the desk in front of him.

He studied it briefly. "It's addressed to Aunt Cornelia, in care of the *Adelina Beach Courier.*"

"I got it this morning. It arrived in a bag of reader mail sent to my employer's address by the editor of the *Courier.*"

Sam glanced at the envelope. "No return address, but it's post-marked L.A. How is this letter different?"

A reasonable question. At least he was paying attention. That was encouraging.

"It's very specific," she said. "Someone appears to believe Aunt Cornelia is responsible for the murder of a woman named Virginia Jennaway."

"Who is Aunt Cornelia?"

"Me, at the moment."

"Your name is Cornelia Lodge?" Sam asked. "I thought you said your name was Margaret Lodge."

"My name is Margaret Lodge. I work for the real Aunt Cornelia, Lillian Dewhurst. She's currently out of the country on a voyage to the South Seas. I've been handling the column for her while she's gone. So, yes, I am Aunt Cornelia for now, but whoever sent the letter has no way of knowing that."

"You're certain the blackmailer didn't aim the letter at you?"

"Of course I'm certain. I have no idea who Virginia Jennaway is—or, rather, was."

"Jennaway," he repeated.

"I realize this all sounds a bit confusing, Mr. Sage."

"A bit," he said.

She sighed. "Obviously I'm going too fast for you."

"Not the first time that's happened to me. I'm used to it. Please continue."

Maybe he wasn't very sharp. That was a depressing thought. She had already concluded she did not want to hire either of the other two private investigators in town. She had interviewed both—briefly—that morning. Adelina Beach was a pleasant community just outside L.A. It was home to a scattering of celebrities and it boasted some exclusive shopping districts. It did not have much to offer in the way of seedy neighborhoods, but Sage's competitors had managed to find the two that did exist.

One step into the offices of the other detectives had been enough to tell her neither man would be a good bet. The first had been intoxicated even though it was nine o'clock. The other had struck her as decidedly shady, the sort who would take a bribe to look the other way.

Sam Sage was not drunk, and he looked reasonably intelligent, or at least competent. He did not appear to be shady, but one could never be sure. She had a spectacularly failed engagement behind her to prove that her talent for lucid dreaming did not give her an edge when it came to judging the trustworthiness of other people.

"Allow me to explain," she said, striving for patience.

"Take your time."

That did not sit well. It was alarmingly close to *calm down*, which, in turn, usually came right before *you're getting hysterical*.

If any of those words came out of his mouth, she would lose her temper and walk out the door. She did not want to do that. She had to get control of the situation and establish herself as the client, the one who was paying the bill and who was, therefore, in charge, because she was out of options. It was Sage Investigations or the Los Angeles phone book.

The thought of trying to find a reliable, trustworthy private investigator in the L.A. phone book was daunting. The town had a well-earned reputation for corruption. The fault line ran from the big studios straight through the police department and all the way to the courts. It was an open secret. Private investigators working in that environment were very likely to be caught up in the system. She needed someone who could not be bought, someone she could trust.

She gave Sam a steely smile, rose to her feet, plucked the copy of the *Adelina Beach Courier* off the desk, and opened it to the Home & Hearth section. She positioned the page directly in front of Sam.

"Let's start at the beginning," she said. "Perhaps that will make it easier for you to follow along."

"Thank you, that would be very helpful."

Reining in her temper, she pointed at the Dear Aunt Cornelia advice column. "This is Aunt Cornelia. As I told you, I have been writing the column recently, but almost no one knows that."

He looked at the column and read the first letter aloud:

Dear Aunt Cornelia,

If a woman discovers three weeks before the wedding that her fiancé is having an affair, should she break off the engagement? This man has apologized and begged for forgiveness. He swears it will never happen again. The woman's parents and friends think she should go through with the wedding.

Signed,
Asking for a Friend

Dear Asking for a Friend:

Leopards don't change their spots. If your friend marries a man who cheats before marriage, she will get a man who will cheat after marriage. You wrote to Aunt Cornelia because your friend has doubts. That is her intuition shouting at her, trying to get her attention. She should listen.

Signed,
Aunt Cornelia

Sam looked up. "You wrote that answer?"

"Yes."

Sam whistled softly. "You're one tough lady. What? You don't believe in giving a guy a second chance?"

"I merely pointed out the obvious to Asking for a Friend."

"Did your advice come from personal experience?"

"That," she said, "is none of your business."

"Thought so. Personal experience."

Maggie sat down. "There is an enormous amount of pressure brought to bear on a bride who cancels the wedding shortly before the ceremony. A woman who abandons a man almost at the altar acquires a certain reputation, you see, regardless of her reasons."

"What kind of reputation?" Sam asked.

"Some will say she had an emotional breakdown and that it indicates she suffers from weak nerves. Others will tell her she is being hysterical and instruct her to *calm down.*"

"I see."

"And then there is the social side of the matter. The bride will be informed that she can't call off the wedding at the last minute because she will embarrass her family. On top of the humiliation, there are the expenses involved. The catering fees. The flowers. The champagne. The wedding gown. And what about all those wedding gifts the guests have already purchased?"

Sam nodded. "Definitely personal experience talking. Think Asking for a Friend's friend will take your advice?"

"Who knows?" Maggie sighed. "People are very quick to ask for advice, but they rarely take it. The truth is, all they usually want to do is whine about their problems. They lack the fortitude and determination it takes to actually do something about them."

"Interesting." Sam leaned back. The chair squeaked. "That's certainly been my experience. Who would have thought the private detective business and the advice columnist profession would have anything in common?"

A flicker of intuition told her he was not being sarcastic this time. Just quietly amused. That was annoying. She was not here to entertain him.

"How would you have answered Asking for a Friend's letter?" she asked.

"Same way you did," he said.

She relaxed a little.

"Don't worry, I am prepared to pay you for your time," she said.

"I am glad to hear that. I appreciate your patience, because until this morning I had never heard of Aunt Cornelia."

"Do you, perhaps, limit yourself to the sports page of the papers?"

"I've been known to read the comics."

She gave him a chilly smile. "That explains why you aren't aware of the Dear Aunt Cornelia column. It happens to be one of the most widely syndicated advice columns in the country. It started in the *Adelina Beach Courier* and it appears six days a week in the Home and Hearth section. That comes right after the society page."

"I only read the Society page when I'm working a case that involves that crowd, which is, frankly, as seldom as possible," he said.

Her curiosity spiked. "You've conducted investigations in society?"

"I was a homicide detective for a few years," he said. "I know you'll be shocked to hear this, but rich and famous people kill each other, too."

"Were you good at your job?"

"Yes, I was, but like you, I found the work frustrating."

"Why?"

"Rich and famous people kill each other but they rarely go to prison."

She nodded. "Money equals power, and power leads to corruption."

"Often enough to be annoying."

"Where did you work when you were in the police?" she asked.

"Started in Seattle. A couple of years ago I moved to L.A."

That jolted her. "You were a police detective in Los Angeles?"

"For a while."

Her spirits sank. "I see."

He eyed her warily. "Is there a problem?"

"No, no, of course not."

His jaw tightened. "There's a problem. What is it?"

"I don't want to insult you—"

"Go ahead, I'm used to it."

She cleared her throat. "It's just that the Los Angeles Police Department is rumored to be in the pockets of the studios and the tycoons who run the city."

"I no longer work in L.A. I was fired."

It was her turn to watch him closely. "Do you mind if I ask why?"

"I arrested the wrong man." He tapped the letter. "Let's return to your case. I assume you did not contact the Adelina Beach police about the blackmail threat?"

"Absolutely not. That letter practically accuses Aunt Cornelia of murder. My employer's career and her reputation would be ruined if it got out that she was in any way linked to a homicide."

"Have you considered the possibility that your employer might have been involved in the death of the Jennaway woman?" Sam asked.

"No. I'm sure Miss Dewhurst did not murder anyone."

"What makes you so certain?"

"Intuition. I've worked for her for over two months now. My office is in her house. I've spent a great deal of time with her. There is nothing about Lillian Dewhurst that would make me suspect she's capable of murder. Read the letter, Mr. Sage. Please. There's a newspaper clipping enclosed."

He extracted the note from the envelope and unfolded it. The clipping fluttered onto the blotter.

He read the letter aloud without inflection:

Dear Aunt Cornelia:

Those who believe that murder by dreams leaves no evidence are wrong. The price of silence is a thousand dollars. Purchase a ticket to the opening conference of the Guilfoyle Institute in Burning Cove and bring the money in cash. You will receive further instructions after you arrive.

Yours in nightmares,
The Traveler

"I see the blackmailer has a taste for melodrama," Sam said. He put down the letter and picked up the yellowed newspaper clipping. His tone turned thoughtful as he read.

Keeley Point—Early this morning the body of Miss Virginia Jennaway was found washed ashore not far from her cottage. A lawyer for the family reported that Miss Jennaway evidently decided to take a moonlight stroll on the beach and was overtaken by a rogue wave that carried her out to sea, where she drowned. The family is devastated and has requested privacy.

Sam set the clipping aside and looked at Maggie. She held her breath. If he turned down her case she would have no choice but to try her luck with the Los Angeles phone book.

"The article is dated four years ago," he said. "Does the name Virginia Jennaway mean anything to you?"

"No," she said.

"Does the Traveler signature ring any bells?"

She hesitated, reluctant to open that particular door. But it had already been left ajar by the extortionist. Sooner or later Sam Sage would have to be told about the Traveler. Might as well get the conversation over with.

"There's an old legend concerning a disembodied spirit called the Traveler that exists on the astral plane," she said. "A sort of psychic assassin. He murders people in their dreams by means of astral projection."

"I see," Sam said, his tone too neutral now. "Do you believe in that astral projection stuff?"

"No, of course not," she said quickly. "Whoever wrote the note was obviously trying to sound ominous."

"Know anything about the Guilfoyle Institute?"

She took a breath and tried for an academic tone. "As you no doubt are aware, dreams are a subject of great interest to the medical and scientific community. Many respected authorities, such as Freud and Jung, are convinced that dream analysis is a useful form of therapy. A great many doctors and researchers are doing groundbreaking research in the field."

"So?"

"In the past year a man named Arthur Guilfoyle has drawn some attention for his approach to lucid dreaming."

Sage reflected briefly. "That's when you dream but you know you're dreaming, right?"

"Yes." She told herself it was a good sign that he at least knew the basic definition of *lucid dreaming*. She dropped the academic air. "About a year ago, Guilfoyle acquired an old celebrity estate on the outskirts of Burning Cove. It was built by Carson Flint back in the late twenties. It is apparently quite impressive."

"Carson Flint, the Hollywood producer?"

"Right. He died about a year and a half ago. Guilfoyle owns the estate now. He has converted it into a research center named the Guilfoyle Institute. The grand opening of the Institute will be in the form of a three-day conference that starts the day after tomorrow."

"Was Lillian Dewhurst planning to attend?"

"We talked about it when we first noticed the ads in the paper several weeks ago," Maggie said, choosing her words with care. "Miss Dewhurst and I share a great interest in the *scientific* study of dreams. But in the end we both decided not to attend the conference."

Sam glanced at the letter again. "The blackmailer wants Dewhurst to show up at the event."

"Yes."

"Why make the extortion payoff during the conference?"

Maggie gave him a cool smile. "That's what I intend to pay you to find out, assuming you take my case."

"Anything else you want to tell me about this note or your boss?"

"No—at least, I don't think so." She paused. "How much more information do you need?"

"I won't know until I start looking around."

Relief splashed through her. "You'll take the case?"

"I'll make some phone calls and see what I can find out about the death of Miss Jennaway. We'll talk about the next step after that."

She had hoped for a little more professional enthusiasm, but it was clear the promise to make the phone calls was all she was going to get, at least for now.

"I suppose that's a start," she said. She opened her handbag and took out her wallet. "You'll be requiring a retainer, of course."

"It's customary. I charge by the day. Expenses are extra."

"I understand. How much is the retainer?"

He told her. She took out the money and leaned over the desk to hand it to him.

He accepted the cash, politely not counting the bills, and unlocked the top drawer of his desk. She caught the dull metallic sheen of a pistol just before he dropped the money inside and closed and locked the drawer.

For some reason the sight of the gun sent a frisson of uncertainty down her spine. She had just hired a man who kept a pistol in his desk drawer. She told herself it was only to be expected. He was a private detective, after all. She was asking him to deal with a blackmailer. She needed someone who could be intimidating if necessary. Sam Sage might not be a prosperous investigator, but she thought he could appear quite dangerous if he bothered to make the effort.

Still, she had never known anyone who kept a pistol in his desk. Yes, her father and brothers occasionally did some hunting, but that was different. There was only one reason a person needed a handgun, and that reason was chilling. Maybe she was making a serious mistake.

Sam did not appear to be aware of her misgivings. "You don't mind using your own money to find out who is blackmailing your employer?"

"My duties as Miss Dewhurst's assistant include paying the household bills while she's away," Maggie said. "Don't worry, Mr. Sage, I am authorized to write checks on her account. Miss Dewhurst is a wealthy woman."

"She obviously trusts you." It was a statement, not a question.

"Yes."

"How do I get in touch with you?"

"I am currently staying in Miss Dewhurst's home on Sunset Lane. I'm looking after the house and gardens while she's gone. She's not in the phone book. I'll give you the number." She jotted down the information on a card and handed it to him. "Will there be anything else?"

"That will do for now." He got to his feet and dropped the card into the pocket of his coat. "I'll be in touch as soon as I have any information."

"Thank you." She rose and glanced at the note on his desk. "What about the letter?"

"Mind if I hang on to it until I finish making the phone calls?"

"It's the only evidence I've got of the blackmail threat. I don't want to lose it."

"You don't trust me to keep it safe?"

"No offense, but I've only just met you."

He refolded the letter, slipped it into the envelope, and handed it to her. "Take the extortion note, Miss Lodge."

She snapped it out of his fingers and dropped it into her handbag. "Call as soon as you have news, night or day."

"I'll do that. Out of curiosity, are you always this prickly?"

She gave him a razor-sharp smile. "I believe so, especially when I'm the one writing the checks. If you have a problem with that, be sure to let me know."

She turned on one stacked heel and marched toward the door.

Sam moved out from behind his desk, crossed the small space in a few long strides, and managed to get to the glass-paned door ahead of her. He opened it.

She tightened her grip on her handbag. She had done what she could. She had hoped to experience some relief after hiring a professional investigator, but the sense of impending disaster was as strong as ever.

She looked at the brass coatrack as she crossed the office—she couldn't *not* look at it. Even from several feet away she sensed the whispers of rage and violence.

Keep your mouth shut, Maggie. You don't want to give him the impression you're one of those people who believes in paranormal energy and psychic visions.

But she couldn't help herself.

"May I ask where you purchased that coatrack, Mr. Sage?" she said.

Sam glanced at it. "Brought it with me from L.A. It was one of the few things left after the divorce."

So he was divorced. So what? She wasn't here to marry the man. She had no intention of marrying anyone. She had already abandoned one groom almost at the altar, and every night when she crawled into bed alone, she vowed never to repeat the near-disastrous mistake. She had come within inches of ending up in an asylum for the second time in her life. She still had nightmares about the very close call.

Nope. Sam Sage's divorce, like the story behind the coatrack, was none of her business. Still, for some reason, it was nice to know he didn't have a wife. Of course, that didn't mean there wasn't a woman in his life.

Keep walking. Do not stop. Just keep going.

With a sigh, she paused in the doorway.

"Would you like some advice?" she asked.

"Depends," Sam said. "What's the advice?"

"Get rid of that coatrack. The sooner, the better."

He eyed the coatrack. "Why?"

She had been afraid he would ask that question.

"It doesn't look right in here," she mumbled.

"What?"

Why had she bothered? Sam was obviously impervious to the disturbing shadows cast by the coatrack. She was the one with the problem. Her family and the psychiatrists and therapists they had insisted she consult had made that perfectly clear to her.

"Never mind," she said, trying for a breezy smile. "It's between you and your decorator."

"Does this office look like I had it furnished by a decorator?"

"I'm sorry I mentioned the damned coatrack." She went out into the hall. "Call me as soon as you have any news, night or day."

"I will," he said. But he was looking at the coatrack, not at her.

She walked briskly toward the stairs. When she went past the door of the secretarial firm she heard the quick, steady clicking of keys that indicated that an expert typist was at work. On the other side of the door there was probably another single woman trying to make her way in the world.

She reached the top of the stairs and hesitated. A tingle of awareness made her glance over her shoulder. Sam was lounging in the doorway, his arms folded. He was watching her now, not the coatrack.

When they locked eyes, he nodded once, moved back into the shadow of the coatrack, and closed the door. She knew then she should not have said anything about the coatrack. The best she could hope for was that he would label her eccentric.

He almost certainly would not get rid of the coatrack. People rarely took good advice. She was the one who would be stuck with the effects of the shadows cast by the thing. It was going to be a long night.

Chapter 3

Sam went to the window and looked down at the street through the slats of the venetian blinds. He watched Margaret Lodge slip into the front seat of a sunset-yellow four-door Packard convertible studded with a lot of sparkling chrome and sharp-looking whitewall tires.

She took off the snappy little high-crowned hat and replaced it with a scarf knotted under her chin. She added a pair of sunglasses and leather driving gloves, put the powerful car in gear, pulled away from the curb, and drove off with a self-confident flair.

Maybe a little too much flair. He got the feeling that on the open road she would have a heavy foot.

He turned away from the window. There was no way she could know the history of the coatrack. She was currently writing a newspaper advice column. Shrewd detective logic told him that meant she had a vivid imagination.

Maybe the problem was his imagination, not hers. He knew exactly what had happened to the coatrack, and the memories were deeply unpleasant. It was conceivable he had misinterpreted her advice. It was possible she had simply given him a decorating tip. A lot of people were passionate about interior design. He was not one of those people, but she looked like the type who cared about that sort of thing—a woman who had been raised in a house that had been furnished by a professional interior designer. He knew about houses like that. He and Elizabeth had lived in one, courtesy of his father-in-law, for a few months.

It was just a coatrack. It was functional. That was the only thing that mattered.

Forget the coatrack.

He had more important things to deal with. He had an actual client and an actual case, his first since he had opened for business a week earlier.

He stripped off his coat, draped it over the back of his chair, and loosened his tie. He sat down, opened a drawer, and took out his notebook.

There was more good news—evidently the client could afford him. Or, rather, she had access to the account of her employer, who could afford him. That worked just as well.

He glanced at the card Margaret Lodge had given him. There wasn't much information on it, just a phone number and the address of her employer's house. Sunset Lane was a quietly expensive neighborhood on the bluffs overlooking the bay. He uncapped the fountain pen and jotted down the details on the card. Then he sat back to consider his impressions.

He had been a good cop because he had good intuition. He could usually get a fast read on people—the living and the dead—but not always. His failed marriage was proof of that.

Lodge was a problem. She did not fit neatly into any of the standard categories. He had, in fact, been blindsided when she walked through the door. Stunned, maybe. Whatever he had expected in the way of his first client, she wasn't it.

She was attractive, but not in the Hollywood way. There were too many strong features and sharp edges. *Compelling* was a more accurate description. She looked like a lady who could take care of herself, one who had been doing exactly that for a while. She didn't need a hero, not the way Elizabeth had. Lodge needed a man who could keep up with her.

The rakish little hat had been tilted at just the right angle to allow the elegantly waved brim to partially veil fascinating eyes, eyes that gave a man the unsettling sensation she could see beneath the surface. That made her both dangerous and interesting.

When she had come through the door he had been afraid she would ask him to tail her husband to get incriminating photographs in preparation for a divorce. He had been dreading divorce work, but he knew he couldn't afford to turn it down, not at the start of his new career. It would take time to build up the insurance, fraud, and missing persons side of the business. When he was established he would be able to turn down divorce work.

But Lodge had not asked him to follow a cheating husband. That should have been a huge relief. And it was. But it didn't explain his reaction to her.

She was obviously intelligent and well-educated, but she did not display the arrogance he often encountered when he had occasion to interview witnesses and suspects in the academic and scientific worlds. Many women her age were married, but she wore no ring and she was working.

Lodge conducted herself with self-confidence, and there was an air of fierce determination about her that told him it would be a very bad idea to get between her and whatever she wanted. She had not tried to flirt with him or make him feel sorry for her. She had been all business.

All in all, Lodge was the ideal client—except for the lucid dreaming stuff. That was an unfortunate twist. The fact that she was interested enough in the subject to be familiar with weird stuff such as astral projection and a legend about a supernatural assassin called the Traveler was definitely cause for serious concern.

None of those observations and considerations answered the big question: Why had it felt as if he had been struck by lightning when Margaret Lodge opened the door and walked into his office? Sure, it had been a while since the divorce, and things had not been good between Elizabeth and him for a long time before she went to Reno. And yes, afterward he had been too numbed by the overwhelming weight of his failure to recognize impending disaster until it was too late. Still, nothing explained why he couldn't fit Margaret Lodge into a pigeonhole and slap a label on her. She was a mystery. And she made him aware that he was no longer numb.

He made a few more notes and then picked up the phone. The Adelina Beach operator came on the line immediately, her voice calm and professional and somehow cheerful and optimistic.

"Number, please," she said.

He asked for the long-distance operator.

"Please hold while I connect you."

He contemplated the coatrack while he waited. It was a solid, substantial piece of furniture. Every office needed a coatrack. His was impressive. It added a classy note to the place. There was no reason to get rid of it just because Margaret Lodge didn't think it looked right in his office.

So he had a client who was interested in lucid dreaming—so what? Occasionally he did read something in the papers besides the comics and the sports pages. The study of dreams was all the rage these days. Yes, there was a seemingly unlimited number of quacks, frauds, and delusional people who were making a lot of money selling fake psychic dream readings and the secrets to astral projection, but there had never been a shortage of swindlers, hucksters, and con artists in the world.

From his point of view—a detective's point of view—a scientific approach to dream research was inherently difficult, if not impossible, because the nature of dreams meant doctors and researchers were forced to rely on the reports of the only eyewitnesses—the dreamers. Every cop knew eyewitnesses were notoriously unreliable.

It looked like he had a screwy client, which meant it would be a screwy case, but it beat divorce work.

A new operator came on the line. "Long distance."

"Keeley Point Police Department, please," he said.

Chapter 4

I hope you know what you're doing," Prudence Ryland said. "Hiring a private investigator is a very serious matter. They're a shady bunch, always sneaking around in the bushes taking pictures of people in compromising situations."

"You know perfectly well I haven't got a clue what I'm doing," Maggie said. "But I can't think of any other strategy. I don't know how to conduct an investigation. I need a professional detective. Mr. Sage is the only one in town who appears to be at least somewhat qualified for the job."

She picked up half of her tuna salad sandwich and took a bite. Pru was munching an egg salad sandwich. They were eating lunch in the Adelina Beach College cafeteria, and they were eating quickly. In precisely nineteen minutes Pru would be rushing back to her desk in the library of the school's recently established Department of Parapsychology. As a very new member of the staff, she could not afford to take the risk of being late.

"You said he's a former police detective?" Pru asked, her eyes bright with curiosity. "That's a good sign, I suppose."

She was wearing what she called a business suit. Maggie had labeled the dark, depressing outfit her Stern Governess costume—a tailored, close-fitting black jacket; a narrow black skirt; and mid-heel black lace-up oxfords. Her hair was pulled back in a prim bun, and she wore a pair of gold-framed spectacles. Her only item of jewelry was a watch. It had a black leather band.

She was doing her best to fit in with the faculty and staff of the college, but in Maggie's opinion anyone with an ounce of perception could see the bright, adventurous spirit and crisp intelligence beneath the dull plumage. In reality, of course, the vast majority of people never bothered to look beneath the surface. They saw what they expected to see, which was a good thing, Maggie thought, because it allowed her and Pru to masquerade as normal.

When Pru had landed the position in the library she had been euphoric, convinced she had found the perfect career. Sadly, it was starting to look like a job in a research library—even one devoted to the study of the paranormal—came with all the customary limitations and challenges that confronted women in every field: male bosses who were slow to promote and obnoxious male colleagues who viewed women on the staff as prey.

Working in an academic institution involved additional challenges, not least of which was that the members of the teaching faculty never hesitated to make it clear they outranked the librarians.

It was obvious that the best way for a determined, independent-minded female to prosper in the world was to start her own business, Maggie thought. She and Pru each had plans for the future, but for now they both had to pay the bills.

"Mr. Sage told me he was fired from the Los Angeles Police Department," she said.

"Really?" Pru's brows shot up. "Did he say why?"

"Something about arresting the wrong man."

"Hah. I'm sure that happens all the time and no one gets fired.

Sounds fishy to me. If Mr. Sage was let go, he must have really bungled the arrest."

"I know, but I got the feeling he did not want to talk about it," Maggie said.

"I'm sure he didn't. It would take a major blunder to get fired from the Los Angeles Police Department. So, we have a disgraced and divorced ex-cop who is barely getting by as a small-time private detective." Pru's eyes glinted with amusement. "Really, Maggie, couldn't you have found a more disreputable investigator?"

"He wasn't drunk at nine o'clock in the morning."

"Wow. You've got to be impressed by a man who holds himself to such high standards."

"I'm trying to remain optimistic," Maggie said. "I'm worried, and I'm short on options."

She took another bite of her sandwich. It was a relief to talk to her best friend. Pru was aware she worked for the reclusive woman who wrote the Aunt Cornelia column. Lillian Dewhurst herself had authorized the disclosure of her identity after meeting Prudence and concluding she could be trusted.

Maggie and Pru were neighbors in an inexpensive apartment house near the beach, but when Lillian had decided on the spur of the moment to sail for the South Pacific, she asked Maggie to move into the mansion on Sunset Lane and look after it while she was gone. "It's never a good idea to leave a big house empty for a couple of months," Lillian said.

Maggie had hesitated to make the move, but Pru encouraged her. "You'll have a nice quiet place to write," she pointed out. "Maybe you'll be able to finish the first draft of your novel if you don't have to listen to the couple upstairs fighting and the nightclub singer next door having sex with her shady boyfriend at three in the morning."

It was true that the walls of the apartment house were very thin. The prospect of having some peace and quiet in which to nail down the rough draft of the book had been too tempting to resist, so for now, Maggie was living on Sunset Lane.

"Anything else you want to tell me about this divorced, fired, failing-but-not-drunk-at-nine-in-the-morning investigator?" Pru asked around the last mouthful of her sandwich.

Maggie brightened. "No, but I do have some good news. I think I've made a breakthrough in my book."

"You've figured out how to fix your hero?"

"After I left Mr. Sage's office today, I suddenly knew what was wrong with him—my hero, I mean, not Mr. Sage. I'm going to go back to the beginning and rewrite the first scene tonight. Once that's done, I'm sure I'll be able to move forward, although I already know I've got to revise the plot a bit, too. It needs more action."

"Action is always good in a novel. Did you get any other inspiration from Mr. Sage?"

"Not the kind I like to get." Maggie made a face. "There's a coat-rack in his office that casts a bad shadow."

"How bad?"

"Pretty bad. Feels relatively recent."

"Think the energy is his or someone else's?"

"Some of it is from Mr. Sage, but the really bad stuff is from another person. Sage appears to be unaware of the shadow, but I wouldn't be surprised if it's affecting his mood and probably his dreams. He just doesn't know it."

Pru narrowed her eyes. "Whatever you do, don't make the mistake of telling him to get rid of the coatrack."

"Too late. I already did."

Pru sighed. "How did he react?"

"How do you think he reacted? He looked at me like I was one of those weird people who believes in paranormal energy and attends psychic readings."

"You just couldn't help yourself, could you?"

"I tried not to mention the coatrack, I really did."

"You should have tried harder."

"Is that right? What would you have done?"

Pru gave her a bright, smug smile. "Kept my mouth shut."

"I couldn't resist. It was for his own good."

"The one reason guaranteed to annoy anyone without fail."

"The important thing is that he took my case," Maggie said. "He's making phone calls about the dead woman, Virginia Jennaway, as we speak."

"What if he doesn't learn anything useful from a couple of phone calls?"

Maggie sat back and tapped her finger on the Formica table. "I reserved a ticket for the conference at the Guilfoyle Institute just in case Mr. Sage isn't able to identify the blackmailer after he makes the phone calls."

"I was afraid of that. You'll be wasting your time."

"The blackmailer will be there, Pru. It's the one thing I can be sure of at this point."

"There will be a couple of hundred people at the conference. How are you going to find the extortionist in that crowd? You're not a detective. You have no idea how to investigate a crime."

"I'll think of something. Besides, you know I've been curious about the Guilfoyle Method."

"Not anymore," Pru shot back. "You lost interest in it after you discovered the guest speaker at the conference was going to be Dr. Emerson Oxlade."

"I admit, now that I know Oxlade is involved in the Institute, I'm not nearly as interested in the Guilfoyle Method, but that doesn't mean there isn't something to it. Oxlade is a dreadful man, but he's serious about his dream research and he enjoys an excellent reputation. It's understandable why Guilfoyle invited him to present a lecture. His presence gives the Method credibility."

Pru leaned forward and lowered her voice. "Have you forgotten that Oxlade laced your tea with a hallucinogenic drug without telling you what he was doing?"

"Of course not. I'm well aware he's a nasty creep."

"What if he sees you at the conference? He's bound to recognize you."

"I'll deal with the problem if it arises."

"It will arise," Pru said. "I don't like the idea of your attending the conference alone. I should go with you."

"We both know the director would never give you the time off. To be fair, no one in his position would. You just started your new job a couple of weeks ago."

"I doubt if he'll ever give me any time off," Pru said. "It's been clear from the start that Attwater doesn't approve of female staff. He thinks women are all right for small-town public libraries but only men are suited for academic and research institutions. I overheard him talking to someone today and discovered that if it hadn't been for Dr. Otto Tinsley, I would not have gotten my new job."

"Who is Tinsley?" Maggie asked.

"He recently joined the faculty, and he's very highly regarded in the field of parapsychology. He's also very nice. Everyone in the department was impressed with the demonstration of his new ESP-sensing machine. He met me when I went in for the interview with the director. Afterward he insisted I get the position of research librarian."

Maggie smiled. "So Attwater had to hire you."

"Yep. Professors, especially stars like Tinsley, are the equivalent of opera divas in the academic world. But Attwater is not happy about the situation. I get the feeling he's biding his time, waiting for me to make a mistake, or maybe he hopes I'll create a scandal of some sort. He's looking for an excuse to fire me."

"I'll bet he's afraid you'll end up making him look bad," Maggie said. "If he realizes just how much you know about the literature of the paranormal and how good you are at research, he'll start worrying about his own job."

"I'm being very careful to appear competent but not too competent. My plan is to make Attwater look good."

"Don't sell your soul just to make the boss appear smart," Maggie said.

"Are you kidding? Making the boss look brilliant is a job requirement regardless of the line of work you're in. As for you, you have no business lecturing me. You're ghostwriting an advice column for a woman who's thousands of miles away in the South Pacific. Aunt Cornelia is getting all the credit for the column."

"Fine by me. I'm not out to take her job." Maggie picked up her coffee cup. "One of these days, Pru."

"Yes," Pru said. "One of these days."

There was no need for either of them to finish the sentence. They had been repeating the words to each other since they had met at a lecture on psychic dreaming a few months ago. They had each concluded independently that the so-called expert giving the presentation was just another fraud in a field studded with cons and fakes.

She and Pru had found a tearoom, ordered a pot of Darjeeling and a tray of tiny sandwiches, and settled in to discuss their observations. Two hours later the hostess had requested that they leave because it was closing time. It was when they got to their feet and collected their handbags that the two talked about their dreams. Maggie explained she was eking out a living writing for the confession magazines while trying to write a full-length novel on the side. Pru had nodded in understanding and confided her own dream: *I want to open a bookstore devoted to the literature of the paranormal.*

Neither had yet realized her dream, but they were making progress financially, at least. They both had jobs that allowed them to put aside a little money for the future. They were on their own because neither of them could look for assistance from their families. The advice from their relatives was to focus on getting married.

Even if they had been inclined to marry, finding husbands would have been complicated, if not impossible. And they were not so inclined. Each of them had an excellent reason to avoid marriage, a reason rooted in that most powerful of all emotions—fear.

"Look at the time." Pru jumped to her feet and slung the strap of her handbag over one shoulder. "I have to get back to the library. Let me know if your investigator solves the case with those phone calls."

"I will," Maggie promised.

Chapter 5

S he delayed going to bed as long as possible because she knew the coatrack would show up in her dreams and she would have to deal with it. That was going to be a problem because she had so little context. All she knew about it was that it was standing in Sage's office and that he and an unknown person had laid down the shadow energy. That didn't give her much to work with.

She was good at ignoring most of the shadows she encountered in daily life. She'd had plenty of practice since her late teens, when her lucid dreaming abilities had blossomed. There had been no choice but to develop the skill and strength of will required to suppress her sensitivity to the energy left on objects that had been handled by people in the grip of some intense emotion.

It was all too easy to blunder into the shadows cast by seemingly innocuous objects—a fireplace poker, a clock, a letter opener. A coatrack. The trial-and-error process of learning how to control her dream world to some extent had been fraught. Early on there had been too many unfortunate occasions when things had gone wrong and she had awakened screaming. Her family had been deeply concerned. She had been whisked off to the offices of a series of psychiatrists and dream analysts.

When she was seventeen, two of the experts had diagnosed her as prone to attacks of hysteria and had recommended eight weeks in a private sanitarium to "calm her nerves." She had learned a valuable lesson during her enforced stay inside the walls of Sweet Creek Manor: She had learned how to keep her mouth shut—most of the time.

These days she was careful to talk about her extreme dreams only with those who understood and accepted her unusual and disturbing ability. She had concluded she would probably always sleep alone. Marriage—a risk on so many levels—could prove catastrophic in her case. It had the potential to doom her to an asylum.

She poured a glass of wine and sipped it while she heated a can of cream of tomato soup and prepared a toasted cheese sandwich. She ate the simple meal at the kitchen table and made some notes for the novel. She did not want to forget the gun in Sam Sage's desk. It would add an intriguing element to the story and to the character of the hero.

She washed the dishes in the kitchen sink and went upstairs to the room she used as an office. She had mailed the questions and answers for two weeks' worth of columns to the editor that afternoon. Tonight she had time to devote to her writing.

She sat down at the desk and pulled out the legal pad. As she had explained to Pru, she knew now why the hero, Bennett North, felt wrong.

> . . . *The house looked as if it had been constructed from the scraps of a graveyard—bits and pieces of discarded headstones and abandoned crypts. The gray rock walls loomed over the dark mirror of Winter Lake.*

The exterior of the mansion was bleak and intimidating, but it was the interior that chilled Grace to the bone. The high-ceilinged room was draped in perpetual shadow, a gloom that could not be chased off by the simple act of opening the heavy curtains.

Flames leaped from the logs piled on the vast stone hearth, but there was little warmth to be had from them. They clawed a path upward through the chimney, seemingly desperate to escape.

There was no escape for Grace. The position of confidential secretary she had been offered was her only hope. If she retreated to her aging Hudson and drove back down the twisted mountain road, she would be dining in a charity soup kitchen that night.

Her future hung on the reception she received from the master of the house, a man with the sculpted features of a fallen angel.

Bennett North rose from behind the expanse of a polished mahogany desk to greet her.

"Welcome to Winter Lake," he said.

His voice resonated with the cool polish and unshakable self-confidence produced by old money and a lineage that stretched back to the Old World. He could have stepped out of the previous century.

Grace knew she was looking at a man who not only accepted but embraced the weight of the traditions and secrets placed on him by family, social status, and money. It was clear he was content to be trapped in the past. It was the source of his strength and his power . . .

No question about it, Bennett North was not only insufferable, he was boring. He was a man who was chained to the past, not one who was capable of carving out a new future for himself.

Maggie uncapped a fountain pen, drew lines through the description of Bennett North, and tried another approach.

. . . There was a sense of resolute determination about him that charged the atmosphere. His fierce will was reflected in his eyes.

Bennett North had found himself in hell, but he would not be defeated by its forces . . .

She put down the pen, sat back, and read what she had written. Bennett was definitely on the way to becoming more interesting, and there was no problem figuring out who had inspired the new version. She wondered if Sam Sage would show up in her dreams.

Thoughts of Sage brought a sharp reminder of the coatrack. He really needed to get the thing out of his office.

She slipped the legal pad back into the drawer and got to her feet. She could usually lose herself in her writing, but that was not going to work tonight. The threatening letter and the coatrack demanded attention. She might as well go to bed and get the dreams over with. She knew they would hover on the edge of her thoughts, tugging at her, until she exorcised them.

Chapter 6

The dream . . .

. . . She walks through the empty white corridors of Sweet Creek Manor, opening the door of each room she passes. She does not know who or what she is searching for, but she will open doors until she finds a room with answers inside.

She opens a door and sees the old version of Bennett North. He gives her a confused, pleading look but he does not speak.

"I never found your voice," she says. "You're free to go. I don't need you."

She closes the door and opens another. This time she sees Sam Sage. He's standing in the shadow cast by the coatrack.

"Are you afraid of me?" she asks.

"No, but we're going to have problems."

"Why?"

"I'm no hero," he says.

"I'm the writer. I'll decide."

She closes the door and moves on to the next room. The extortion letter and a postcard are on the floor.

40 . . .

She knows in the way dreamers do that someone is hiding in the corner of the room, but she can't see the person.

She also knows, as she usually does, that she is dreaming and that it is time to take control of the script.

She contemplates the extortion letter. Only some of the words are legible in this dreamscape.

Murder

Burning Cove

The Traveler

She turns away from the letter. There is nothing more to be learned from it in this dream. Experience has taught her that if she studies it any longer she will become anxious and frustrated. If she pushes too hard for comprehension she will awaken in a full-blown anxiety attack.

She examines the postcard. It is picture-side down. There is some writing on the back. She can discern two words.

Guilfoyle Method

She picks up the postcard and turns it over to see the picture.

There is an illustration of a charming Mediterranean-style town on the front. Whitewashed buildings topped with red tile roofs line palm-shaded streets. The ocean sparkles in the sun. The scene is almost too perfect to be real, a movie-set town.

There are words written across the picture postcard. She can read them clearly.

WELCOME TO BURNING COVE, CALIFORNIA

She sees the shadow that hangs over the town. Anxiety unfurls its dark wings. She knows she needs to end the dream. Now.

She drops the postcard on the floor and hurries toward the door, her exit from the dreamscape. But just before she steps into the safety of the hallway, she senses motion in the room.

This is not part of the script.

She turns and sees Emerson Oxlade lunging toward her, a syringe in one hand.

"You belong to me," he says.

Panic sweeps through her. She is losing control of the dreamscape. She runs for the door. It is like trying to move through quicksand . . .

She yanked herself out of the dream, opened her eyes, and sat up on the edge of the bed. Her pulse was beating too quickly, and she could not seem to take a deep breath.

"Breathe," she whispered into the darkness. "Your nerves are fine. You know how to breathe. Just breathe."

After a few minutes she grew calm. When she was satisfied she had her nerves under control, she switched on the lamp and reached for the dream journal on the nightstand. She wrote down what felt like the important elements of the dream before they could slide away; before she could convince herself she was imagining things.

When she was finished she studied her notes. Her intuition was telling her that the answers she sought were in Burning Cove and that she needed Sam Sage to find them, but she already knew that.

All in all, not one of her more useful dream journeys.

Chapter 7

The phone on Sam's desk rang at five minutes after eight o'clock the following morning.

"I have a collect call for Mr. Sage from Detective Flynn of the Keeley Point Police Department," the operator said. "Will you accept the charges?"

Sam winced and then reminded himself he would be putting the cost of the collect call on his bill.

"Yes, I'll accept the charges," he said.

"Go ahead, Detective Flynn," the operator said.

"Sage? This is Flynn. I got your message when I walked into the office a few minutes ago. Why are you looking into the Jennaway drowning?"

Sam got the familiar whisper of certainty that told him he was on the right track. The fact that Flynn had phoned as soon as he received the message answered the key question. A homicide cop a hundred miles away had better things to do than return a call to a private investigator—a stranger—unless the detective had a few questions of his own about the death.

"I've got a case of blackmail here in Adelina Beach that appears to be tied to Miss Jennaway's death," he said.

"The name Sage sounds familiar. Are you the cop who arrested Chichester for the Bloody Scarf Murders a while back?"

"Unfortunately, yes."

"What do you want to know about Jennaway?"

Sam hung up a few minutes later and studied his notes. He was reaching for the receiver when the phone rang again. Two phone calls before eight thirty in the morning. Business was picking up at Sage Investigations. He could think of only one person besides the Keeley Point detective who would be calling at that hour. He got a pleasant little jolt of anticipation when he picked up the receiver.

"Sage Investigations," he said.

"Have you seen this morning's paper?"

Right caller, but Margaret Lodge was not in a good mood. She was furious.

"Miss Lodge?" he said, trying to play it cautiously.

"Yes, of course it's me. Who else would be calling you at this hour?"

"As a matter of fact—"

"By the way, as we're going to be working together, you might as well call me Maggie. Did you read the *Adelina Beach Courier* this morning?"

He glanced at the paper on his desk. "Not yet. Why? Is there—"

"Open it. Turn to the Celebrity Confidential column. Hurry."

He braced the phone between his shoulder and his right ear and reached for the paper.

"Where is the Celebrity Confidential column?" he asked.

"Bottom half of the Society page."

Impatience sharpened her voice. He decided not to ask for further instructions. He had a feeling she had already concluded he was not Sam Spade or Nick Charles.

He found the Society page, located the column beneath the fold, and read it aloud:

> What famous advice columnist was seen drinking an endless stream of Manhattans at the Paradise Club in Burning Cove, that vacation destination of the rich, famous, and shady? None other than the notoriously reclusive Aunt Cornelia. Yes, that Aunt Cornelia, the one who appears six days a week in newspapers across the country.
>
> Who would have guessed the trusted adviser to thousands is not the prim and proper matron of our imaginations but rather a glamorous redhead with a wardrobe any Hollywood actress would cheerfully kill for?
>
> We're told Aunt Cornelia is in town to attend the opening conference at the new Guilfoyle Institute. Perhaps she hopes to learn how to use her dreams as a resource for advice she can pass along to her faithful readers.

He put the paper down on the desk. "I'm assuming you did not know your employer was in Burning Cove."

"Lillian most definitely is *not* in Burning Cove." Maggie's voice was tight with outrage. "I told you, she is on an extended voyage in the South Pacific. Also, she is not a redhead, and she drinks martinis, not Manhattans. She does not go out to hot nightclubs. Do you understand what I'm telling you, Mr. Sage?"

"Sam," he said automatically.

"What?"

"If I'm supposed to call you Margaret, you had better call me Sam."

"Maggie, not Margaret. My ex-fiancé called me Margaret. You do not want to remind me of him."

"Okay. Right." The conversation had lurched violently off topic. Sam forced himself to focus on the case. "I understand you think someone is pretending to be Aunt Cornelia."

"It's quite obvious a fraud has discovered the real Aunt Cornelia is out of the country and is now impersonating her in Burning Cove."

"Why?" he asked, grasping at a frail strand of logic that appeared to be dangling in midair.

"I have no idea," Maggie said. "But we have to do something about this immediately."

It was the *we have to do something* that alarmed him.

"Don't worry," he said, trying to sound professional and reassuring. "If you're prepared to pay for a trip to Burning Cove, I'll drive there and talk to the woman who is claiming to be Aunt Cornelia. But maybe you'd like to hear my report on the death of Virginia Jennaway first?"

"What? Oh, yes, of course. I was so shocked by the Celebrity Confidential piece about Aunt Cornelia I almost forgot the Jennaway situation. What did you find out?"

"I just got off the phone with a detective who works homicide in Keeley Point. He said Jennaway's death was ruled accidental but afterward there were rumors."

"Of what?"

"Evidently Virginia Jennaway ran with a fast crowd of bored socialites. They were rumored to use drugs. A relative found the body washed up on the beach one morning. The gossip was that Jennaway most likely died of an overdose and the family covered it up."

"And now, four years later, someone blames Aunt Cornelia for the tragedy?"

"No, someone is looking to make a profit. Blackmail is about money, not justice or revenge." Sam paused, thinking. "Does Lillian Dewhurst have any connection to Keeley Point?"

"I have no idea. Lillian has never talked much about her past. All I know is she is the last of her family line and she inherited a great deal of money. The important thing is that whoever wrote the extortion letter obviously knows Lillian Dewhurst is Aunt Cornelia."

"Not necessarily," Sam said. "If the blackmailer knew Dewhurst was Cornelia, the letter would have been sent directly to her address here in Adelina Beach. You said it was delivered in a bag of reader mail that came from the editor of the *Courier*."

"That's right." Maggie's voice brightened. "An excellent observation, Mr. Sage."

"Believe it or not, this isn't my first investigation."

She ignored that. "You're saying the extortionist has reason to believe that the woman who is Aunt Cornelia was involved in Jennaway's death but doesn't know Aunt Cornelia's real identity."

"Yes."

"Seems rather odd, don't you think?"

"Not necessarily," Sam said. "It indicates the blackmailer may have come by the incriminating information secondhand. Knows something about what happened but doesn't know the players personally."

"Hmm. I see what you mean."

"Mind if I ask how you got the job as Aunt Cornelia's assistant?"

"We met at a seminar on lucid dreaming," Maggie said. "We both have an interest in the subject. Why?"

More screwy dream stuff. Sam suppressed a groan and reminded himself it still beat divorce work.

"Here's what strikes me as strange," he said. "Miss Dewhurst has been a near recluse for years, but she suddenly decides to go on a long ocean voyage where she will be stuck on a ship with a lot of other passengers."

"Your point?"

"It's hard to be a recluse on a ship."

There was another beat of silence on the other end of the phone.

"Several weeks ago Lillian began to come out of her shell," Maggie said.

"Was there a reason for the change?"

"That is none of your business, Mr. Sage."

"Did you perhaps suggest she throw out a perfectly good piece of furniture? A nice chair? A lamp? A coatrack?"

"We are not going to discuss the matter," Maggie said. Icicles hung on each word. "You have made it clear you are not a student of meta-physics. Let's return to the subject of the investigation I hired you to carry out."

"Sure. I'll leave the physics to you."

"Metaphysics."

"Moving on. I assume that, as Dewhurst's assistant, you handle her correspondence. Has she received any unusual mail addressed directly to her lately?"

"Nothing of a personal nature. She gets bills in her own name and bank statements. She also subscribes to some magazines and scientific journals."

"What kinds of scientific journals?"

"Journals that focus on metaphysics." Maggie's voice was gla-cial now.

"Forget I asked."

"That won't be difficult."

"Notice any long-distance calls on the latest phone bill?"

"No."

Sam thought for a moment. "Any chance she might have an anony-mous mailbox at the post office?"

"Not that I know of." Maggie paused. "That's an interesting idea, though. A post office box would be an excellent way to keep certain types of correspondence a secret from others in the household. In this case, however, the question is, why bother? Miss Dewhurst lives alone."

Sam got the ghostly whisper of awareness. "You appear to be one of the very few people who are close to Lillian Dewhurst."

"Trust me, that did occur to me," Maggie said, her voice sharp but not defensive. "The only secret I'm aware of is that she is Aunt Corne-

WHEN SHE DREAMS

lia. I'm not the one blackmailing my employer. If I was, I wouldn't have hired you."

"It would be an interesting way of diverting suspicion from yourself."

"Hmm."

He thought he heard paper rustling. It was a small, insignificant sound, but it set off warning bells.

"Miss Lodge? What are you doing?"

"Just making a few notes," she said a little too smoothly. "Please go on."

She was taking notes? That did not sound good. He wasn't sure why it didn't sound good, but his intuition told him it was ominous.

"You've worked for Dewhurst for a couple of months and now you're writing the columns," he said.

"I didn't get rid of her in order to get her job, if that's what you're implying."

"Just trying to establish the facts."

"I don't want her job. It's a good career but it's not my calling. It is Miss Dewhurst's calling, however. She has a talent for giving the right advice."

"Why isn't it a calling for you?" he asked, distracted.

"One never knows how the story ends."

"What?"

"An advice columnist almost never finds out if the person who asked for help took the advice and, if so, how things worked out," Maggie explained. "I find the work somewhat unsatisfying. I want to know the outcome."

So do I, Sam thought. Back to business. "Why Burning Cove?"

"Pardon?"

"The extortionist thinks the conference at the Guilfoyle Institute will be a good place to collect the blackmail payment. You said that Dewhurst had thought about attending the event?"

"We talked about it, but in the end we both changed our minds."

"Why?"

"Lillian decided to take the voyage to the South Pacific instead. I changed my mind after I discovered that Dr. Emerson Oxlade would be the guest lecturer."

"You consider him a quack?"

"Not in the usual sense. He's a real doctor and he is serious about his research in the field of lucid dreaming, but he is extremely unethical. Knowing he was involved with the Guilfoyle Institute put me off the notion of attending."

It was his turn to take notes. Sam picked up a pencil and jotted down the name *Oxlade*.

"How did you come to that conclusion about Dr. Oxlade?" he asked.

"Long story. It's not relevant."

He scrawled the word *personal* and followed it with an exclamation point.

"What are you doing, Mr. Sage?"

"Just making a few notes."

"Oh." She went silent.

He smiled, pleased at having been able to stop her cold, at least for a couple of beats, by throwing her own words back at her. The moment of satisfaction was fleeting, however, because he immediately went back to wondering why she had been making notes earlier. There was definitely something worrisome about it, but he couldn't figure out why it made him uneasy.

He reminded himself to stay focused on the case.

"Everything about this situation appears to be linked to the conference at the Guilfoyle Institute," he said.

"Exactly." Energy infused her voice again. "I have come to the same conclusion."

"I'm happy to continue to investigate, but it won't be cheap. I'll need a hotel room in Burning Cove, and there's the cost of gas, meals, telephone calls, et cetera."

"Money is not a problem, Mr. Sage. I agree the next step is to attend the dream conference at the Institute. It opens tomorrow evening with a formal reception. Would you prefer to take your own car, or would you like to accompany me? There's the train, of course, but it will be more convenient to have our own vehicle once we're in Burning Cove. We don't want to have to call a taxi every time we need to follow a suspect."

He tightened his grip on the phone. "No offense, Miss Lodge, but I don't think it would be a good idea for you to accompany me."

"Maggie, remember? Of course I have to go with you. I'm your cover."

"Excuse me?"

"To slip into the crowd without calling attention to ourselves, we will have to appear to be ordinary conference attendees. I know a lot about lucid dreaming. I can talk the language, if you see what I mean."

"Not really."

"I'll be able to blend in and provide you with a believable reason for being there."

"I don't think—"

"I'll take care of the hotel reservations and the conference tickets," Maggie concluded. "Don't worry about the cost."

It occurred to him he was losing control of the conversation, the case, and the client. He forced himself to concentrate.

"What about your job?" he asked. "You're supposed to be writing the advice column. How can you take off for Burning Cove?"

"It's very thoughtful of you to be concerned about my work, but there's no need to worry. The next two weeks' worth of Dear Aunt Cornelia advice is on the way to the editor as we speak. I'm a very efficient person. We'll need a good story to explain why you're with me at the conference. Don't worry, I'll think of something."

"I have to tell you, the very thought of you cooking up a cover story strikes fear in my heart."

Maggie either didn't hear him or wasn't paying attention.

"The more I think about it, the more it makes sense to take only one car," she said. "Miss Dewhurst insisted I use her lovely new Packard while she's away. I'll pick you up at nine tomorrow. What's your address?"

He wondered if he should panic.

"Eleven Beachfront Drive," he heard himself say.

"Got it. Do you have an evening jacket? You'll need one."

"An evening jacket?"

"It's Burning Cove. Of course you'll need an evening jacket. Don't worry if you don't have one. I'm sure you'll be able to rent something suitable when we get there. See you tomorrow at nine. Burning Cove is about a hundred miles north of L.A. We will be there in time for lunch."

There was a click. The phone went dead. He took the receiver away from his ear and stared at it for a moment. No question about it. He had lost control of the conversation, the case, and the client.

Definitely time to panic.

Chapter 8

The Packard's white leather seats were buttery soft. The polished wood inlay on the instrument panel gleamed. There was far more power under the mile-long hood than could be justified by any reasonable driver who was not on a racetrack.

Maggie Lodge drove like Wilbur Shaw roaring around the Indianapolis Motor Speedway. All she lacked was a pair of racing goggles.

The top was down, so Sam had to raise his voice to be heard above the whipping wind and the howl of the engine.

"Are you sure your employer won't mind you driving her car all the way to Burning Cove?" he asked.

"I told you, she insisted I use the Packard as much as possible," Maggie called back. "Isn't it gorgeous?"

"It's a lot of car," Sam said.

"What?"

"Never mind."

The car was beautiful, and under other circumstances—if he had been at the wheel, for example—he would have been enjoying himself.

AMANDA QUICK

The day was perfect for a drive up the coast—crystal clear blue skies and a diamond-bright ocean. But the lady at the wheel was transforming what should have been a pleasant road trip into a roller-coaster ride.

Maggie's shoulder-length hair was once again secured with a scarf that had been folded into a triangle and knotted under her chin. She wore a white silk shirt and a pair of high-waisted dark green trousers. Sunglasses and leather driving gloves added a dashing touch. She was the kind of woman a man's mother was supposed to warn him about: smart, independent, bold, reckless, unpredictable—downright scary.

He gripped the armrest and braced himself as Maggie accelerated out of another tight curve. He needed a distraction.

"About our cover story—" he said.

"Don't worry, I've got it all figured out."

"Is that right?"

"I'm going to tell people I'm doing research for a book on lucid dreaming and that you're my assistant. It will give both of us reasons to ask questions and interview people."

"You have an excellent imagination," he said.

"I know."

"Want some advice from a professional investigator?"

"Of course," she said. "I hired you for your expertise."

"If someone inquires, go ahead and tell them you're writing a book. That won't make people suspicious. Everyone thinks they can write a book. But let me ask the questions that relate to the investigation."

"Probably better to play it by ear, don't you think?"

"No," Sam said. "What do you know about the Guilfoyle Institute?"

"I told you, Arthur Guilfoyle is making a name for himself in the field of lucid dreaming. He says he can teach people to use his Method to open a pathway to their psychic senses."

"Is that so?"

"I hear skepticism."

"Yes, you do."

"Guilfoyle is not alone in his belief," Maggie said, launching the Packard out of another curve. "His theories are strikingly similar to those of Edgar Cayce, for instance."

"That does not reassure me."

"You've made it clear you are not a believer when it comes to the paranormal."

Some of the enthusiasm seeped out of her voice. It was replaced with the cool wariness he had detected two days before when she had walked into his office. He was surprised to realize he missed the warmth.

"In my experience, anyone claiming to have paranormal powers is a fraud or a quack or delusional," he said.

"What about intuition?" she asked.

He glanced at her, annoyed. "That's different."

"You're sure?"

"Positive. Every cop I know believes in intuition. Forget it. What else can you tell me about Guilfoyle?"

"Guilfoyle claims he can teach almost anyone how to become a lucid dreamer," Maggie said. "For those of us who do it naturally, he claims his Method will help us achieve greater control over our dreams."

"You do this lucid dreaming frequently?"

"Ever since my teens," she said. "I've got fairly good control, but it's far from perfect. Things sometimes go off script."

"Meaning you lose control of the dream?"

Her mouth tightened a little. "Yes."

"When that happens, I assume the dream becomes a regular dream?"

"Not exactly. Well, who knows what a regular dream looks like for someone like me?"

"What does that mean?"

"Never mind, it's not important," she said.

"Is there a practical application for the Guilfoyle Method, assuming it works?" he asked.

"Certainly." Enthusiasm sparked again in Maggie's voice. "A person who is plagued by nightmares, for example, might be able to use the technique to rewrite the scripts of the bad dreams."

He heard the ghostly whisper of his intuition and knew that for Maggie, the possibility of rewriting a nightmare was more than a matter of curiosity or academic interest. It was personal.

"I can see the appeal," he said, trying not to sound like a skeptic. "Who wouldn't want to be able to rewrite a bad dream?"

"Exactly." She braked for a curve. "I do find that my lucid dreams are often quite helpful when it comes to generating plot ideas."

He went cold. "Plot ideas? You're a writer?"

"I'm working on a novel of suspense, but so far I've only been able to sell short stories to the confession magazines. Not much money in that kind of publishing, and to be honest, I'm not very good at it. That's why I'm assisting Lillian Dewhurst. I need the extra cash."

He closed his eyes for the next curve. "Why aren't you any good at writing confessions?"

"The stories all have the same theme—sin, suffer, repent." Maggie downshifted. "It's the female protagonist who gets to do the sinning, of course, and it almost always involves sex. Illicit affairs, that sort of thing. I'm good with that part. It's fun to write. But it's incredibly boring to do the suffer-and-repent bits."

He gripped the edge of the window frame in preparation for another curve. "Let me guess—you're not writing from personal experience."

"Of course not. No one could rack up that many interesting experiences no matter how hard she tried. What success I've had in the magazine market is a tribute to my creativity, if you ask me. You'd be surprised how difficult it is to come up with a lot of fake confessions."

"I am, of course, shocked to hear that those magazines are printing fiction."

She laughed. "The same way the detective and police magazines print fake crime stories."

Sam gazed straight ahead at the two-lane highway and considered the fact that he had a writer for a client, one who wrote fake true confessions. Could this case get any screwier?

It was time to change the subject.

"Where are we staying in Burning Cove?" he asked.

"Sadly, not the Burning Cove Hotel." She stomped on the gas as they came out of a curve. "Two reasons. First, I doubt if I could have gotten reservations on such short notice. Second, the Institute recommends that conference attendees stay at a nearby hotel, the Sea Dream, which is affiliated with the Institute and is within walking distance of the grounds. I was able to get us connecting rooms. That way we'll be able to discuss our findings in private."

Our findings. The words chilled his gut. Or maybe he was getting carsick.

"There are two formal receptions," Maggie continued. "I believe I mentioned the champagne event scheduled for tonight. The other event is a farewell cocktail party on the third night of the conference. Did you bring an evening jacket, or should we go shopping in Burning Cove?"

He held his breath as Maggie braked for another curve. Distraction was no longer working.

"You'd better pull over," he said.

"Why?"

"Two reasons. The first is that it's my turn to drive."

"I don't mind driving. I enjoy it."

"The second reason is that if you don't pull over and change places with me, I am going to be ill all over these nice leather seats."

"A delicate stomach?"

"Oh, yeah. Very delicate."

She slowed the Packard and pulled into a turnout. He opened his door with a sense of relief and extricated himself from the depths of the seat. Maggie got out on her side of the car. Without a word they changed positions.

He put the convertible in gear, pulled out onto the highway, and drove toward Burning Cove at a sedate pace.

"I guess you aren't accustomed to fast cars," Maggie ventured after a moment.

"Guess not."

"I'm sure you'll get used to this one soon," Maggie said encouragingly. "It's exciting to drive."

"Uh-huh."

"About your evening jacket," she said.

"Don't worry. I've arrested a few mobsters in my time. I know how to dress for a town like Burning Cove."

Chapter 9

ooks like they intend to sell the hell out of the Guilfoyle Method," Sam said. "This place must have cost a fortune, not to mention the money it took to remodel it so it could be used for commercial purposes."

"I must admit I'm a little surprised, myself," Maggie said. "Guilfoyle is a rising star in the dream analysis world, but I didn't realize he was this successful."

They were standing in an alcove on one side of the vast room, champagne glasses in hand. Together they watched Arthur Guilfoyle and his wife, Dolores, welcome guests to the champagne reception. There were at least a hundred people so far, and more were arriving by the minute. The women floated around the room in beaded gowns and sparkling jewelry. As Maggie had predicted, the men wore evening jackets.

Sam figured that between his career as a homicide detective in L.A. and his short-lived marriage to the daughter of a wealthy tycoon, he had seen the interiors of enough mansions to be able to judge the old

Carson Flint estate. No question about it, the sprawling complex of Spanish Colonial–style buildings that was now the Guilfoyle Institute was impressive even by Southern California standards.

The estate had been constructed on a large chunk of property situated above the rugged cliffs just outside Burning Cove. Some of the smaller structures that had probably once housed caretakers and household staff were still awaiting renovations. It was clear the new owners had poured cash into the main building, a couple of guest villas, and the vast gardens.

The proportions inside the lobby of the Institute were on a grand scale. Every doorway and window was oversized, arched, and framed in dark wood. Massive wrought iron chandeliers hung from heavy wooden beams. The floor was covered in warm terra-cotta tiles. The area rugs were done in deep, rich Mediterranean colors. Sam knew he was no expert on art, but the paintings hanging on the plastered walls looked expensive.

Maggie had brightened immediately when he'd joined her in the hall outside their hotel rooms wearing the white jacket and the bow tie and the rest of the evening outfit. She had looked so relieved he had immediately decided not to mention that every item, including the gold cuff links, was a leftover from his doomed marriage. Like the coatrack.

Elizabeth had done her best to try to make him blend in with L.A. society. She had failed. It wasn't her fault. He had known from the start he would never be more than an observer in her world, and a disinterested one at that. The more he had observed, the less he had wanted to become a part of the upper-class social set in which Elizabeth moved.

It struck him that being here with Maggie was different. He was comfortable standing in the alcove with her for a couple of reasons. The first was that she wasn't asking him to become something he wasn't. She had been concerned about the evening jacket only because she thought it constituted the camouflage he needed to go undercover for the investigation.

So yes, she was enthusiastic when it came to telling him how to do his job, but he had no problem with that. He already knew how to do his job. He found it entertaining to have her instruct him in the art of investigation. Okay, it was also irritating. Why did it amuse him? One of the mysteries of the universe, probably. Make that one of the mysteries of Maggie Lodge.

As for the second reason why he was happy to stand here with her—well, he wasn't sure what it was yet, but there was another reason, of that he was positive.

Her own camouflage this evening was entirely satisfactory, as far as he was concerned. She wore an emerald-green number with short, fluttery sleeves. The dress was demure in front and cut low in back, and it clung to her feline curves. The silky fabric flowed over her hips and stopped just short of her very nice ankles and green evening sandals.

Her hair was parted in the center and clipped back behind her ears with a couple of combs. It fell in soft waves to her shoulders. Her jewelry was limited to a pair of simple gold earrings and a tiny evening bag studded with gold sequins. Classy. He would have been content to stand in the alcove with her all evening, sipping champagne and studying the crowd.

Studying the crowd.

That was it—the second reason why he liked being here with Maggie. She was an outsider—an observer—like him. He wasn't sure how he knew that, but he trusted his intuition. Maybe, deep down, they actually had a few things in common. But probably not.

"Guilfoyle may be a fake psychic selling dreams, but judging by the size of this crowd, it's obvious he's got a real talent for promotion," he said.

Maggie sipped a little champagne, but she did not take her attention off the people milling around the grand room. He knew she was searching the faces of those around them, trying to spot the woman who was posing as her employer.

"I told you, Guilfoyle has some interesting theories and techniques," she said. "That's why I originally planned to attend this conference."

Sam watched Arthur and Dolores Guilfoyle play the role of gracious hosts at the entrance of the lobby. They made a handsome, glamorous couple. Dolores was a striking, sophisticated blonde. She wore a pale pink gown that glittered with what must have been a million pale pink sequins. Long pink gloves, a dainty pink bag, and a lot of jewelry completed the outfit.

Arthur had the dark eyes and chiseled profile of a leading man. He deployed a polished charm that seemed to work as well on men as it did on women. His black-and-white evening clothes fit his tall, lean frame with a perfection that could be achieved only through hand-tailoring. His dark, collar-length hair was brushed back from a dramatic widow's peak and gleamed with just the right amount of oil.

In addition to the Guilfoyles, four attractive young people—two male and two female—circulated around the room offering champagne and a warm welcome. They wore name tags identifying them as dream guides. They all looked as if they had been borrowed from a movie studio for the evening.

"Do you think there's something wrong with Guilfoyle's eyes?" Sam asked in low tones.

"His eyes?" Maggie was obviously surprised by the question. "No, what makes you ask that?"

"I noticed a weird look in them when he kissed your hand."

"Oh, right." Maggie smiled. "Mr. Guilfoyle possesses what is called a smoldering gaze."

"I thought maybe he had a vision problem. Does the smoldering thing work on you?"

"Under other circumstances, I might find it entertaining, but I have other interests at the moment."

"You take this dream research stuff seriously, don't you?"

Maggie shot him a steely smile. "Yes. I do."

"Why?"

She blinked. Apparently she had not expected the question. A cool, considering expression lit her eyes.

"I told you, I frequently have lucid dreams, so naturally I'm very interested in the research that is going on in that field."

It sounded like the truth, but not the whole truth. He was used to dealing in half-truths. You got a lot of experience with them when you worked in law enforcement. They came from victims, suspects, and witnesses. Now that he was in the investigation business, it looked like he would be getting them from clients.

"I understand your interest is personal," he said. "I was just wondering—"

She shot him a warning smile. "Enough about me. Let's talk about you."

"What do you want to know?"

"We can start with the coatrack in your office. Did you get rid of it?"

"No."

She nodded in a knowing way. "I was sure you wouldn't."

"It's not like I've had a lot of time to redecorate the office. Don't I get some credit for showing up in an evening jacket tonight?"

"Yes, you do." She studied the jacket. "It's very nice. You don't look like a mob boss at all."

"Have you ever met a mob boss?"

"Well, no. But I go to the movies and read the papers like everyone else."

"It's good to know I don't look like Dillinger or Capone."

"Much classier," she assured him.

Was she teasing him?

Before he could decide, she turned back to her survey of the room.

"There are a lot of people here tonight. I'm worried we won't be able to spot the imposter in this crowd."

"Don't worry, we'll know when she arrives."

That got Maggie's attention. She glanced at him, intrigued. "What makes you think so? We're too far away from the Guilfoyles to hear the names of the guests when they are introduced."

"Judging by the fact that the imposter managed to get herself into the celebrity gossip columns of the newspapers, I don't think she's trying to hide. She wouldn't have gone to that local nightclub and had her picture taken if she hadn't wanted to be noticed."

Maggie narrowed her eyes. "I see what you mean. That is very good thinking. Logical."

"I read *The Maltese Falcon*."

"So did I." Enthusiasm warmed Maggie's voice. "What do you think of Mr. Hammett's portrayal of the private detective? There are those in the literary world who have called that book a quintessentially American novel and an important work of modern fiction. Gertrude Stein is said to be a great fan of Hammett's mysteries."

Maggie paused with an expectant air. Sam looked at her.

"What?" he said.

She smiled encouragingly. "You are the first person I've met who is in a position to judge the character of Sam Spade in *The Maltese Falcon* from an insider's point of view. What did you conclude?"

By now he should know better than to resort to wisecracks with Maggie, Sam thought.

"Hammett's detective is an arrogant, egotistical, narcissistic ass," he said. "I'd say he has the moral code of an alley cat, but that would be unfair to cats. He isn't interested in justice. His only goal is to prove to himself and everyone else that he's the strongest, smartest guy in the room, and he doesn't care who gets hurt in the process."

Maggie stared at him, her mouth open in shock.

"Too many big words?" he asked.

She blinked a couple of times, closed her mouth, and got a thoughtful expression.

"I knew there was something wrong with that character," she said. "I couldn't put my finger on it, but it was obvious he wasn't good hero material."

"Also, he's a lousy detective," Sam said.

Maggie's eyes widened. "Really?"

"Every investigator makes mistakes, but drinking a cocktail the bad guy mixes for you at a critical point in the case is not a real smart professional move," Sam said.

"You're right," Maggie said, clearly impressed. "I never thought of that. Sam Spade knows Gutman is a criminal and yet he drinks the cocktail that Gutman serves him. The drink is laced with a drug that renders Sam unconscious. I must tell you, however, that from a writer's point of view, sometimes one needs a plot twist that allows—"

"Miss Smith. What an astonishing coincidence."

Maggie froze. Sam turned to see a distinguished-looking man with thinning hair, spectacles, and a gold signet ring bearing down on them.

"Damn," Maggie said, her voice barely above a whisper. "You're about to meet Dr. Emerson Oxlade, manipulative liar and pathetic dream analyst."

"Why did he call you Miss Smith?" Sam asked.

"I'll explain later."

She was furious, Sam decided, not fearful. Another Maggie mystery.

Before he could ask any more questions, Dr. Emerson Oxlade was upon them. Sam decided that even if he hadn't been aware Maggie did not like Oxlade, he would have found the man annoying. Oxlade radiated pompous arrogance, but it was the sheen of unwholesome excitement in his eyes that set off alarm bells. It looked a lot like obsession, and it was fixed on Maggie.

Oxlade stopped in front of her. Looming.

Maggie deliberately took a step back. "Dr. Oxlade."

"I had no idea you would be here tonight, Miss Smith." Oxlade closed the distance between them. "I assume you are attending the conference because you are still seeking therapy for your disturbing dreams. I did warn you it was a mistake to end treatment, my dear."

Maggie gave him a pitying smile. "You are obviously having memory problems, Dr. Oxlade. My name is Miss Lodge, not Miss Smith, and I never saw you for treatments of any kind. I booked a couple of professional consultations with you. Unfortunately, you had no idea what you were doing. You were clearly out of your depth."

Sam realized they had both forgotten about him. He moved toward Oxlade, just a step. Oxlade did not appear to notice him, but he automatically retreated, the way a person did when a stranger got too close. The small maneuver gave Maggie some breathing room.

Oxlade got a concerned expression. "I was afraid of this, my dear. You are suppressing your lucid dreams rather than learning how to control them, and the result is that you are allowing them to distort memory and reality. You need therapy."

"No," Sam said. "She doesn't need your therapy. She's got me."

Maggie and Oxlade looked at him as if they had suddenly realized he was present.

"Are you an expert in lucid dreams, sir?" Oxlade's expression made it plain he doubted that possibility. "Perhaps I've heard of you. I know everyone of importance in the field."

"Allow me to introduce you to my research assistant," Maggie said. "Mr. Sage, this is Emerson Oxlade."

"*Dr.* Emerson Oxlade," Oxlade corrected smoothly.

"Oxlade," Sam said. He did not offer his hand.

Irritation sparked in Oxlade's eyes but he suppressed it immediately. "What sort of research do you do, Sage?"

Maggie took charge. "I'm writing a book about quacks and charlatans in the dream analysis business. Mr. Sage is an expert on exposing frauds."

Oxlade's brows bunched together in deep concern. "You are hardly qualified to write that sort of book, Miss Smith. Or Lodge."

"I disagree," Maggie said. "I have had a great deal of experience identifying quacks. They are amazingly common."

Rage flashed in Oxlade's eyes. "Sadly, it appears your failure to accept professional guidance has led you down a dangerous path, Miss Lodge. I advise you to be very careful. There is considerable risk involved in slandering respected members of the medical profession. Annoy the wrong people and you will find yourself swamped with lawsuits."

"Are you threatening Miss Lodge?" Sam asked, keeping his tone politely inquiring. "It sounds like you're threatening her, but I like to be sure before I jump to conclusions."

"I am giving Miss Lodge some professional advice," Oxlade snapped. "I'll give the same advice to you. Research assistants can be sued, too."

He turned and stalked off into the crowd.

Sam watched him for a moment. "Care to tell me what that was all about?"

"That was about me letting my emotions get the best of my common sense."

"Thought so. Generally speaking, professionals in the detective business do not recommend a loss of temper when you're trying to stay undercover. It attracts attention."

"I'm aware it was a mistake," Maggie said, her voice tight. "Unfortunately, I lack experience in this sort of thing."

"What's done is done, so forget it, but you had better fill me in. What happened between the two of you?"

"About five months ago I made a couple of consultation appointments with Oxlade to discuss my dreams."

"Why?"

"It requires a lot of skill to achieve control over a dream script. Gaining and keeping the techniques is an ongoing process, at least for me. I'm good, but far from perfect."

"You do realize how odd that sounds to someone like me," he said.

"You are not the only one who finds the subject of lucid dreams odd. That's why I generally refrain from discussing the subject with people who are not interested in metaphysics."

"Tell me more about Oxlade."

"The first session went well. He understood what I was talking about. To give the devil his due, he really has studied lucid dreaming. I didn't like the man or his office, but I thought I could work with him."

Sam decided to ignore the comment about Oxlade's office. Probably another furniture problem.

"What happened?" he asked.

"At the second meeting Oxlade slipped a drug into the tea he served me. He called it his *enhancer.* I got the impression he concocts it himself. It was odorless and tasteless. The session started out as usual. I was in the middle of describing my most recent dream experience when I suddenly found myself falling into a waking nightmare."

"What does that look like?"

"I began hallucinating. The walls and ceiling of the office appeared to dissolve. The furniture floated. It was all very bizarre. Thankfully I realized what was happening. I managed to suppress the hallucinations and get out of the office." Maggie paused to take a sip of her champagne. "There was a struggle."

"With Oxlade?"

"He came after me with a syringe full of a sedative. Claimed I was hysterical. Having a nervous breakdown."

"I take it Oxlade lost the struggle?"

"I threw a few things at him. I remember a glass ashtray and a large vase of flowers."

Sam nodded, impressed. "Nice work."

Maggie glanced at him as if she didn't quite know what to make of the compliment. "You believe me?"

"Why wouldn't I?"

"Maybe because my story sounds like the imaginings of a hysterical woman? Among other things, Oxlade said I was prone to hysteria. Weak nerves, you see."

"Oxlade wants you."

Maggie sputtered on a sip of champagne and coughed once or twice. "Just to be clear, Oxlade's interest in me isn't personal. Well, it's personal, but not—"

"Sexual? I could tell. What does he want?"

"I've thought about that a lot in the past few months. Pretty sure he wants to run experiments on me using his stupid enhancer drug."

"Because of the way you dream?"

"Yes."

"Why does he care that you are a lucid dreamer?"

Maggie tightened her grip on the champagne glass. "I can't prove it, but I think he's got some crazed notion of controlling my dreams."

"Controlling your dreams?"

"That makes me sound paranoid, doesn't it?"

"Well, sure, but I'm fine with paranoia. Sometimes it's warranted. What would be the point of controlling your dreams, assuming such a thing would even be possible?"

"That," Maggie said, "is a very good question. There is a theory that when we dream we are in a trancelike state that is similar to what happens when a person is hypnotized. I suspect Oxlade is convinced that if he can induce a lucid dreamstate with his drug, he will be able to control the dreamer."

"By implanting a hypnotic suggestion while the person is dreaming?"

"Yes, I think so. I can't imagine any other reason for wanting to control another person's dreams. I think he selected me for his experiments because I frequently have lucid dreams naturally. He probably thought it would be easier to test his theories on someone like me."

"Let me see if I've got this case doped out. In addition to chasing an imposter advice columnist and someone who is trying to blackmail the real columnist, we're also dealing with a mad scientist who wants to run bizarre experiments on you?"

"In fairness, I don't think Oxlade is mad—just obsessed," Maggie said. "But yes, this case is complicated by his presence. You can understand why I wanted to employ a professional such as yourself."

"Absolutely," Sam said, his tone grave. "This is not a job for an amateur."

Maggie chuckled. "Luckily for the sake of our partnership, I've read Hammett and I've seen enough detective movies to know that the wisecracks are an important aspect of your professional image."

"That's swell, but let's get something straight here. We don't have a partnership. I'm the detective. You are the client."

"Yes, of course, but I didn't want to point out that distinction, because it underscores the fact that I'm the one in charge."

"It does?"

"Well, yes," Maggie said. "I'm the one who will write the check for your services."

She had a point. He decided not to pursue that angle. "I've got to say this private investigation work is turning out to be different from what I expected when I set up shop last week."

"What did you expect?" she asked.

"When I opened the doors of Sage Investigations, I figured I'd be spending most of my time hiding in the bushes taking photos of men cheating on their wives or wives cheating on their husbands. Divorce work. Never thought I'd wind up in an evening jacket at a ritzy champagne reception for a bunch of people who want to learn how to control their own dreams."

"You didn't become a private investigator to do sleazy divorce work."

The absolute certainty in her words made him take his eyes off the crowd long enough to glance at her.

"I didn't?" he said.

"No. I realize there's probably some money to be made in that line, but I advise you not to take those sorts of cases."

He watched her for a moment, unaccountably fascinated. "Why did I open Sage Investigations?"

"I'm still working on that. I'll let you know when I figure it out. Then I'll be able to advise you on how to conduct your business. I've learned a lot as Aunt Cornelia's assistant. I'm quite skilled at giving good advice."

He was about to tell her he did not need business advice when a burst of flashbulbs lit up the night outside the entrance of the Institute. A ripple of awareness fluttered across the crowd. It was not the heated excitement that announced the arrival of a major Hollywood star, but it was clear someone of note was about to enter the room.

A moment later a woman swept through the door, pausing just long enough to make an entrance. Her bright red hair fell in deep waves around her shoulders. Her slinky red gown was cut very low in front. The glittering necklace draped around her throat looked heavy enough to sink her if she had the misfortune to fall into a swimming pool.

Sam listened to the low voices of nearby guests.

"That's her, the advice columnist, Aunt Cornelia," a woman whispered. "The paper had a photo of her at the Paradise."

"I never imagined she would be so glamorous," another woman remarked. "I always assumed she was older. More mature."

"So did I," the first woman said.

Arthur and Dolores Guilfoyle moved forward to greet "Cornelia."

Arthur raised his voice, projecting it so that everyone in the suddenly hushed room could hear him.

"My dear Aunt Cornelia, it is an honor to have you with us this evening. A glass of champagne, perhaps?"

"That sounds lovely." The woman calling herself Cornelia offered Guilfoyle a graceful hand sheathed in a red lace, elbow-length glove. "I am looking forward to attending your introductory lecture tomorrow. I'm convinced we can all benefit from the profound insights concealed in our dreams if only we can master the Guilfoyle Method."

"I hope you will find my talk and the other sessions that will be held here at the Institute helpful."

"I'm sure I will," Cornelia said.

One of the dream guides offered her a glass of champagne. She accepted it and was immediately surrounded by a throng of people.

The noise level of the crowd climbed back to its pre-Cornelia level. Sam turned to Maggie.

"Interesting," he said. "Looks like the fake Cornelia is working with the Guilfoyles to help promote the Method. Maybe this imposter business is nothing more than a marketing gimmick."

Maggie's eyes narrowed like those of an Old West gunfighter. She set her champagne glass down on the alcove table with an ominous clink. "How dare that woman pretend to be Cornelia? I'm going to have a talk with that fraud right now."

"Has it occurred to you that you will have a problem if you confront her and accuse her of being an imposter?"

"I can't let this go on."

"The *problem*," Sam said evenly, "is proving she's a fraud without revealing Lillian Dewhurst's real identity."

Maggie tapped one red-tipped fingernail on the table. "Damn."

"People who are cornered are dangerous and unpredictable. Also, keep in mind it would be awkward to prove she is not the real Cornelia in front of a crowd."

Maggie considered that briefly and finally sighed. She accepted the advice, but she didn't like it. "Have you got another plan?"

"Yes."

"What?" she asked, immediately perking up.

Her enthusiasm, as usual, made him nervous.

"We need more information," he said, trying to sound cool and competent. *You know, like a professional detective, Sage.* "You're paying me to deal with this situation. Let me do my job."

"Damn," Maggie said again.

"I'm giving you good advice."

"People almost never take good advice."

"I've noticed," Sam said.

Chapter 10

Beverly Nevins stopped in front of a door at the end of a long, shadowed hall, her chest tight, her pulse racing.

She was about to execute the first step of the plan, and she was stunned to realize she was suddenly terrified. She told herself she could not turn back now. There was too much at stake.

She was standing in a dimly lit wing of the main building. She could no longer hear the noise of the champagne reception going on in the lobby. The walls of the old estate were thick. According to the brochure she had picked up in the lobby, they were riddled with old corridors that had once been used by the household staff and by Carson Flint's houseguests, who took advantage of them to make clandestine visits to other people's bedrooms.

She took a deep breath, opened the door, and moved into the small theater. She stopped just inside, startled by the wildly flickering lights. The source was a strange, disturbing version of a nightclub mirror ball on the stage. The device spun around. Instead of showering the space with pretty colored droplets, it emitted rapid flashes of harsh white light. *Black-white-black-white-black-white.*

The effect was disorienting. It created strange afterimages. She wanted to look away but for a moment she was transfixed. She did not sense the other presence in the room until she heard movement behind her.

She knew then that things had gone terribly wrong. She had to get out of the theater, back to the safety of the lobby.

The door closed.

"What?" she said. "Who's there?"

There was no answer. With the door shut there was no light from the hall to modify the flickering lights. She tried to scramble backward, away from the shadowy figure, and nearly lost her balance.

"Stay away from me," she warned.

She came up hard against the aisle seat in the last row. The shadow moved toward her. She could not make out a face. She continued to retreat, using the backs of the seats in the last row to guide her. If she got to the aisle on the far side of the theater, she could run toward the stage and perhaps escape into the wings.

The shadow closed in quickly. Beverly reached the last seat and turned to make a dash for the stage.

The needle burned when it struck her shoulder from behind. The sedative took effect quickly. She collapsed into the aisle seat.

She was unconscious when the killer injected another drug into her arm, the drug that stopped her heart.

Chapter 11

The reception was at its height. The lobby was packed, but Maggie knew the crowd would soon start to dwindle. People would be departing for dinner and a night on the town. This was Burning Cove, after all. Tomorrow the conference attendees would be listening to lectures and attending demonstrations, but tonight there would be dancing and cocktails in shadowy nightclubs and hotel lounges.

"The imposter will probably leave soon," she said. "We should go out to the car and prepare to follow her."

"What's the point?" Sam kept his attention on the crowd. "She's obviously in town with the goal of being noticed. She'll be going to dinner at a fashionable restaurant and will then drop into a hot club. We won't learn anything watching her drink and dance for the rest of the night."

"What do you suggest?" Maggie asked, irritated but also curious.

"She's a celebrity. Everyone in town is aware she's here. It shouldn't be hard to find out where she's staying."

"Right." Maggie experienced a rush of excitement. "We locate her hotel and search her room while she's out on the town tonight. I should have thought of that myself."

"You just did. Consider the idea your own, because that wasn't what I had in mind."

She glanced at him, intrigued. "What's your plan?"

"We'll get the name of her hotel and call on her tomorrow morning when she's likely to be alone."

"What good will that do? You said yourself she'll deny everything."

"Maybe," Sam said. "But we'll learn a lot, not just by talking to her but by having an opportunity to catch her when she's not playing Aunt Cornelia. She'll be off balance."

"Hmm."

"Trust me, finding us at her door early tomorrow morning will make her very nervous," Sam said. "She won't have the safety of a crowd. She'll be alone."

"So?"

"Nervous people tend to panic. They make mistakes."

"I suppose that is one approach to this situation. Nevertheless, I prefer my plan. We've got a perfect opportunity to search her hotel room tonight, assuming we can find out where she's staying."

"A perfect opportunity to get arrested for breaking and entering," Sam said. "We're sticking to my plan. I'm the expert, remember?"

"I know, but—"

"Well, now, this is interesting," Sam said quietly.

Maggie realized he was focused on the other side of the room. She followed his gaze and was just in time to see the fake Cornelia disappear through the arched entrance of a dimly lit hallway.

"Maybe she doesn't know the ladies' room is in another wing," Maggie said.

"She knows where she's going." Sam set his unfinished champagne on the console table. "Stay here. I'm going to follow her."

"I'll come with you."

Sam hesitated but evidently concluded he did not want to waste time arguing. The fake Cornelia was already out of sight.

"All right," he said, "but we don't want anyone to notice us."

"Don't worry, the only person in the room who might pay attention to me is Oxlade, and he left some time ago," Maggie said.

Oxlade aside, it was clear she and Sam had not drawn the interest of anyone else at the reception. She was proud her cover story had worked. The Guilfoyles had greeted them politely when they'd arrived, but they had spent the rest of the evening mingling with attendees who evidently ranked much higher on the social ladder. The four attractive dream guides were doing the same thing—charming the obviously more affluent guests.

"Let's go," Sam said.

They made their way around the edge of the crowd and went into the shadowed hallway the imposter had entered. The main light fixtures were off, but a wall sconce glowed at the far end of the corridor where it intersected with another wing.

Maggie heard the crisp click of fashionable high-heeled evening sandals echoing from the far end of the hall. She saw the shadowy figure of the fake Cornelia turn the corner and vanish into the adjoining wing.

Sam stopped and opened one of the French doors. "We'll cut across the courtyard. It will be faster."

Maggie followed him out into the darkened garden. They went quickly along a flagstone path lit by a nearly full moon. A fountain murmured softly in the shadows.

"What if the doors on that side of the courtyard are locked?" she asked.

"I doubt if they are," Sam said. "Why bother? The courtyard is secured on all four sides. But even if they are locked, it won't be a problem."

"Meaning you can pick a lock?"

"You learn things when you arrest bad guys."

"I'll bet. You were definitely right about one thing—the imposter seems to know where she is going. If she was looking for the ladies' room she would have turned back by now."

The windowed doors that lined the hallway on the far side of the courtyard were, indeed, unlocked. Maggie followed Sam into the gloom of another dimly lit corridor. He drew her to a halt and touched her lips with one finger. She got the message.

The imposter was nowhere to be seen. Maggie was starting to fear they had lost their quarry when a woman's scream echoed from the far end of the hall. The primal sound raised the hair on the back of Maggie's neck.

"Sam," she whispered.

"Stay here," he ordered.

He started forward just as the door at the end of the corridor slammed open. The imposter flew out, silhouetted by bursts of flashing lights. She was no longer screaming. She appeared to be running for her life. Her long skirts whipped around her ankles.

She did not notice Sam until he loomed in her path. She scrambled to a stop, stricken.

"Please don't hurt me," she gasped. "I won't tell anyone. I swear, I won't tell anyone."

"Don't move," Sam said.

The imposter froze, automatically obeying the command. He stepped around her and disappeared into the room.

Maggie hurried forward and stopped directly in front of the fake Cornelia. "What's wrong? What happened?"

Her sharp tone of voice broke the momentary spell cast by Sam's order. The woman took a rasping breath.

"I don't know," she whispered. "I had nothing to do with it."

"Are you all right?"

"I have to get out of here," the imposter said.

She dodged around Maggie and fled down the corridor, heading toward the lobby.

Maggie went to the doorway and looked into the disturbing storm of flickering lights.

"Sam."

"Stay where you are," he said. "I just need to find—got it. Hang on."

The flickering lights abruptly ceased. A second later a bright spotlight came on, illuminating the stage at the front of the room. The heavy red velvet curtain had been pulled aside. She took a few steps into the space and realized she was standing at the back of a small ornate theater.

She shivered. Shadows—visible and invisible—cloaked the rows of seats. Something bad had happened in the room.

Out of long habit she suppressed her senses.

More lights came on, softly glowing wall sconces this time. Sam appeared from the wings and walked out into the spotlight.

"Found a bank of light switches back there," he said. He studied the metal canister sitting on top of the phonograph turntable. The device was dark and still now that it had been turned off. "What the hell is that thing?"

"It's a kind of flicker machine." Maggie walked down the aisle toward the stage, intrigued. "There's a strong light inside. When it's on, the light flashes out through the cutouts in the canister rotating on the turntable. People who study dreams sometimes use flickering lights to induce hallucinations or a trance. But, generally speaking, you have to sit quite close to the device to get the full effect. That one is an unusually large and powerful version. It must have frightened the imposter. That's why she ran out of here."

Sam shielded his eyes with one hand and looked toward the back of the theater. "No, that's not what sent her into a panic."

He went down the side steps and loped up the aisle on the far side of the theater. Maggie turned to see what had riveted his attention.

The invisible shadows that seethed in the theater were anchored to the seat at the end of the last row, where a woman in a cocktail gown was slumped, unmoving.

Sam touched the woman's throat with two fingers.

"She's dead," he said quietly.

Chapter 12

etective Brandon pushed his battered fedora back on his head and surveyed the contraption sitting on the stage. "What the hell is that gadget? Looks like a Halloween lantern on top of a phonograph."

"I'm told that's exactly what it is," Sam said. "It creates a lot of flickering lights that can induce a trance in some people."

He and Brandon, the head of Burning Cove's small homicide division, were standing on the stage of the theater. They were not alone in the room. A doctor was concluding an examination of the body in the last row. Arthur and Dolores Guilfoyle waited in the aisle near the entrance. When Sam had informed them of the death, they had both appeared stunned. Now their faces registered anxiety and tension.

It didn't require psychic talent to know what they were thinking. Having a conference attendee die on the premises would not make for good publicity.

Maggie was watching the scene from behind the last row of seats. Sam was sure he knew what was going through her head, as well. Her case had been complicated enough as it was. The discovery of the dead woman threatened to send things in a new and far more dangerous direction.

Brandon squinted at Arthur Guilfoyle. "You hypnotize people with that gadget?"

"I do not practice hypnosis," Arthur Guilfoyle declared coldly. "That's for charlatans and quacks. I am engaged in serious dream research and analysis. I designed the dream generator to induce a state of lucid dreaming."

Brandon continued to eye him with a dour look. "So there's nothing dangerous about that thing?"

Arthur's jaw was rigid. "No, of course not. It's a purely therapeutic device. Detective, I realize this is a tragic situation, but there is nothing to indicate that a violent crime took place in here. Is there any reason why the body can't be removed immediately? My staff has a very full program scheduled for tomorrow. They need time to prepare."

Brandon switched his attention to the doctor, who was in the process of latching his leather medical satchel.

"What do you say, Doc?" he asked.

The doctor shook his head. "No signs of violence. Miss Nevins's death may have been the result of natural causes—an underlying heart condition or an aneurysm, perhaps. But there is a recent injection mark in her right arm. I suspect an overdose. Intentional or accidental, I can't say."

"Drugs?" Brandon asked.

"Given the injection site and the fact that the body was found in this rather isolated location, I think that's the most likely explanation," the doctor said. "However, there is no sign of a syringe. It might have rolled under the seats."

Brandon looked at the two uniformed officers. "Search the theater for a needle. Be careful. Use gloves."

"Yes, sir," one of the officers replied. He switched on a flashlight.

AMANDA QUICK

Sam silently cataloged the facts that were available. Thanks to the contents of her evening bag, the deceased had been identified as Beverly Nevins. She had arrived in Burning Cove on the train from L.A. Dolores Guilfoyle had confirmed that Nevins was registered for the conference and that she was staying at the Sea Dream Hotel, but that was all anyone seemed to know about the dead woman.

Her cocktail gown and heels looked expensive and fashionable, but her jewelry didn't fit with the rest of the outfit. Nevins's chandelier earrings, stacks of bracelets, and chunky necklaces were stylish enough, but they appeared to be Bakelite and paste. No one had stepped forward claiming to be acquainted with Nevins.

Sam told himself there was no evidence the death had anything to do with his case, but his intuition was not happy with that observation. Dead bodies did not show up by accident in the middle of an already screwy case. In his professional experience, the law of no coincidences was as reliable as the law of gravity.

"Can we keep this out of the press?" Dolores Guilfoyle asked sharply. "This is clearly a tragedy but hardly a crime."

"Any idea why Nevins was in this room?" Brandon asked.

Dolores sighed. "I imagine she wanted to experience the dream generator. There is information about it in the brochure we give out to our guests. If she did, indeed, inject herself with some drug, she may have believed that the atmosphere in here would enhance the experience."

"If that's true it was a terrible idea," Arthur said. "To have a successful therapeutic experience with the machine, one must be guided by an expert in the Guilfoyle Method. I do those sessions in here because the atmosphere in this room is conducive to engaging the psychic senses."

"Yeah?" Brandon looked around. "Why is that? Feels like any other room to me."

"This is the old séance room," Dolores explained, her voice tight with irritation.

Brandon grimaced. "You're summoning ghosts and spirits in here?"

"No, of course not," Arthur said. "The man who built the estate, Carson Flint, was rumored to be fascinated with the occult. He hired mediums to hold séances for himself and his guests. As you can see, we have converted the room into a theater."

"How would Nevins have found this room?" Brandon asked.

"All of the guests can pick up brochures in the lobby," Arthur said. "There's a floor plan of the Institute inside. It's designed to help conference attendees find the correct lecture halls and seminar rooms. This place is quite large, as you can see. Some wings have not yet been remodeled. We don't want people stumbling into an area that is still undergoing construction."

Dolores Guilfoyle gripped the back of a theater seat. "Detective, we have no idea how Miss Nevins came to be in this wing of the Institute." She glared accusingly at Sam. "For that matter, we don't know why you and Miss Lodge were here, either."

Brandon raised bushy brows. "I was going to ask that question, myself."

Maggie spoke up from the doorway. "I wanted to talk to Aunt Cornelia. I'm a fan of her advice column. I never miss it. I was thrilled to discover she was here tonight. Mr. Sage and I followed her, hoping to catch up with her. We had begun to think she was lost and were about to offer to assist her when she opened the door of this room, disappeared inside for a moment, and then came running out. She was very upset. Obviously she had seen the body."

Not a bad version of events, Sam thought, especially considering that Maggie was making it up on the fly. Brandon and the others seemed satisfied. Aunt Cornelia was a celebrity, after all. Fans chased after celebrities.

Brandon surveyed the small group gathered in the room. "Where is Aunt Cornelia?"

"She left in a taxi shortly before you arrived, Detective," Dolores said. "She was distraught. I escorted her out to the cab."

Brandon reached inside his jacket and took out a notebook and a pencil. "Got a last name for Aunt Cornelia?"

Arthur and Dolores exchanged bewildered glances. Sam looked at Maggie and knew she was holding her breath.

Dolores shook her head. "No. She's registered as Aunt Cornelia. She said she preferred to use what she called her stage name. She's a celebrity, after all. That's what celebrities do. Hollywood actors all have screen names that are different from their real names. We are thrilled to have Aunt Cornelia among our guests, so we didn't insist on a last name."

"How did she pay for her ticket?" Brandon asked.

"Cash," Dolores said.

"Where is she staying?" Brandon asked.

"She told the cab driver to take her to a cottage on Rose Beach," Dolores said. "It's off Cliff Road, a couple of miles from here."

Well, that was easy, Sam thought. He glanced at Maggie and saw the glint of understanding in her eyes. They had an address for the fake Cornelia. With luck Maggie would take that as an indication that he knew how to do his job. Then again, that probably wouldn't stop her from offering advice.

Brandon finished jotting down the address and looked at the doctor. "I'll get a statement from her in the morning. Meanwhile, I'll take a look around Miss Nevins's room at the hotel. If everything is in order, I'll tell the staff to pack up her things tomorrow and put them in safe-keeping until someone claims them." He looked at the doctor. "Anything else for me, Doc?"

The doctor shook his head and hoisted his satchel. "Not unless you come up with something that warrants an autopsy."

"Doubt the family will authorize one," Brandon muttered. "Especially if it might indicate an overdose."

Maggie cleared her throat. "What about the possibility of a seizure caused by the dream generator?"

Sam and everyone else looked at her. The Guilfoyles were shocked. The doctor rubbed his jaw and got a thoughtful expression. Detective Brandon frowned and turned to Arthur.

"Is it possible for someone to suffer a seizure from that thing?" Brandon asked.

"Absolutely not." Arthur's jaw tightened. "Some people are disturbed by rapidly flickering lights, but I assure you the dream generator experience is not harmful."

Brandon grunted. "That's that, then. Time to track down next of kin. I hate this part of the job." He angled the fedora over his eyes and looked at Sam. "I'd like a word with you before we leave. Outside."

"Sure," Sam said.

The doctor motioned to two men waiting with a stretcher. "Take the lady to the morgue."

Sam followed Brandon out of the theater and through the French doors into the courtyard garden. Brandon stopped.

"Cop?" he asked.

"Ex," Sam said. "Homicide."

"Thought so. You've got the look." Brandon took out a pack of cigarettes, extracted one, and stuck it in the corner of his mouth. He did not light it. "Trying to quit. Wife says it's bad for the health."

"Yeah? The ads say smoking is good for the nerves."

Brandon shook his head. "Who you gonna believe?"

"Your wife is probably more honest than the people who sell cigarettes."

"That's what I figure. Where did you work homicide?"

"L.A."

"You're too young to be retired."

"Fired."

"Don't tell me you got caught taking bribes. Nobody gets fired for that, not in L.A. Bribes are considered one of the benefits of the job. Part of the pension plan."

"I arrested the wrong man. The family was not happy."

"Yeah, that'll do it every time," Brandon said. "Who'd you arrest?"

"John Harris Chichester the Third."

"The Bloody Scarf Murders. Right, that explains it. So, what are you doing here in Burning Cove?"

"I'm in the private investigation business now. My office is in Adelina Beach. Miss Lodge is a client. I'd rather that information did not get out while I'm working the case. The situation is somewhat delicate. Blackmail. People will get hurt if I'm not careful."

Brandon snorted in disgust. "And your case will fall apart if the Guilfoyles and everyone else discover you're a private detective."

"The extortionist will disappear if that happens. At this point I'm going on the assumption that whoever it is doesn't know who I am or what I'm doing here."

Brandon angled his head in the general direction of the hallway behind them. "You think the extortionist is attending this dream conference?"

"That's what it looks like."

"You've got everyone convinced Miss Lodge is writing a book about dreams and you're her research assistant." Brandon grimaced. "Sounds like a real screwy case."

"Beats divorce work."

"Anything would." Brandon thought for a couple of beats. "You'll give me a call if there's anything I need to know, right?"

"Yes. And thanks."

"For what?"

"Your discretion," Sam said. "It's appreciated."

"That's me. Fucking discreet."

Without another word they walked back inside. Brandon summoned his officers and headed toward the lobby. The Guilfoyles and Maggie were the only ones left in the corridor outside the theater.

Arthur Guilfoyle eyed Sam with suspicion. "If you don't mind, I'm going to lock up now."

"Right," Sam said. He took Maggie's arm. "We'll be on our way."

Maggie waited until they were out in the parking lot before she spoke.

"What did Detective Brandon want?" she asked.

"He doped out that I used to be a cop." Sam opened the passenger side door of the Packard. "Asked a few questions."

Maggie stopped. "He knows you were a police detective?"

"Cops usually recognize each other. Don't worry, Brandon won't be a problem, at least not for a while. I told him enough to keep him satisfied. We agreed I'll call him if I come across anything he ought to know."

Maggie looked anxious. "Did you tell him about Lillian Dewhurst?"

"No. At the moment his only concerns are Nevins's death and the possibility that someone is dealing drugs here at the Institute."

Maggie relaxed. "Good." She slipped into the front seat of the convertible and looked up. "You don't think that Beverly Nevins died of an accidental overdose, do you?"

"I can't rule it out, but I doubt it."

"I agree," Maggie said. "Something terrible happened in that little theater tonight, Sam."

"I know," he said.

He closed the door, rounded the long hood of the Packard, and got behind the wheel. He fired up the big engine and drove toward the road.

"What are you thinking?" Maggie asked.

"I'm thinking we had better have our chat with the fake Cornelia tonight," he said.

"You told me it was too soon to confront her. You said we needed more information and that I had no way to prove she's a fraud."

"The death of Beverly Nevins changes things. The imposter was shocked and badly frightened when she came running out of the theater tonight. Frightened people don't think clearly. They make mistakes. Sometimes they tell you more than they realize. You just have to know how to listen."

"That theory actually works?"

"According to *Detective Magazine*, it never fails."

Chapter 13

There were three cottages scattered across the bluffs overlooking the moonlit Pacific. It wasn't hard to figure out which one belonged to the fake Cornelia. Two of the three were dark, with no cars parked in the driveways.

The door of number three was open and the lights inside were on. There were two suitcases on the front steps. The imposter was busy stuffing a third grip into the trunk of a Ford sedan. She was no longer wearing the glamorous evening gown and her hair—now brown—was tightly pinned. She had on a pair of wide-legged trousers and a pullover sweater. Dressed for travel.

"I knew that red hair was a wig," Maggie said. Outrage shot through her. "She's leaving town."

"I had a feeling she might be running," Sam said.

He pulled into the drive and brought the Packard to a halt behind the sedan, effectively blocking the path to the main road. The fake Cornelia was trapped in the glare of the headlights. She whirled around. The expression on her face was all too easy to read.

"She's scared to death," Maggie said.

Sam shut down the engine and the headlights. He opened the car door. "The question is, what is she scared of?"

He climbed out from behind the wheel and stood beside the front fender. "Take it easy—I'm not a cop, and we had nothing to do with Beverly Nevins's death."

The imposter stared at him. "She was murdered, wasn't she? I knew it. Someone killed her."

"They're calling it a probable accidental overdose," Sam said. "But it's obvious you aren't buying that story. Neither are we. We want to ask you a few questions."

Maggie jumped out of the convertible. "He's right. Just some questions, that's all."

"Who are you?" The imposter retreated a step. "What do you want? I don't have any money. The clothes aren't mine. I didn't pay for the cottage. It's just a job, damn it."

Sam reached inside his jacket. The imposter's eyes widened in horror.

"No," she squeaked. "Please, don't shoot me."

"My business card," he said. He held it out to her. "Sam Sage, Sage Investigations. Miss Lodge is my client."

The imposter looked at the card as if she had never seen one before. After a few seconds she moved forward, snatched it out of Sam's hand, and hastily retreated a few paces.

She shook her head. "I don't understand."

"Let me clarify a few things for you," Sam said. "We know you're impersonating the real Aunt Cornelia."

"You can't prove that," the woman said. But there was no energy in the denial. "No one knows the identity of the real Aunt Cornelia, not even me."

"I know who she is," Maggie said. "I work for her. I'm her assistant. The real Cornelia is out of the country on an extended ocean voyage.

She's not due to return for another month. But you already knew that, didn't you?"

"Prove it," the woman whispered.

"That would take time," Sam said. "We don't have a lot of that because you are obviously in a hurry to get out of town."

"I've got news for you—stumbling over a body is hard on the nerves," the imposter shot back.

"I agree," Maggie said gently. "Let's start with something simple. What is your name?"

The imposter seemed to sink in on herself. "Phyllis Gaines."

"Why did you go into the theater tonight?" Sam asked.

"I was looking for the ladies' lounge."

"No," Maggie said.

Phyllis did not argue.

"Did you go to the theater to meet Miss Nevins?" Sam asked. "Or someone else?"

"I don't—" Phyllis closed her eyes. When she opened them again, she looked at Maggie. "Do you really work for the woman who writes that advice column?"

"Yes," Maggie said. "And speaking on her behalf, I can assure you that she would advise you to tell us what is going on here."

"Look, it was just a publicity stunt. A job." Phyllis sighed. "I'm an actress, see? Haven't worked much lately. I was sent money to buy the clothes and the jewelry I needed to carry off the role. I was told I could keep everything. I'm doing exactly that, by the way. I'm not stealing this stuff. It was part of the arrangement."

"Someone hired you to play Aunt Cornelia here in Burning Cove?" Sam asked.

"The plan was to promote the opening of the Guilfoyle Institute," Phyllis said quickly.

"What were you supposed to do if the real Aunt Cornelia showed up and objected?" Sam asked.

"I was told she would never know because she was traveling in the South Pacific. Look, I realize it all sounds a little shady, but—"

"A *little* shady?" Maggie said.

Phyllis took a step back. "I really needed the work, and there didn't seem to be any harm in it."

"You're telling us that whoever hired you knew the real Aunt Cornelia was out of the country?"

"I was assured she would never find out," Phyllis said. "All I had to do was play the role for a few days at the conference and then disappear."

"Who hired you to impersonate Aunt Cornelia?" Sam asked.

Phyllis frowned. "Someone from the Institute. Why?"

"I need a name," Sam said. "Guilfoyle? His wife?"

Phyllis shook her head. "No, it was a woman in the marketing department. Miss Finley. I never met her in person. The arrangements were all done on the phone. There was an envelope full of cash waiting for me when I checked into the cottage. I was supposed to get the second half of the money when I finished the job. But I got a message telling me to meet someone in that theater tonight. I was afraid I was going to be fired. When I saw the body, I panicked. If the cops decide it's murder, I'm going to be at the top of the suspect list."

"You may be right," Sam said. "But you've got a couple of eyewitnesses who can testify that you weren't inside the theater long enough to murder Miss Nevins."

"You two?" Phyllis grimaced. "Thanks but no thanks. I don't like my odds. I'm going to disappear until this mess blows over."

"You said you got a message telling you to meet someone in the theater this evening?" Maggie asked.

"Someone slipped it to me when I went to the ladies' room. It was shoved under the stall door. All I saw were a pair of evening sandals and a hand. The note said: *Meet me in the theater. Tell no one.* The floor plan of the Institute had been torn out of a brochure. The location of the theater was marked."

"Was the note signed?" Sam asked.

"Just an initial," Phyllis said. "It looked like the letter *T*, not *F* for *Finley*, but I figured maybe it was poor handwriting."

"On the basis of that you went to meet a stranger?" Sam asked.

Phyllis grimaced. "I told you, I thought the note was from the woman who hired me to play the part of Aunt Cornelia."

"What happened when you opened the door of the theater?" Sam asked.

"It took me a moment to see anything because of all those horrible flashing lights. They made me nervous. I was going to leave but I finally noticed the woman at the end of the last row. I assumed it was Miss Finley. I started toward her. When I got close I spoke to her. She didn't respond. I had a feeling something was wrong, but I didn't know what to do."

"Go on," Sam said.

"I thought maybe she was asleep or had fainted, so I tried to shake her awake," Phyllis continued. "That's when I realized she was dead or unconscious. I screamed. I thought I heard someone on the stage or in the wings."

"Did you see anyone?" Sam asked.

"No. I turned around but I couldn't see anything because I was looking straight at the flickering lights. I was terrified. All I could think about was getting out of there. I had to feel my way using the backs of the seats in the last row."

"When you saw me in the hall you thought I had something to do with the death of the woman you discovered in the theater," Sam said.

"I didn't know what to think. I was terrified."

"Tell me about the person you heard on the stage," Sam said.

Phyllis made a face. "I heard footsteps in the wings. That's all I know. Oh, and a door closed somewhere backstage."

"Man or woman?" Sam asked.

"I have no idea. I was not paying close attention. All I cared about was getting out of that horrible place. Do you think the police will want to talk to me?"

"Detective Brandon said he planned to get a statement from you in the morning," Maggie said.

"I knew it," Phyllis said. She went back to the front step and hoisted a suitcase. "I've got to get out of town tonight."

"I'm sure the woman in marketing who hired you over the phone, Miss Finley, will explain everything to the police," Maggie said.

"I doubt it." Phyllis tossed the suitcase into the trunk and went back to the front steps for the last grip. "It's starting to look like a setup. Someone murdered that woman in the theater and figured they could make me take the fall."

"It's a possibility," Sam said.

Phyllis slammed the trunk shut. "I should have turned down the job, but the money was too good to pass up, not to mention all the nice clothes."

"A setup for what, exactly?" Maggie asked.

"Who knows?" Phyllis said. "But there's obviously a lot of money involved in that Institute. Just look at the place. It must have cost a fortune. Wherever there's that much cash, there's always someone who will do whatever it takes to get it."

"Good point," Sam said. "Where are you going?"

"As far away from Burning Cove as I can get." Phyllis opened the driver's side door of the Ford. "Unless you point a gun at me, I'm leaving right now. If you don't move that nice Packard, it's going to sustain some major damage when I pull out of here."

"I'll move the car," Sam said. He opened the driver's side door. "If you think of anything else that would be helpful, you can leave a message at the Sea Dream Hotel. No need to tell the operator why you're calling. Just say you're a friend from out of town and would like to get together for a drink. Leave a number. We can meet you anywhere, anytime, and we'll pay you for your trouble."

"Yeah, sure, I'll be in touch."

Phyllis climbed into the front seat of the Ford and slammed the door. The engine rumbled.

"I won't hold my breath," Sam said.

He got into the Packard and backed it out of the way. Phyllis stomped on the gas. The Ford roared out of the drive, heading for Cliff Road. Maggie watched the headlights vanish around a curve.

Sam eased the Packard back into the driveway, turned off the ignition, and got out. He contemplated the open door of the cottage.

"What are you thinking?" Maggie asked.

"That Phyllis Gaines is probably exactly who she claims to be," Sam said. "An out-of-work actress who took a short-term job playing Aunt Cornelia for a few days, found herself caught up in something very dangerous, and wisely decided to disappear."

"I agree. What do we do now?"

"I'm going to take a quick look around the cottage. People in a hurry often leave something behind."

He went to the front steps and disappeared through the open door. Maggie rushed after him and arrived on the threshold just as he was retrieving a crumpled slip of paper from the wastebasket under the small console in the hall. She watched him unfold it.

"Is that the note that Phyllis Gaines got tonight?" she asked.

"Yes. I think it's safe to say it was sent by the blackmailer. The initial is definitely a T, not an F."

"The Traveler." Maggie shuddered. "That settles it. The extortionist doesn't know the identity of the real Aunt Cornelia and doesn't know what she looks like. What now?"

"I don't know about you, but I could use a drink," Sam said. "I would also like to eat dinner. Let's go back to the hotel. I saw a sign that said there would be piano music in the lounge. No need to waste this evening jacket."

She watched him turn off the lights and close the door of the cottage. He did not speak as they walked back to the car. Her intuition stirred.

"You've got a plan, don't you?" she said.

"I'm working on it."

"Is it illegal?"

"Let's just say I won't be phoning Detective Brandon to ask his permission."

"Thought so." She opened the door on the passenger side of the convertible. "We're sure now that Beverly Nevins was murdered, aren't we?"

"Yes, we are." Sam paused beside the driver's side door and looked at her. "Which means there is a strong possibility that four years ago Virginia Jennaway was murdered. We're looking for a connection that ties the two deaths together."

Satisfied, Maggie slipped into the front seat. "Excellent."

"What's that supposed to mean?" Sam asked.

"I like the *we're looking for a connection*. I think we are developing a true working relationship, don't you? A partnership."

Sam got behind the wheel. "I was afraid of that."

Chapter 14

T his is a fucking disaster." Arthur Guilfoyle took a long, deep swallow of his scotch and soda, lowered the glass, and sucked in a breath. "The news of Nevins's death will be in the local papers tomorrow. What are we going to do? We'll be ruined."

"Calm down," Dolores said. She picked up the silver lighter on the coffee table and lit her cigarette, giving herself a moment to decide how to handle Arthur's seething panic. It wasn't the first time he had lost his nerve at the hint of a crisis. He was an actor, after all—high-strung, impulsive, easily rattled. "The death of Miss Nevins is unfortunate. However—"

"Unfortunate? It could destroy me."

Us, Dolores corrected silently. It could destroy *us.* Arthur had a way of forgetting they were a team. Yes, he was the star of the show, but she was the producer and director. It was her inheritance that was paving the way into the big time for the Guilfoyle Institute and the Method.

She walked to the window of the villa and looked out over the moonlit Pacific. The private villa was on the grounds of the Institute.

It had originally been one of four lavish guesthouses. Designed in the same Spanish Colonial style as the main building, it was perched high on the cliffs overlooking the restless waves that lashed the rocks below.

There had been only enough money to remodel two of the guest villas. The others were still empty and shuttered. The villas and the rest of the estate were her inheritance, the birthright that had long been denied her because the bastard who had fathered her had refused to recognize his illegitimate daughter.

Carson Flint had planned to leave Summer House to his legitimate son and heir. But Carson Flint the Second had succeeded in killing himself on a motorcycle shortly before his father died. Distraught at the realization that he had no legal heir, Carson had done what any self-centered mogul would do—he had left all of his worldly possessions to his only surviving offspring. She might be illegitimate, but at least his blood ran in her veins.

Sadly, while Flint had not been wiped out by the crash, he had lost a large portion of his fortune in the Depression that had followed. In addition to the run-down estate, Dolores had received barely enough money to renovate the main building and the two guest villas. From now on, the Institute had to start paying for itself.

"It's not as bad as it looks," she said, careful to use a soothing, reassuring tone. What she really wanted to do was scream at Arthur. "There will be a small mention of a tragic event here at the Institute, but that will be the end of it. Trust me, the death of a woman from out of town—a nobody—is not front-page material. It's not as if Beverly Nevins was a movie star or the daughter of a tycoon."

"You'd better be right."

Some of the panic was seeping out of Arthur. Dolores considered how to move on to the disturbing questions that had been raised that evening. She decided to go with a straightforward approach.

"Were you sleeping with her, Arthur?" she said. "Was she one of your devoted acolytes?"

"*No.*" Arthur sputtered on a mouthful of scotch and soda. "I never met the woman until tonight, when she came through the reception line. I forgot her name as soon as she was introduced."

Dolores decided to give him the benefit of the doubt. Arthur's movie-star looks combined with his talent for seduction and his promise to help a woman access the psychic side of her dreams was irresistible. Hell, back at the start she had leaped into bed with him, just like all the others over the years.

Eventually the novelty of their affair had worn off for Arthur, but by then he had found her useful because she had a head for business, and he knew he desperately needed a business manager.

Eighteen months ago she had come into her inheritance. That had cemented the relationship as nothing else could have done. Arthur had begged her to marry him. She had agreed because she had discovered he was as useful to her as she was to him. His gift for seduction was not limited to individuals. Arthur could seduce an entire audience. His talent had never translated to film, but it was amazing to behold in person.

His acting ability combined with a complete lack of conscience made him a consummate liar, but she was almost certain he was not lying tonight. She did not need to watch his face to know when he was trying to con her. They had been together long enough for her to be able to hear the truth or lack thereof in his voice. He was definitely unnerved by Beverly Nevins's death. He was far more concerned with the future of the Institute than with covering up a meaningless affair.

And they were all meaningless. That was the one thing she could be sure of when it came to Arthur. No woman mattered to him, not for long. He was the most self-absorbed individual she had ever met. As-tonishingly, his lovers, including her, never realized that until he lost interest in them. When that happened—and sooner or later he always lost interest—it was as if he had switched off a light. Probably a tribute to his acting talent.

"You heard the doctor," Arthur said. "The Nevins woman might have died of an overdose."

"Relax," she said. "This is Burning Cove. No one is going to be shocked by rumors of drugs."

"What if someone connects the Nevins overdose to Jennaway's death?"

It was her turn to take a deep breath. "That could be a problem. But it's not going to happen."

"You're sure?" Arthur finished his drink. "When you think about it, there are some similarities."

"No," Dolores said. "The two incidents are very different."

"You're sure?"

"Positive. For one thing, there is no way Nevins could have gotten hold of Oxlade's drug. He's the only one who knows the formula."

"He brought a supply with him," Arthur said.

"Yes, but you know as well as I do he treats the stuff like liquid gold. He refuses to sell it. Why would he waste any of it on a random stranger in uncontrolled conditions? He's a scientist. All he cares about is his research and his reputation."

Arthur grimaced. "I know."

"There are plenty of common drugs out there that can be lethal. Heroin, sedatives, morphine, cocaine. Besides, Oxlade swears the new version of the enhancer isn't as dangerous as the old one. He says the worst that could happen with an overdose would be severe hallucinations for a few days."

"During which time a person could walk out a window or try to fly off a cliff." Arthur went to the drinks cart to mix another scotch and soda. "Or maybe take a midnight stroll on the beach and get swept away by a rogue wave."

"Stop talking like that." Dolores tapped ashes into the elegantly molded glass ashtray. "That was four years ago. There is absolutely no indication that Nevins got hold of the enhancer. The doctor said it looked like she injected herself, remember? The enhancer is always taken orally."

Arthur took a calming breath. "You're right. Of course, you're right. I didn't think about that aspect."

"We may, however, have another problem involving Oxlade."

Arthur gulped some of his drink. "We need him, Dolores."

"I admit he's useful, but—"

"He gives the Institute credibility. He's a respected doctor. He's got credentials. Having him promote the Guilfoyle Method will do wonders for our image. It separates us from the quacks and the frauds."

"Oxlade has convinced you he can make the Institute successful, but you saw the crowd tonight. Those people bought tickets because of you, not Oxlade. No one paid any attention to him. He needs us, not vice versa."

"I know you don't trust the guy," Arthur said.

"You're wrong. I trust him because I know exactly what he's after. As you said, he's obsessed with his research. All he cares about is getting published in the most prestigious journals. He has concluded he can use us and the Institute to provide him with a well-equipped lab and an unlimited number of test subjects—the things he needs to enhance his reputation. That's the only reason he's willing to cooperate with us."

"He may be a little obsessive about his work, but I'm telling you, he's onto something with his lucid dreaming drug," Arthur said. "I'm the living proof. Every time I've used the enhancer I've had the most amazing experience. I've seen things. I've had genuine visions."

Dolores sighed. "You hallucinated, Arthur. Oxlade hypnotizes you when you are under the influence of the drug. Or maybe you hypnotize yourself. Who knows? Whatever happens when you take the enhancer, it's not a genuine psychic experience."

"You're wrong." Arthur's eyes heated with excitement. "I'm able to access my latent psychic talents. Yes, it's disorienting and hard to explain, but the experience is genuine, not a hallucination. Oxlade says not everyone has the talent for it, but I am a natural lucid dreamer. The drug takes me to the next level. I just need time to learn how to control the experience."

This was not good. Dolores pulled hard on the cigarette. The situation was worse than she had realized. Arthur had crossed the line. He had become a true believer in Oxlade's theories and the drug. It was a worrisome turn of events.

"We got into this business to make money," she said quietly. "We told each other we could never go wrong selling dreams."

"But think of the possibilities," Arthur said. There was a feverish energy about him. "Thanks to Oxlade's drug we can offer a unique, incredible dream experience. People will pay fortunes for the Guilfoyle Method."

Money always got her attention. She had been focusing on the realization that Oxlade had gained too much influence over Arthur. Maybe she needed to step back and consider the situation from a purely financial perspective. No, they wouldn't be selling a genuine psychic experience. But what if they could sell something that felt like the real thing? Arthur was right. People would pay any amount for a drug that made them believe they could tap into their psychic senses.

She took another drag on the cigarette while she considered the possibilities. "Tell me the truth. Do you really feel as if you are able to experience psychic visions when you take Oxlade's drug?"

"If it's not real, it's as good as the real thing," Arthur said. "It's an incredible experience every time. You should try it."

"Forget it," she said automatically. It was the same answer she always gave whenever he suggested she experience the drug. She knew a lot about drugs, more than enough to make her nervous about taking them. "The plan will work only if we control the enhancer."

"As long as we control Oxlade, we control the drug," Arthur said.

"I'm worried about his insistence on running an endless number of experiments."

"Oxlade says he needs to conduct more tests before he can guarantee the results," Arthur said. "We will insist he does his testing here at the Institute. If we don't take advantage of this opportunity, some other smart operator is going to realize there's a fortune to be made off the drug. Whoever it is will offer Oxlade whatever he wants."

"One of the things he wants is Miss Lodge," Dolores said. "You heard what he said tonight. He's insisting we get her to cooperate with his experiments. How are we supposed to do that?"

Arthur's shoulder rose and fell in casual dismissal of the problem. "I'll handle Margaret Lodge."

Dolores stifled a groan. She knew Arthur better than he knew himself. The careless shrug was an example of his acting skill. What mattered was the all-too-familiar hint of sexual excitement in his voice. He was intrigued by Margaret Lodge. As if things were not complicated enough at the moment.

It certainly wasn't the first time he had been distracted by a woman who had drifted into his net, but Lodge was not his usual type. She wasn't a glamorous blonde. There was no indication she possessed connections in society or Hollywood. She appeared to be exactly what she claimed to be—a writer doing serious research for a book on lucid dreaming. Definitely not the kind of female who usually caught Arthur's eye. So why was he so interested?

"What makes you so sure you can convince her to let Oxlade run experiments on her?" she asked.

"Oxlade told us she used to be a patient of his, remember? She suffers from weak nerves and is prone to attacks of hysteria. I can work with that."

"What about that man who accompanied Lodge? The research assistant?"

"He's nobody. He won't be a problem." Arthur smiled his slow, seductive smile, the one that had come within inches of landing him a Hollywood contract. "Remember what we told ourselves back at the start."

She ground out the cigarette in the glass ashtray. "No one ever went broke selling dreams."

Chapter 15

"Phyllis Gaines misinterpreted the message she received at the end of the champagne reception," Sam said. "She assumed she was being summoned by the woman in marketing who hired her to play Aunt Cornelia. But what she actually got was a note from the blackmailer who believed she was the real Cornelia."

"It was the follow-up to the threatening letter that was sent to Aunt Cornelia in Adelina Beach," Maggie said. "The extortionist expected Phyllis to understand she was to follow instructions, go to the theater, and make the payoff. By playing the role of Aunt Cornelia, Phyllis Gaines unwittingly made a target of herself."

They had eaten dinner in the hotel dining room, and now she and Sam were sitting in a booth in the lounge. There were two glasses of brandy on the table. The shadowy space was lightly crowded. As promised by the sign in the lobby, there was piano music. The musician, dressed in a white evening jacket and black bow tie, was playing a moody jazz piece.

The lounge, like the restaurant, wasn't trying to compete with the more glamorous establishments in town, such as the Burning Cove Hotel or the Paradise Club. It was a quiet refuge for the convenience of guests who, for whatever reason, did not want to venture out in the evening. It was also perfect for couples seeking a low-key club for a clandestine rendezvous.

The words *clandestine rendezvous* sent a little thrill across her senses. Under other circumstances she could create a very pleasant fantasy that involved a clandestine rendezvous with Sam Sage/Bennett North. It would make for an interesting scene in the novel.

"A case of mistaken identity, but with a twist, because the extortionist didn't know what the real Cornelia looks like," Sam said.

It was obvious he was not thinking about a clandestine rendezvous.

"Past tense?" Maggie said. She picked up her brandy. "Do you think Beverly Nevins was the blackmailer?"

"It's a possibility. Extortion is a dangerous occupation. Blackmailers sometimes get themselves killed by irritated victims. The letter sent to your employer indicated there was more than one individual responsible for the death of Virginia Jennaway. If the other targets were instructed to attend the conference and make the payoffs here, one of them may have gotten to Nevins before Phyllis Gaines walked into the theater."

"That makes sense," Maggie said.

"But it's also possible Nevins herself was one of the targets," Sam pointed out. "Perhaps she refused to pay or threatened to expose the extortionist."

"Who murdered her to keep her quiet."

"We also need to talk to the woman who hired Phyllis Gaines to play the part of Cornelia," Sam said. "Miss Finley in marketing."

Maggie sighed. "There are so many questions here."

Sam looked at her, his brows slightly elevated. "Including one about the real Cornelia."

"What do you mean?"

"The more I think about it, the more I find Lillian Dewhurst's sudden decision to take a long voyage to the South Pacific one month ahead of the dream conference an interesting coincidence."

She smiled. "It's not really, not when you know the whole story behind her decision to board that ocean liner."

Sam drank some brandy and lowered the glass. "Explain."

"All right, but you probably won't believe me. No, that's not true. I think you'll *believe* that I think I'm telling you the truth, but you'll probably conclude that Lillian and I are gullible or mildly delusional."

Amusement glinted in Sam's eyes. "So long as it's only mildly delusional."

"Right." She sipped some brandy and set the glass down with great care. "I told you that Lillian and I share an interest in dream analysis, and lucid dreaming in particular."

"Dewhurst is a lucid dreamer?"

"Yes. Unfortunately, she is prone to nightmares. I've had considerable experience with bad dreams."

Sam had been about to swallow more brandy. He paused. "Are you saying you suffer from nightmares?"

She went quiet, taking a moment to consider just how much to tell him.

"I need information," Sam said. He was not demanding a response; he was asking quietly, sincerely. "I'm trying to fit pieces of a puzzle together. I could use some help. You're the one who keeps telling me we're working this case together."

She studied him for a moment. This was probably one of those occasions when she ought to keep her mouth shut or, alternatively, sidestep a straightforward response. There were ways to finesse questions such as the one he had asked. She was very experienced at evasive answers. *Everyone occasionally has nightmares. Lots of people have particularly intense dreams, which can be unnerving. Haven't you ever had a disturbing dream, one that wakes you up? A dream you can't forget?*

She rarely used the most truthful response, not with those who did not take dreaming seriously. *Have you ever had dreams that bring you awake in a full-blown panic? The kind in which you try to scream and can't? Worse yet, the kind in which you do come awake screaming? Nightmares that are so powerful and so real they make you think you're going to be trapped forever in a dreamstate? Dreams that are guaranteed to doom an intimate relationship? Dreams that make you fear sleep? Dreams that could land you in an asylum?*

No, she kept the honest answers for people who understood extreme dreaming. But this was Sam. He might not take dream analysis seriously, but she was sure he was very serious about his work. She had hired him for his expertise. The least she could do was give him the information he seemed to think he needed.

He might conclude she was naïve or overly imaginative or even inclined toward hysteria, but she sensed he would see the case through to the end. Afterward they would go their separate ways. She was safe because he wasn't in a position to have her committed to a hellish place like Sweet Creek Manor.

"Ever since my late teens I've been prone to dreams that seem so real they can be terrifying," she said. "Sometimes I woke up screaming or in the midst of an anxiety attack. Sometimes I was so exhausted from my dreams that I would drift off at my desk in school, go into another bad dream, and come awake in class in the middle of a nightmare."

"Awkward," Sam said. He sounded sympathetic but not shocked.

"Very awkward. My teachers and the other students were alarmed, to say the least. Actually, they were frightened. My parents took me to a series of doctors and dream therapists. After some of them recommended a stay in a sanitarium so that I could be treated for shattered nerves, my parents decided to give it a try. I spent two months in a private clinic. Sweet Creek Manor."

Sam watched her intently. "That must have been tough."

"Let's just say I still have nightmares about my time there." She swallowed some brandy, lowered the glass, and kept going, determined to finish what she had started. "I did learn some survival skills, however."

"Such as?"

"It became clear at Sweet Creek that I would have to learn how to control my dreams if I wanted to get out and stay out. If I failed, there was a very real possibility I would spend the rest of my days in an asylum." She paused. "I make some people quite nervous, you see."

"Is that right?"

She leaned forward. "Does it make you anxious to know you've got a client who, according to certain experts, ought to be locked up in a psychiatric hospital?"

"Beats divorce work."

She blinked and then, like the morning coastal fog, much of her inner tension dissolved. Or maybe the brandy was taking hold.

"I told you that you should not do divorce work," she said.

"I've made a note. So, you learned to control your dreams?"

"For the most part. But sometimes I still wake up thinking I'm going to get trapped in that other world."

"Other world?"

"That's what dreaming is like for me. When I sleep, I enter another dimension or world." She sighed. "I should have known better than to try to explain."

Sam's brows rose. "Why did you?"

"Call it a calculated risk. I agree you need all the information you can get in order to make progress on my case."

"What was the risk?"

"Giving you the information you wanted means you might conclude I'm unbalanced. You could drop my case. I don't want to have to find another private detective, but quitting is the worst thing you could do to me."

He put his glass down on the table with just enough cool precision to signal his anger. "What the hell is that supposed to mean?"

"You don't have the power to have me committed to an asylum," she said. She swallowed the last of her brandy and set down the glass. "It's not as if you're my husband."

Sam went very still. Understanding heated his eyes. "Your dreams are the reason you're not married, aren't they?"

She was shocked speechless for a few seconds. And then she found her voice. "You are a very astute detective, Mr. Sage."

His mouth twisted in a wry smile. "Thanks, but there was no Sherlock Holmes work involved in that deduction."

"I disagree. I can count the number of people who have arrived at that conclusion on one hand, and I wouldn't need all five fingers. No one in my family has figured it out. Neither have the various dream analysts and therapists I've seen over the years."

"Haven't they been curious about your aversion to marriage?"

"Sure. But when I refuse to give them a straight answer, they come to their own conclusions."

"And you don't bother to correct them," he said.

"Nope."

"Just how close did you come to getting married?"

"Too close." She shuddered. "I still have nightmares about that, as well."

"What happened?"

"It's a long and rather harrowing tale that ends with me terminating the engagement in a somewhat abrupt fashion."

Sam smiled a little. "You went for a dramatic touch."

"I would just like to point out that I ended the engagement *seventeen days* before the ceremony. Contrary to the gossip, I did not abandon my fiancé at the altar."

"Got it."

"Also, the rumors about the fire in his office were greatly exaggerated."

Sam looked interested. "There was a fire?"

"Forget it."

"All right. I'll put it aside for now. I would like an answer to my question, though."

"What?"

"You never explained exactly why Lillian Dewhurst took off on that long voyage," Sam said.

"Oh, right. I got sidetracked, didn't I?" Maggie winced. "Sorry about that. Lillian had trouble with nightmares that caused her to walk in her sleep. I advised her to get rid of a certain object in her bedroom that was casting a bad shadow. She did as I suggested and was able to use her natural lucid dreaming talent to rewrite the scripts of her dreams. When the nightmares stopped, so did the sleepwalking."

"She was afraid to get on board a ship because she might walk in her sleep?" Sam asked.

"She wasn't just alarmed by the possibility of waking up in a public place wearing her nightgown," Maggie said, "although that would have been bad enough. Lillian was terrified she would go overboard in her sleep and drown. I think something about the object that was giving her nightmares was linked to water."

"You're saying that once she was confident she wouldn't walk overboard, she felt free to book the voyage?"

"Right," Maggie said. "I told you that you probably wouldn't believe me."

"Huh."

"Changing your mind?" She gave him a thin smile. "Worried I might be delusional after all?"

"No, just contemplating the power of suggestion."

"You think I somehow hypnotized Lillian into believing she was cured?"

"Doesn't matter. If it worked, it worked. Let's get back to the case." Sam leaned forward and folded his arms on the table. "Here's what we've got. We don't know if Beverly Nevins was the blackmailer or one of the victims, but we do know that she is dead under circumstances that are strikingly similar to the Virginia Jennaway death."

Startled, Maggie frowned. "I'm not sure I agree with you."

"Somehow that does not come as a surprise."

She pretended she hadn't heard him. "It's true they are both dead and they both appear to have had a link to other people who are interested in dream analysis, but beyond that, their deaths are not all that similar. Jennaway drowned. The verdict on Nevins looks like natural causes or accidental overdose. She certainly did not drown."

"Jennaway's death was ruled accidental, but there were rumors of a possible overdose," Sam pointed out.

Maggie thought about it. "True."

"The details vary but the result is the same. Two women are dead. Both had links to groups that study dreams, and there were rumors of an overdose in each case."

Maggie got the unpleasant icy-hot frisson that one gets when one narrowly avoids a close brush with disaster.

"There's another constant in this case," she said quietly. "The Traveler."

Sam's eyes tightened. "You're talking about that old legend you mentioned when you hired me?"

"Yes. I told you the Traveler supposedly murders people by invading their dreams."

"Such a murder, if it were possible, would leave no evidence of foul play."

"Like an overdose," she pointed out.

"I'm not buying the possibility of murder by supernatural means."

She raised her eyes toward the ceiling. "Of course not."

"I can, however, go for the theory that the killer used the legend of the Traveler to stage a death that looked as if it had been caused by astral projection. It's an interesting idea. The murderer would have to be someone very familiar with the tale."

Encouraged, she gave that some thought. "My friend Prudence Ryland works in a research library that is dedicated to the study of the paranormal, including dreams. She's an expert on legends. If you think it might help, I'll telephone her in the morning and ask her to find out what she can about the Traveler."

"That might be useful."

At least he wasn't dismissing her suggestion out of hand. She lowered her voice. "Meanwhile, you're going to do something illegal, aren't you?"

"Only sort of illegal."

Chapter 16

Margaret Smith was attending the conference.

No, her name was Lodge. Margaret Lodge. Not Smith. It didn't matter. She was here, and he had recognized her immediately.

Emerson Oxlade could scarcely suppress the feverish excitement that threatened to consume him. He loosened his tie and gulped some of the whiskey he had poured for himself. He was dazzled by his good fortune. He had literally dreamed of finding Smith-Lodge again, and now his dream had come true.

He had been afraid he had lost her forever when she had suffered the attack of hysteria and stormed out of his office. He had dared to hope she would show up at the conference—after all, she was an astonishingly talented lucid dreamer, and the Guilfoyle Method was focused on lucid dreaming. There had been a chance she would buy a ticket, but no guarantee. He had known it was a long shot, yet here she was.

It was as if he had willed her to attend through the power of his own dreaming. After he had spent all these months searching for her, she was finally within reach again.

He opened the windowed doors of the guest villa and went out onto the front steps. He was too restless to sleep, torn between excitement and dread. There was so much at stake. He had sensed from that first meeting in his office that Lodge was the key to the success of his life's work. Now the Guilfoyles had the power to give her to him. Tonight he had made it clear she had to be part of the arrangement. They were not pleased, but he intended to stand firm.

It wouldn't be difficult to manage the Guilfoyles. He had learned everything he needed to know to manipulate them when he had met them all those years ago.

Admittedly, the realization that Lodge was attending the conference in the company of a man had come as a jolt. Sam Sage did not look like a scholarly research assistant—there was nothing bookish about him. Sage was in the way. He posed a problem, but surely not an insurmountable one.

Oxlade swallowed some more whiskey and considered the death of the Nevins woman. It was obvious the discovery of the body had alarmed the Guilfoyles. They were worried about the image of the Institute. That made three of them.

Yes, Arthur Guilfoyle had some lucid dreaming talent, and the enhancer had allowed him to access some of his latent psychic talent, but that didn't change the fact that he and his wife were con artists. They didn't care about the astonishing potential of his drug. They wanted to use it to make a great deal of money.

But when it came to lucid dreamers, Margaret Lodge put Arthur Guilfoyle in the shade. Oxlade's euphoria spiked. Lodge was the one who would make him famous and cement his reputation as a true genius. He would be known worldwide as the brilliant scientist who could unlock psychic doorways.

Chapter 17

S am peeled off the evening jacket, removed his shoes, and loosened his tie. He stretched out on the bed to try to catch a few hours of sleep and set his mental alarm clock for three in the morning. Hotel hallways were quiet at that hour, and the hotel dick would most likely be napping or reading the paper.

He needed sleep—he hadn't been sleeping well for a while now—but he lay awake for some time, thinking about Maggie on the other side of the connecting door. Her fascination with dreams and metaphysics probably ought to worry him. Maybe the fact that it didn't was what should alarm him.

But what really concerned him were two dead women and the obsession in Dr. Emerson Oxlade's eyes.

After a while he drifted off . . .

. . . and woke with the realization that he needed to do something important. He sat up on the side of the bed, turned on the lamp, and checked his watch. Five minutes to three.

He pushed himself to his feet and paused for a moment to contemplate the rumpled bed. He had slept more solidly in the past few hours than he had for a long time. There had been no disturbing dreams involving a madman trying to crush his skull with a coatrack.

Interesting.

As he had anticipated, the hotel was asleep. The lounge was closed. The guests had retired to their beds. Most were attendees at the dream conference. They had a full day of seminars and lectures ahead.

He went down the stairs to the front desk. There was no sign of the clerk. A quick glance at the guest register told him Nevins had been given room 357. He went behind the counter, took the key off the board, and headed back upstairs.

When he reached the third floor, he walked down the empty hallway, his evening jacket draped casually over one arm to conceal the flashlight he had brought with him. Just another guest returning from a late night on the town.

He stopped in front of the door marked *357* and checked the corridor to make sure there was no one in the vicinity.

Satisfied he was alone, he started to insert the key into the lock.

The knob turned easily in his hand. The door was unlocked.

He hesitated, running through the possibilities. There were a couple of logical reasons why the door would not be locked. Detective Brandon had stopped by earlier to take a look around Nevins's room. Maybe whoever had opened the door for Brandon had neglected to lock up afterward. The death of a hotel guest and the presence of a police detective would be enough to make a clerk nervous.

Maybe a bellhop or a housekeeper had already been sent to pack up Nevins's things and had forgotten to lock up afterward. But it seemed more likely that project would have been delayed until morning. There would have been no rush.

There was, of course, a third possibility—someone else had gone into the room before him, someone who, like him, had no right to be there.

He eased his way into the darkened space and closed the door as quietly as possible. He gave himself a moment to adjust to the deep gloom. The lamps were off and the blinds were closed, but a rectangle of hall light glowed through the transom window over the door.

The room felt empty, but he had learned he could not depend on that sensation. He had encountered killers who were so cold inside, they did not give off the warmth of normal human beings—or so it seemed.

No one lunged out of the shadows with a knife. He decided to take that as a good sign. He draped his coat on the doorknob, switched on the flashlight, and surveyed the scene. Whoever had searched the room had made a neat job of it. The dresser drawers and the closet doors were closed, but there were small signs that someone had gone through the room in a hurry. The bed was rumpled and the mattress was slightly askew.

There were two suitcases on the luggage racks. Both were empty. The clothes that Nevins had brought with her were still in the drawers and hanging in the closet. They looked expensive, fashionable, and very new.

The small jewelry box proved more interesting. It was still full of bracelets, earrings, and pins, none of which looked expensive. The pieces were scattered haphazardly around the interior, however. It looked as if someone had dumped out the contents, gone through the items, and then tossed everything back inside. A cat burglar would have taken the lot and sorted through the haul later. It looked as if someone had been searching for a specific piece of jewelry.

Sam went to the doorway of the bathroom and splashed the beam of the flashlight across the pink and jade-green tiles. The towels were neatly folded, and Nevins's toiletry items were precisely arranged on the shelf above the sink. The searcher had not spent much time in here, probably because there were no obvious hiding places.

But the searcher had not had much experience looking for items that had been concealed by people who had limited options when it came to hiding places. Hotel rooms offered extremely limited options.

He found what he was looking for taped to the underside of the lid of the toilet tank.

Chapter 18

Maggie was not surprised to find herself walking through the endless corridors of Sweet Creek Manor. She had hoped to get some solid sleep, but evidently her intuition had other plans for the night.

She is looking for someone or something. She opens the first door. Phyllis Gaines stands in the center of the featureless room.

"I'm not looking for you," Maggie says. "Why are you here?"

"That's the wrong question," Phyllis says.

"What is the right question?"

"Where is the real Aunt Cornelia?"

"On a ship in the South Pacific. Is there anything you want to tell me?"

"Wherever there's money, there's someone who will do whatever it takes to get it," Phyllis says.

"This is a waste of time," Maggie says. *She closes the door, walks down the hall, and enters the next room. She sees Arthur Guilfoyle.*

"I'm not looking for you," she says. "What are you doing here?"

"Come with me. I will teach you how to travel on the astral plane," Arthur says.

WHEN SHE DREAMS

"You're a fraud. There is no such thing as astral projection."

She closes the door and opens the next. Dolores Guilfoyle is inside the room.

"Stay away from my husband," Dolores says.

"I don't want him," Maggie says. "I'm looking for someone else."

She closes the door and moves on to the next one. Emerson Oxlade stands alone in the room.

"You need me to achieve your full potential for lucid dreaming," Oxlade says. He reaches for her. There is a syringe in his hand.

"You are extremely annoying," Maggie says.

She tries to walk out the door but she discovers she can't move. She opens her mouth to scream but she can't make a sound. Oxlade is coming closer. The glittering lust in his eyes is no longer annoying—it is terrifying. She is trapped in a room with a man who wants to possess her and control her dreams.

She knows she is dreaming, but she has lost control of the script. She reminds herself that she has the ability to yank herself out of a nightmare. She must get through the door.

She becomes aware of a muffled rapping. Someone is knocking on the door of her dream . . .

She wrenched herself out of the nightmare and sat up on the edge of the bed. She was breathing hard, and her heart was pounding. She was in the middle of a full-blown anxiety attack. It wasn't the first time.

"Breathe," she whispered.

It was impossible to focus on her breathing because *someone was rapping on the door of her room.*

That was not right. There was no reason why anyone would be knocking at this hour. Another burst of panic shot through her. Sam would know what to do. He was right next door.

She leaped out of bed, grabbed her robe, and hurried to the connecting door. She made a fist and prepared to rap sharply. She paused when she heard another soft knock and realized it was coming from the other side of the door.

Dazed with relief, she unlocked the door and opened it. For a few seconds she simply stared at Sam, trying to come up with an explanation for the fact that he was wearing the shoes, trousers, and white dress shirt he'd had on earlier. But she could not concentrate on the problem of why he was dressed because she was distracted by the acid energy of anxiety still coursing through her veins.

"What's wrong?" Sam asked.

"Can't . . . can't talk now," she said. "Give me a minute."

"Hang on."

He disappeared. She didn't try to understand why. She started to pace the room, struggling to rid herself of the poison created by the anxiety attack.

"Breathe," she muttered. "Just breathe. You know how to do this. It was just a nightmare."

Sam reappeared. He had a glass in his hand. It was filled with an amber liquid. "Here you go. Good for what ails you."

She didn't argue. She grabbed the glass and downed a healthy swallow of the whiskey. Too much, too fast. But the burn shattered the spell that had gripped her senses. She coughed and took a deep breath. The nerve-rattling energy began to dissipate. She resumed pacing. Drank some more whiskey. Took another breath.

Gradually she regained control. She realized Sam was still there, watching her from the doorway between the two rooms. She groaned. Now he really would conclude that she was not entirely balanced.

"Feeling better?" he asked.

"Yep. Just great."

Sam smiled but he did not comment.

At least he wasn't looking at her as if he was afraid she was hysterical. That helped settle her rattled nerves as nothing else could have done.

"Sorry you had to witness that," she said.

"Bad dream?"

"My fault. I lost control of it. Got the feeling I couldn't escape. It happens from time to time. I told you, I'm good, but I'm not perfect."

"And this is why you've never married," he said. "You're afraid a husband would witness you waking up in an anxiety attack and conclude you were unstable."

She glared at him. "Yes, not that it matters. What are you doing here?"

"I went to Beverly Nevins's room a few minutes ago."

"Oh, right. The mildly illegal job. Well?"

"Someone else got there first."

"Really?" She frowned, trying to make sense of that news. "A burglar?"

"Didn't look like the work of a professional. I don't think whoever it was had any success."

She discovered she could concentrate now. "Why do you say that?"

"Because I found something interesting."

He held up a gold bracelet. A charm in the shape of a crescent moon dangled from it.

Maggie stared at it, a fresh tide of anxiety igniting her nerves and her senses.

"Damn," she whispered. "This is not good."

Sam watched her closely. "Recognize it?"

"I told you I advised Lillian Dewhurst to get rid of an object that was casting a bad shadow. I worried it was disturbing her dreams."

"I remember," Sam said.

"It was a bracelet that was identical to the one you're holding."

Chapter 19

"There were initials on the back of the crescent moon on Lillian's bracelet," Maggie said. "*ATS*. Lillian said they stood for *Astral Travelers Society*. It was the name of a group she and some of her friends joined a few years ago. They were all interested in dream analysis."

She and Sam were sitting across from each other at the table in her room. She had turned on a floor lamp, hoping some strong light would make the situation feel less intimate. She had been wrong. She was in her nightgown and robe and she was alone with Sam in a hotel room at three thirty in the morning.

There was no escaping the sense of intimacy—at least, she could not ignore it. Sam, however, was focused solely on the bracelet sitting on the table. Maggie tried to concentrate on it, too.

She wasn't sensing the same sort of shadow energy she had picked up from Lillian's bracelet. The bracelet Sam had found looked somehow ominous, but the primary sensation emanating from it felt more like melancholia.

"The initials *ATS* are on the moon on this bracelet, too," Sam said.

He examined the inside of the band. "But there's an additional inscription. *To EN, the woman of my dreams.* It's signed *Dream Master.*"

"*EN?*" Maggie raised her brows. "Beverly Nevins's initials would be *BN.*"

"This bracelet may have belonged to someone else."

"True."

Maggie touched the bracelet gingerly with a fingertip. Sam watched intently, but he didn't say anything.

"Hmm," she said.

"Well?" he asked.

She raised her eyes to meet his, wondering if he was going to make a crack about her dream talent. But one look at him told her he was in a very serious mood.

"It looks exactly the same as Lillian's except for the inscription," she said. "But it doesn't affect my senses the way hers did. There's a faint tingle of sadness on this bracelet. Depression, perhaps. But that's all."

"What does that tell you?"

"Not much, I'm afraid."

"No sense of violence?" Sam pressed.

"No." She narrowed her eyes. "Don't tell me you are taking my sensitivity seriously."

"I'm taking your intuition seriously," he said.

"Right. My intuition."

She was not sure what to make of that.

"Did Dewhurst go out of her way to hide her bracelet?" Sam asked.

"No. She kept it with the rest of her jewelry. It wasn't a dime-store trinket, but it wasn't especially valuable, either, certainly not as expensive as most of her other jewelry. She never wore it."

"How did she react when you informed her she ought to throw it away?"

"She didn't argue or try to convince me that it was harmless. She said I might be right. The next morning when I arrived for work, we walked to the bluffs. She threw the bracelet into the ocean. A few days later she told me she was sleeping better than she had in a very long time."

"What happened to the Astral Travelers Society? Does it still exist?"

"I don't think so. Lillian didn't go into the details but I got the impression most of the members of the Society were upper-class socialites who viewed the group as a form of fashionable entertainment. They soon lost interest and moved on to other social activities."

"Yet Dewhurst kept the bracelet," Sam said.

His eyes were cold and razor-sharp. The man was born to hunt bad guys, Maggie thought. Born to be a cop. It was sad that his career as a police detective had ended so abruptly.

"Are we going to tell Detective Brandon about this bracelet?" she asked.

"Yes. I'll telephone him in the morning. There's not much he can do with the bracelet or the information that someone searched Nevins's room tonight, but I've got a feeling he'll ask me to continue to keep him informed."

"In other words, he's got his suspicions, so he's decided to take advantage of your presence and professional expertise." Maggie smiled. "You're his undercover detective."

"Has anyone ever told you that you've got a tendency to view everything from a very dramatic viewpoint?"

"A common character flaw in writers."

"I'll keep that in mind."

She tried to switch to a more businesslike tone of voice. "Things are starting to happen, aren't they? We need a plan."

"We do," Sam agreed. "At the moment all roads lead back to the Institute. I think it's time to put a little pressure on the Guilfoyles."

"Great idea. How do we do that?"

WHEN SHE DREAMS

"No offense, but your enthusiasm makes me nervous."

"Think of it as encouragement and support."

Sam eyed her with deep suspicion. "You're wondering how you can work this new development into the plot of your novel, aren't you?"

"A writer is always open to inspiration."

"I was afraid of that." Sam got to his feet and went toward the connecting door. "The opening lecture at the Institute takes place at ten o'clock tomorrow. We want to be there early so that we can catch one or both of the Guilfoyles. I want to see their reaction when they find out the woman they hired to play Cornelia has left town."

"Right," Maggie said.

He glanced at his watch. "We've got time for a few more hours of sleep. See you at breakfast? Eight o'clock?"

"I'll be ready."

She rose and trailed after him. Now that his business was over, he seemed in a great rush to leave her room. Just as well. She should not say another word. There was nothing more to be said, not tonight. She really should keep quiet.

"Sam?" she whispered.

He paused in the doorway, looking amused. "Are you going to tell me I should chuck a piece of furniture out the window before I try to sleep?"

"Some other time, maybe. I wanted to thank you for not panicking when you caught me in the middle of an anxiety attack tonight."

"Takes a lot more than that to make me panic," he growled in a tough-guy voice.

For some reason she suddenly felt much lighter. She was almost floating. She folded her arms. "Is that right? What, exactly, would it take to make you panic?"

"Finding myself in that novel you're writing would do it."

"Don't worry, I always change the names to protect the innocent. And also to avoid getting sued for libel."

...129

He moved into his own room and turned to look at her. "I have to tell you that is not exactly reassuring."

"You're a tough private detective. You can handle it."

She closed the door and listened carefully. Sam did not turn the key on his side. She decided not to lock her side, either.

Chapter 20

This doesn't make any sense," Dolores Guilfoyle said. "There is no one named Finley in marketing or anywhere else here at the Institute. I don't understand why that woman, Phyllis Gaines or whatever her name is, would tell you she was hired to pretend to be Aunt Cornelia."

"She was very upset," Maggie said. "Finding the body of Beverly Nevins was a shock to her nerves. It certainly rattled mine."

The news of the death had appeared on page two of the *Burning Cove Herald* under the headline *Tragedy Mars Opening of Dream Conference.* Nevins's death had been attributed to natural causes. There was no mention of the dream generator or drugs. There was also no indication the death had dampened enthusiasm for the conference. Eager attendees thronged the lobby of the Institute.

It had not been difficult to track down Dolores Guilfoyle. At a quarter to ten they had found her stationed at the entrance to the main lecture hall, greeting people as they filed into the large room to take their seats. There was no sign of her husband.

When Maggie had mentioned that Phyllis Gaines had left town during the night, Dolores had not appeared to recognize the name. Sam's casual observation that Gaines had been masquerading as Aunt Cornelia, however, had hit Guilfoyle like a jolt of electricity.

"That can't be right," she hissed. "I don't believe it."

Sam shrugged. "That's what she told us. Gaines could have been lying, but it didn't look that way. Why would she be?"

"This . . . this is shocking," Dolores whispered.

As far as Maggie could tell, the alarm in her eyes was genuine.

Dolores raised a finger to get the attention of a nearby dream guide. The attractive young woman hurried forward. When she got close, Maggie was able to read her name tag: *Valerie Warren.*

"Yes, Mrs. Guilfoyle?" Valerie said.

She was polite; an employee showing the proper degree of respect to her boss. But it struck Maggie that she was a little too polite and deferential—as if she was trying to conceal her dislike of the other woman.

"Please welcome the rest of our guests to Mr. Guilfoyle's lecture," Dolores said. "I have some business to discuss with Miss Lodge and her research assistant."

There was a glacial edge on her words. Evidently she didn't like Valerie any more than Valerie liked her.

A scene from last night's dream flashed through Maggie's memory. She saw herself opening a door and finding Dolores Guilfoyle inside the room. Dolores's words echoed faintly in the shadows: *Stay away from my husband.*

"Yes, Mrs. Guilfoyle," Valerie said.

She rushed back to the entrance of the lecture hall.

Dolores looked at Maggie and Sam. "Please come with me."

She led the way to a quiet alcove and then turned to confront them.

"Are you absolutely certain Phyllis Gaines was impersonating Aunt Cornelia?" she said.

"There is no doubt about it," Maggie said.

"Damn." Dolores's elegant jaw tensed. "May I ask what made you drive to that woman's cottage last night?"

"We were on our way into town to find a restaurant," Sam said. "We took Cliff Road. When we passed the cottage where Aunt Cornelia was staying, we noticed she was putting suitcases into her car. It was obvious she was about to leave."

Maggie was impressed with the smooth way he delivered his lines. She was determined to give an equally good performance. It wasn't as if she hadn't had a lot of practice deceiving people into thinking she did not belong in an asylum. She was a rather skilled liar herself.

"I couldn't resist the opportunity to tell Aunt Cornelia how much I enjoy her columns," she said. "We stopped to talk to her, and that's when she told us she wasn't the real Cornelia."

"Bizarre." Dolores shook her head. "Absolutely bizarre. I realize there is no shortage of frauds in the world, but this is astonishing. I can't understand why she would do such a thing. All I can tell you is that Phyllis Gaines convinced my husband and me, as well as the local press, that she was the real Aunt Cornelia."

"It did make for some great publicity for the Institute," Sam said.

Fury blazed in Dolores's eyes. "I can assure you no one affiliated with the Institute hired anyone to impersonate Cornelia for marketing purposes or for any other reason. That's not how we do things here." She paused, eyes widening. "When word gets out that the Institute was taken in by a charlatan, we will become a laughingstock."

Maggie summoned up a reassuring smile. "I assure you, Mr. Sage and I have no reason to gossip about Phyllis Gaines."

That much was true, she thought.

"Thank you." Dolores sighed. "I would take it as an enormous favor if you would not mention your conversation with Gaines, but I'm afraid it will be impossible to keep this news out of the papers. People are bound to notice that Aunt Cornelia has suddenly disappeared. There will be questions. Rumors. If a reporter gets curious, we will be doomed."

"Would you like some advice?" Maggie asked.

Dolores hesitated, wary but curious. "What is it?"

"I agree with you," Maggie said. "The news of the imposter is bound to get out sooner or later. But if the Institute moved fast and took credit for unmasking the fake Cornelia, it might actually enhance the reputation of the Guilfoyle Method."

Dolores appeared to have been struck by electricity for the second time. An instant later, excitement lit her eyes.

"That is a brilliant idea, Miss Lodge," she said. "I should have thought of it myself. If Arthur announces in his opening lecture that during the night he experienced a lucid dream that allowed him to detect the deception, we can take control of this situation. He will be able to offer proof of the effectiveness of the Method. Excuse me. I must speak to him immediately. He is scheduled to go onstage in a few minutes."

She started to turn away.

"One more thing," Sam said. "Ever heard of the Traveler? He's supposed to be a sort of dream assassin."

Dolores stopped suddenly and turned back to stare at him. "I don't understand. Who told you about that old legend?"

"Someone mentioned it recently," Sam said. "I was just curious. Part of my job as Miss Lodge's assistant is to note interesting tales that circulate in the world of lucid dreamers."

"Forget the Traveler," Dolores said. "It's just a silly myth that has been floating around the dream research community for years. I don't have time to go into the details now—I must speak to Arthur before he goes onstage."

Sam watched thoughtfully as Dolores vanished around the corner. "I got the impression she's a little more concerned about the legend of the Traveler than she let on."

"She certainly recognized the story," Maggie said. "But anyone who is as familiar with dream theories and analysis as she is would have heard about the Traveler."

"She wasn't just familiar with the legend; she was worried about it," Sam said. "Trust me."

"I hired you for your professional intuition," Maggie said. "I'll take your word for it."

"My professional intuition got me fired from my last job."

"Obviously you were working for the wrong employer."

They walked out of the alcove, heading for the doors of the lecture hall. Sam's mouth kicked up at the corner.

"You know, that was a very sharp suggestion you gave Dolores Guilfoyle," he said. "If her husband takes your advice and pretends he uncovered Phyllis Gaines's deception in a lucid dream, the Institute might end up with some great publicity."

"I didn't offer the advice to help the Guilfoyles polish the image of the Institute. I'm hoping my version gets into the newspapers because it will ensure that everyone knows the redhead seen partying at a nightclub in Burning Cove was not the real Aunt Cornelia."

"Got it," Sam said. "You're trying to protect your employer's reputation. Smart move."

"Thanks, but it will only work if the Guilfoyles take my advice."

"Five will get you ten Dolores Guilfoyle convinces her husband to go along with the plan."

"No bet," Maggie said. "Speaking of Dolores Guilfoyle . . ."

"What?" Sam asked.

"I think she's the jealous type."

"Who isn't?"

"Good point."

"Your point is valid, too," Sam said. "Mrs. Guilfoyle has a lot at stake. Regardless of her personal feelings about her husband, she knows he's vital to the future of the Institute."

"True," Maggie said. "He's the box-office draw."

Chapter 21

Arthur Guilfoyle stalked onto the stage radiating drama in a high-collared black coat that looked as if it had been borrowed from the wardrobe Bela Lugosi had used in *Dracula*.

Guilfoyle moved into the glare of the spotlight, head bowed as though he was gathering strength for what lay ahead. A breathless hush gripped the lecture hall. Maggie was impressed. He had spoken not a single word, but everyone was on tenterhooks. Well, not Sam, she decided. It would take a lot to put him on tenterhooks. But there was no doubt everyone else in the auditorium was excited, including her. In spite of her misgivings about the Guilfoyle Method, she was interested to hear what Guilfoyle had to say.

You had to hand it to the man, she thought. He might or might not be a fraud, but he had what it took to command the room. It wasn't just his extraordinarily handsome appearance. Onstage, he exuded a compelling energy.

Arthur seized the edges of the podium with both hands and flung up his head as though he had just sunk his fangs into a lady's throat and was savoring the thrill of fresh blood. He was wearing stage makeup. A lot of it. His magnetic eyes had been rendered even larger and more intense by the application of dark eye shadow and eyeliner.

She slanted a sideways glance at Sam, who was lounging in the seat beside her. In the shadows it was difficult to be certain, but she thought he was amused.

"I am here to welcome you to the first annual conference of the Guilfoyle Institute of Dream Analysis," Arthur said. His resonant voice, enhanced by a microphone, rolled across the auditorium. "You are about to embark on a journey that will open your minds to new planes of awareness and a new kind of knowledge. You will begin your climb up the ladder of the Guilfoyle Method and glimpse the astonishing things that await you when you reach the top. But before we begin, I have unpleasant news to report."

A murmur of alarm swept through the crowd. Sam took the opportunity to lean close to Maggie. He put his mouth to her ear.

"Looks like the Guilfoyles decided to take your advice."

"Once in a while people do," she whispered.

"Last night I was inspired to journey into a lucid dream of the highest order," Arthur intoned. "I employed the Guilfoyle Method to open my other senses and discovered there was a fraud among us, a person who was engaged in a grand deception."

This time the auditorium buzzed with curiosity.

"In the course of my dream the truth was revealed to me," Arthur continued. "I am saddened to report that the woman who claimed to be the celebrated columnist who writes the Dear Aunt Cornelia advice column was an imposter. She was intent on deceiving not only the Institute and those of you in the audience but the entire town of Burning Cove and the press."

Shock and amazement rippled across the audience.

"When the imposter was confronted with the truth, she immediately packed up and left town," Arthur continued. "We will never know why the imposter chose to carry out such a scheme. It's possible she is a practiced con artist. Perhaps she is mentally unstable. There are those who impersonate famous people simply because it gives them a thrill. Whatever the answer, rest assured she is no longer among us and can no longer deceive us."

A round of enthusiastic applause greeted that news.

"I would remind you that it was the Guilfoyle Method that uncovered this astonishing deception," Arthur said. "You, too, can gain this extraordinary ability to discover the truth by studying the techniques we teach here at the Guilfoyle Institute."

An hour later Maggie and Sam filed out of the lecture hall and headed for the coffee and tea bar that had been set up in the lobby. They collected cups and saucers and sat down at a small round table that overlooked the lush gardens.

"I did have one psychic revelation during Guilfoyle's lecture," Sam said. "He's a con, just as I thought."

Maggie stirred her coffee with a small silver spoon. "What makes you so sure of that?"

"There's no big mystery to it. Guilfoyle made it clear how the Institute will rake in the cash. It's not about selling inexpensive tickets to introductory seminars and conferences like this one. Those are designed to get people hooked. Once they are in the program, they will find themselves buying their way up to higher and higher levels in order to learn the secrets that are only available to those who pay for the privilege of enlightenment."

"There is definitely a financial angle, but that is only to be expected," Maggie said. "We know it must have cost a fortune to purchase this old estate and convert it into the Institute. It will be very expensive to keep it operating. The Guilfoyles obviously have to turn a profit, but it doesn't mean the program is a complete con."

"The Guilfoyle Method is a con. Trust me."

Maggie waved that aside. "All right, I agree Guilfoyle's claims for his Method are rather extravagant, but that doesn't mean he doesn't sincerely believe he's having a psychic vision when he's engaged in a lucid dream. The experience can feel very unsettling." She broke off. "Damn."

Sam raised his brows. "Something wrong?"

"I'm getting that feeling you get when you think someone is watching you."

Sam's gaze shifted to a point behind her left shoulder. "Probably because someone is watching you."

"Emerson Oxlade?"

"Good guess. He was on the other side of the room, staring at you. He left when he saw me looking at him."

She shivered. "Such a creepy man. Straight out of a horror film."

"But you said he takes a genuine scientific approach to the study of dreams."

"Yes, I'm sure of it."

"Yet he's hooked up with a couple of cons like the Guilfoyles."

"Serious researchers need money like everyone else," she pointed out. "And publicity. The Guilfoyles can provide both."

"Which brings us back to Phyllis Gaines's observation last night. She was right. Where there's a great deal of money, there is always someone who will do whatever it takes to get it."

Maggie shivered and quickly lowered her cup. "I'm getting that feeling again. Who is watching me this time?"

"Dolores Guilfoyle," Sam said.

He got to his feet just as Dolores materialized at the table.

"I'm so sorry to interrupt your conversation," Dolores said. "Please sit down, Mr. Sage. I won't be long. Very busy day."

Sam took his seat. Dolores turned to Maggie.

"Arthur and I are very grateful for your advice on dealing with the unpleasant situation this morning, Miss Lodge," she said. "As a way of expressing our appreciation, Arthur would like to invite you to observe an exclusive dream-reading demonstration tomorrow evening."

"Exclusive?" Maggie said. "You mean it's not part of the regular program?"

"No, this event will be presented to only a few very special guests. It will take place in the old séance room here at the Institute."

"The theater where Miss Nevins died?" Maggie asked.

"Yes," Dolores said. "My husband responds to the aura in that room."

"He believes in ghosts and spirits?" Sam asked.

"No, of course not," Dolores said, irritated. "It's simply that Arthur finds the atmosphere in the theater conducive to allowing him to enter the trance state. It was remodeled for the purpose of presenting private demonstrations and small-group dream experiences."

"You said only a few guests would be invited?" Sam asked.

"Just those who have shown a keen interest in discovering the secrets of the Guilfoyle Method," Dolores said. She spoke without looking at Sam.

"How many other guests?" Sam continued, undaunted by the fact that he was being given a very cold shoulder.

"Twelve in all, if you must know," Dolores said, her tone sharpening. "Our guest of honor, Dr. Oxlade, will serve as guide and dream interpreter for the audience."

"Arthur Guilfoyle needs an interpreter?" Sam asked a little too politely.

Maggie decided to step in before the situation could deteriorate further.

"It all sounds absolutely fascinating," she said quickly. "Mr. Sage and I would be pleased to observe one of Mr. Guilfoyle's readings."

Dolores blinked a couple of times, glanced at Sam, and then turned back to Maggie. "I'm afraid it won't be possible for your assistant to accompany you, Miss Lodge. This will be a very exclusive reading."

Sam's eyes tightened at the corners. Maggie knew he was preparing to interrupt again. She shot him a warning look and then smiled at Dolores.

"I understand," she said. "Thank you so much for this amazing opportunity. I shall look forward to the event tomorrow night."

"Excellent." Dolores was clearly relieved. "I'll see that you receive a proper invitation with the details."

She hurried away.

"Well, that was interesting," Sam said. "You have been invited to a private demonstration of a Guilfoyle dream reading."

"I appear to have catapulted up several rungs on the Guilfoyle social ladder," Maggie observed.

"The question is, why?"

"And why go to great lengths to make sure you don't accompany me?"

"I think the plan is to separate us," Sam said.

"Why would Dolores Guilfoyle do that?"

"You're writing a book intended to expose fraudulent dream analysts and you are here to study the Guilfoyle Method. The Guilfoyles have a big investment to protect. They want to ensure that you make the Institute look good. I'm just a lowly research assistant. It's not me they have to impress. You're the writer, so you're the one who matters."

Maggie raised her brows. "And maybe the Guilfoyles really are grateful for the excellent advice I gave them this morning."

"Maybe. Either way, this is a very convenient opportunity."

"For what?"

"Your old pal Emerson Oxlade will be at the demonstration."

"Unfortunately."

"Fortunately," Sam said. "With him out of the way for the evening I'll be able to take a look around his villa."

Maggie cheered up at that news. "That is an excellent plan."

"Not to brag, but I came up with it all by myself."

At five o'clock that afternoon they walked back to the hotel.

"If I have to sit through any more lectures from perky dream guides informing me about the wonders of the Guilfoyle Method and suggesting I sign up immediately, I'm going to need a large bottle of whiskey," Sam said.

"Have you been a skeptic all your life?" Maggie asked, amused but also curious.

"I was raised on a farm, and I went into a career of police work. The combination teaches you to take a realistic approach to life. Psychic powers can't ensure a good harvest, and lucid dreams don't solve cases."

"I understand your objections to the Guilfoyle Method," Maggie said. "But you should keep an open mind."

She smiled at the doorman who was ushering them into the lobby of the Sea Dream Hotel. He touched his fingers to his hat.

The last conference event of the day had been conducted by the dream guides named Valerie and Gloria. Following a detailed explanation of the various levels of lucid dreaming that could be achieved through the Guilfoyle Method, Valerie had explained that an exclusive discount on a package of ten private sessions designed to impart the secrets of the Method was available to attendees who signed up before the end of the conference. Gloria had made it clear that those who registered would receive a monthly magazine and a monthly bill.

While the women carried on enthusiastically about the promise of the Method, the two male guides, Larry and Jake, sat at a table at the side of the room signing up those who decided to embark on the program.

"If the Method is as good as the Guilfoyles claim, it shouldn't be necessary to give it such a hard sell," Sam said.

"Shush," Maggie said.

She stopped at the front desk and smiled at the clerk. "Room two fifteen, please."

"Certainly, Miss Lodge," the clerk said. "And two seventeen for you, Mr. Sage."

"Thanks," Sam said.

The clerk plucked the room keys off the hooks and then reached into the little cubbyhole marked *215*. He took out two envelopes.

"A couple of messages for you, Miss Lodge," he said.

"Thank you." She glanced at her name on the envelopes as she walked toward the stairs with Sam. "One is from the office of the Institute. The invitation to the private demonstration, no doubt."

"Who's the other one from?" Sam asked.

"I don't know. I'll open it when I get into my room."

They went up the stairs and down the hall to 215 and 217. Maggie hurried into her room, dropped her handbag on the dressing table, and unsealed the envelopes. The first one was, as she had expected, an invitation to the dream reading.

She was opening the second envelope when Sam rapped on the connecting door.

"Come in," she called.

He opened the door. "Is it personal, or do I need to know what's in the second envelope?"

Maggie glanced at the message and drew in a sharp breath. "You need to hear it." She read aloud. *"The parking lot at the Carousel Club. Ten o'clock tonight. Flash the lights twice. I can tell you about the Traveler. Bring twenty-five dollars. Cash."*

"That's a lot of money for details of an old legend," Sam said. "Is there a signature?"

"No," Maggie said. "But the note is obviously from someone who wants to sell us inside information. I'll bet it's a member of the Institute staff. This is a big break for us, Sam."

"Maybe. Have you got twenty-five bucks to waste on what might be a useless tip?"

"Yes, I brought a fair amount of cash with me in case something like this happened," Maggie said. "It's just too bad the person who sent the note didn't suggest the parking lot at the Paradise Club."

"Why?"

"I would love to see the Paradise. I've heard it's the hottest night-club in Burning Cove."

Chapter 22

think we can guess why our helpful informant didn't suggest that we meet in the parking lot at the Paradise," Sam said. He glanced at the two goons lounging around the entrance of the Carousel as he drove past. "It probably has more impressive security."

The neon sign above the Carousel Club sparked and flickered erratically, spitting shafts of light into the night. The random flashes reminded him of the dream generator in the theater at the Institute. If he believed in omens, he would consider the sign a bad one.

Meeting informants was always a risky business, but in this case it was about as safe as such ventures got. The top was up on the convertible to add some additional privacy. The Carousel's security wasn't first-class, but it looked tough enough to handle anything unpleasant that might take place in the parking lot.

Maggie studied the two men guarding the front door. "They don't look like they are there to offer gracious valet service, do they?"

She had dressed for the meeting in a pair of dark trousers and a snug pullover sweater. Classy and sporty, Sam thought, amused. She looked as if she was about to go out for lunch at a country club. He, on the other hand, was properly dressed for the occasion. There was a pistol in the shoulder holster under his coat.

"Their primary job is to warn management if someone from law enforcement shows up," he explained. "The secondary job is to handle misunderstandings."

Maggie looked at him. "Can I assume that in this context, *misunderstandings* refers to fistfights among the patrons?"

"As well as the failure to pay bar tabs, gambling debts, or management's commission on transactions that take place in the parking lot."

"Do you mean they will expect us to pay them off for letting us meet with whoever sent the message?"

She didn't sound concerned, just curious. Probably taking notes for her novel.

"We're from out of town," he said. "I'm sure there will be a special price for tourists. It will be worth it because they are providing security for us."

"How?"

"No one is going to risk doing anything too dramatic here in the parking lot within view of those two."

"They are carrying guns under their jackets, aren't they?"

"I certainly hope so. We might need backup."

He parked the Packard, flashed the lights a couple of times, and took the pistol out from under his coat.

For the first time Maggie looked alarmed. "I didn't know you brought your gun."

"Didn't want to show up empty-handed. It was either the pistol or cupcakes. I didn't have time to bake."

Maggie reached into her handbag and took out a notepad.

"Put that away," he warned.

Reluctantly she dropped the notepad back into her bag. "It was a great line."

"Thanks. I worked on it."

She eyed the gun. "Your pistol is rather small, isn't it?"

"Some men might be offended by that comment."

"Really? I apologize. I never meant to insult you."

He sighed. "A snub-nosed .38 fits better under a coat than a Colt revolver."

"I see. That makes sense."

"A small pistol can be just as scary as a big one at close quarters."

Maggie slid a hand surreptitiously toward her handbag.

"Forget your notebook," he said.

Another car pulled into the parking lot, headlights glaring. A couple got out and hurried toward the entrance of the club. When they were gone, a figure moved toward the Packard, slipping through the deep shadows cast by two nearby vehicles. A moment later a face appeared at the passenger side window. A woman in a wide-brimmed hat trimmed with netting rapped on the glass.

Maggie rolled down the window. "You're Valerie, one of the dream guides."

"Valerie Warren. I wasn't sure if you would show. Did you bring the twenty-five bucks?"

"Yes," Maggie said. "But I need to know what's going on before I hand over the cash."

Valerie glanced over her shoulder and then turned back. "I can't stand around out in the open. Some of the other members of the Institute staff might show up here tonight. It's not like any of us can afford the Paradise."

"Get in back," Sam said.

Valerie stared. "You've got a gun. Why do you have a gun? You're a research assistant."

"Don't worry about the gun," Maggie said quickly. "It's a very small one. Please get into the back seat. No one will see you."

Valerie glanced around. "Well, okay. I guess."

She straightened away from the window and grasped the rear door handle.

Maggie leaned closer to Sam and lowered her voice to a stern whisper.

"Let me ask the questions," she said. "You've already frightened her."

"Sometimes a little fear can be helpful."

"Not in this situation."

He shrugged. She might be right.

Valerie opened the back door and got into the car. Sam and Maggie turned to watch her.

"Please tell us about the Traveler," Maggie asked.

"Where's the money?" Valerie asked.

Maggie plucked several bills out of her handbag and held them up so that Valerie could see them.

"Thanks," Valerie snapped the cash out of Maggie's fingers. "I'll make this fast." She leaned forward and kept her voice low, even though no one outside the car could have heard her. "I'm leaving town tonight. I don't want to drive the highway back to L.A. after dark, but if I wait until dawn there will probably be fog like there was this morning."

"You're leaving town?" Maggie asked.

"As fast as I can," Valerie said. "We don't get paid until the end of the week, but I'm not going to stick around, not after what happened to that Nevins woman in the theater last night. They used to hold séances in there, you know. That room gives me the creeps."

"We're here for information," Sam said. "We're not interested in ghost stories."

"Right, okay," Valerie said. "I couldn't hear everything you said to Mrs. Guilfoyle this morning, but I know you asked her about the Traveler."

"That's right," Maggie said. "What do you know about the legend?"

"He's some sort of spirit that lives on the astral plane. Murders people in their dreams. The other dream guides are saying it might have been the Traveler who murdered Beverly Nevins."

"Who, exactly, is saying the Traveler murdered Nevins?" Sam asked.

"I just told you, the other dream guides—Larry, Jake, and Gloria. But they all smoked some of Larry's reefers last night after everyone left, so maybe they just imagined the story about the Traveler."

"It's a minor legend in the dream analysis community," Maggie said. "I wonder how your friends heard about the Traveler."

"Mr. Guilfoyle told us about the Traveler during one of the training sessions we took after we were hired," Valerie said. "We figured he was just trying to impress us. None of us really believe in that psychic dreaming stuff, you see. But we're pretty sure Arthur Guilfoyle does believe in it."

"What do you think happened to Beverly Nevins?" Sam asked.

"I wouldn't be surprised if one of the Guilfoyles murdered her," Valerie said, her voice fierce with rage.

"Why?" Sam said.

"That bastard Guilfoyle probably slept with her and then got bored and ended things," Valerie muttered. "That's what he does, you see. Seduces a girl and then drops her when he gets tired of her. I bet Nevins showed up at the conference and threatened to make a scene, so they got rid of her."

"Which Guilfoyle did it?" Maggie asked.

Valerie shrugged. "I don't know. Could have been either one. She's mean as a snake and he's a lying, cheating son of a bitch. Also, I think he's unbalanced."

"Because he believes in the connection between lucid dreaming and the paranormal senses?" Maggie asked quietly.

"Yes," Valerie said. "You have to be cuckoo to really believe that stuff, right?"

Sam knew Maggie was about to lose her temper. He touched her hand, willing her to keep her mouth shut.

She appeared to get the message.

"You said Guilfoyle has a habit of sleeping with women and then dropping them," Maggie said. "Are you speaking from personal experience, Valerie?"

"Yes, if you must know." Valerie clenched her hands on her lap. "He's a real creep. Makes you think you're special. Says you have a natural talent for psychic dreaming. Says you can fly with him on the astral plane. Calls you his soul mate. Then he dumps you."

Maggie looked at Sam, evidently uncertain how to respond. He kept his attention on Valerie.

"How did you get the job as a dream guide?" he asked.

"The Guilfoyles put an ad in one of the Hollywood papers. Said they were looking for people with acting experience. It sounded a lot more interesting than working at a lunch counter, and we get to live rent-free at the Institute. I figured being a dream guide was the same as working in a magic show or a theater, plus I'd be in Burning Cove. I told myself there would be plenty of opportunities to meet important people in the movie business in this town."

"At what point did Arthur Guilfoyle seduce you?" Maggie asked.

"Each dream guide gets some one-on-one sessions with Guilfoyle. It's part of the training process. In my first session he went into a trance. When he came out of it, he told me some things about myself he couldn't possibly have known. For a while I actually believed he was psychic. I was a fool."

"Did he tell you the sort of things you would hear from a fortune-teller?" Sam asked.

"No. Well, not exactly. He didn't just tell me stuff about the past. He told me he could help me achieve my full potential as a lucid dreamer." Valerie hesitated. "That's when he told me that I had a special talent for dreaming. He said if I followed his techniques and allowed him to guide me, I could develop real psychic powers. But first I had to expand my dream experience and learn to access other planes of consciousness."

"What did that require?" Maggie said.

Valerie snorted. "Ever hear of the casting couch?"

"What an appalling man," Maggie said.

"Yeah," Valerie said. "And I fell for his line."

"When did you figure out he was just using you?" Sam asked.

"When he hired another dream guide," Valerie said. "Her name was Betty. She moved into the Institute about a month ago and started her training. After she and Guilfoyle had a couple of one-on-one sessions, Guilfoyle told me he and I wouldn't be doing any more sessions together because I had reached my limits as a psychic dreamer."

"I don't remember seeing a dream guide named Betty," Maggie said.

"That's because she didn't last long," Valerie said. "I found Betty crying in the bathroom one day. She said Mrs. Guilfoyle had caught her in the old caretaker's cottage with Mr. Guilfoyle and fired her on the spot. Betty packed up and left that afternoon."

"Has Arthur Guilfoyle tried to seduce Gloria?" Maggie asked.

"No, she's not his type," Valerie said. "Lucky for her, he likes blondes. Gloria isn't interested in him anyway. She and Larry are dating."

"All right," Sam said. "Arthur Guilfoyle is a womanizer. That's interesting but not surprising. We're here to talk about the Traveler. So far you haven't told us anything we didn't already know. We expected a little more information in exchange for the cash."

"This is the part that's worth the twenty-five bucks," Valerie said. She leaned forward. "Last night after the police, the doctor, and everyone else was gone, I went into the gardens to have a smoke. I overheard the Guilfoyles and Dr. Oxlade talking as they walked back to their villas. I could tell they were discussing the dead woman, so I didn't light the cig. I knew they couldn't see me, because I was on the other side of a tall hedge. I stayed real quiet and listened."

"What did you hear?" Sam asked.

"Oxlade said something about Nevins's death looking like the death of someone else. Jenny Something."

"Jennaway?" Maggie asked.

"That's it, Jennaway," Valerie said. "Oxlade told the Guilfoyles he was worried there might be rumors of the Traveler. That really rattled Dolores Guilfoyle. She got angry and ordered him to stop talking about the old legend. Rumors like that would be bad for the image of the Institute, she said."

"How did Oxlade respond?" Sam asked.

"He agreed with her," Valerie said. "He was worried about bad publicity, too. He was afraid the Institute might get a reputation for being some kind of cult. He said he couldn't afford to lend his good name— that's what he called it, *his good name*—to an organization that would be laughed at by the scientific community. That's when he mentioned you, Miss Lodge."

Maggie clutched the back of the leather seat. "Oxlade talked about me? What did he say?"

Valerie opened her mouth and then appeared to rethink whatever she had intended to say.

"Professor Oxlade is not what you'd call real stable," she said instead. "That's not just my opinion. All the dream guides think he's strange."

"What did Oxlade say about Miss Lodge?" Sam asked, keeping his voice very even.

Valerie flinched and sat back against the seat. "Never mind—it's not important."

"If you want to leave this car with your twenty-five bucks, you'll tell us exactly what Oxlade said."

Maggie reached over the seat and touched Valerie lightly on the hand. "Please. I have to know."

Valerie grabbed the door handle and visibly braced herself.

"Oxlade told the Guilfoyles the only reason he was sticking around is because of you, Miss Lodge. He said you were the most powerful lucid dreamer he had ever encountered, and if they couldn't persuade you to cooperate in his experiments he would no longer allow himself to be associated with the Guilfoyle Method. He said he would leave and take the enhancer with him."

Maggie stared at Valerie, evidently speechless.

"Do you know what Oxlade meant by *the enhancer*?" Sam asked.

"No," Valerie said. "But after he stomped off and went into his villa, I followed the Guilfoyles for a while. I heard Arthur tell Dolores they needed the enhancer. *Everything depends on it*, he said. That's all I know, I swear."

Valerie opened the door and leaped out of the back seat. She vanished into the shadows of the parking lot. A moment later an engine rumbled. A set of headlights blazed. A sedan flashed past and careened toward Cliff Road.

"She's definitely in a hurry to get out of town," Maggie said. "She's terrified."

Chapter 23

"Lucky for you, I don't believe in that astral projection nonsense," Sam said. He started the engine, switched on the headlights, and drove slowly through the nightclub parking lot. "Otherwise I might be a little concerned about our connecting-rooms arrangement."

"That is not funny," Maggie said. She had not been this angry since the day she had battled her way out of Oxlade's office. "This is too much. It's appalling. He's a monster."

"Oxlade's not going to get his hands on you, so don't worry about it."

"Easy for you to say."

"Which is why I'm saying it. We already knew he was obsessed, at least when it comes to you. Right now we need to sort through the facts we have."

"Like the fact that Arthur Guilfoyle is a womanizer?"

"That doesn't come as a shock. What's really interesting is that all three of them—Oxlade and the Guilfoyles—are not only aware of the rumors of the Traveler and the Jennaway death, they're concerned about the potential bad press from those two things."

Maggie forced herself to focus on the case. "You're right, that is interesting. Fascinating, in fact."

She stopped talking, because the club's two badly dressed security people had left their posts at the doors and were strolling forward to block the exit.

"This could be a problem," she said.

"Just routine," Sam said.

"Do you think you'll need your little pistol?"

"No. There are two of them and one of me. I don't like the odds."

"Oh. Right."

Sam braked to a stop and rolled down the side window. "Good evening, gentlemen. Nice night."

The larger of the two guards leaned down to speak through the open window. "Couldn't help noticing that you and the lady never took advantage of the amenities of our fine club. Looks like you conducted a meeting in the parking lot instead."

"We did," Sam said. "A short business transaction. We purchased some information, not goods." He took his wallet out from under his jacket, extracted a couple of bills and handed them through the window. "Appreciate you two keeping an eye on the situation. You never know when a business meeting might go bad."

"Sadly, that is very true. Happy to hear we were able to provide you with some peace of mind." The security guard slipped the money into the front pocket of his jacket. "You say you came here to purchase information?"

"That's right," Sam said.

The guard squinted. "Cop?"

"Not anymore. Private now."

"I see." The guard glanced at Maggie, angled his head in a polite nod, touched a finger to the brim of his fedora, and stepped back. "You two drive carefully. Cliff Road is tricky at night. Lot of sharp curves."

"Thanks for the advice," Sam said.

He put the Packard in gear and motored down the long drive.

"Do cops and tough guys always recognize each other?" Maggie asked.

"Usually. Probably a psychic thing. You know, like lucid dreaming all the way to the astral plane."

"I will not lower myself to respond to that poor attempt at a joke."

"Sorry," Sam said. "Couldn't resist."

"Let's get back to my case. We seem to have acquired a lot of interesting facts but no answers. It's as if the more we learn, the murkier everything becomes."

"I'd say you got your money's worth from Valerie tonight." Sam slowed for the turn onto Cliff Road. "We need more information, though. I'm going to have to make some phone calls tomorrow. That will be complicated."

"Why?"

"I don't want to make the calls from the hotel room phone," Sam said.

"Don't worry about putting them on the bill."

"That's not the problem."

She glanced at him. "You're worried the hotel operator might eavesdrop, aren't you?"

"Hotel operators are in an ideal position to listen in on conversations, and the Sea Dream Hotel is owned by the Institute. That means the operator works for the Guilfoyles."

"If she heard you asking questions about them, she might decide to give that information to her employers. At the very least she would probably tell other people what was going on. I see what you mean. But if you disappear from the conference tomorrow for an extended period of time, we'll need a reason. Someone is bound to ask why my research assistant isn't with me."

"We'll think of something."

"Yes." She watched the moonlight splash silver on the surface of the Pacific. "I've been thinking about what you said about Lillian."

"You're starting to wonder if Dewhurst's sudden decision to take that voyage to the other side of the world might not have been a coincidence after all?"

"Yes. Maybe she knew someone was threatening the former members of the Astral Travelers Society and decided to get as far away as possible."

"How much do you know about Lillian Dewhurst?"

"Not as much as I thought," Maggie admitted. "But, then, how well do we ever know someone else? She is a very private person. She never mentions her family. I think Lillian is the last of her line. She inherited a lot of money."

"Has she lived in Adelina Beach all of her—" Sam broke off and started to brake.

Startled, Maggie glanced at him. "What's wrong?"

"I don't know yet."

She realized he was focused on the scene through the windshield. She turned back and saw what had riveted his attention.

The hellish glow of a fierce fire illuminated the night. The flames swept up from the bottom of the cliffs.

Sam brought the Packard to a halt in a turnout. He had his door open before Maggie could comprehend what was happening. She climbed out of the passenger seat and hurried to join him at the edge of the road. They both looked down at the beach. There was a broken vehicle on the rocks. It was engulfed in flames.

Maggie got a queasy, light-headed feeling. "That's the car Valerie was driving when she left the Carousel, isn't it?"

"Yes," Sam said. "It is."

Chapter 24

W hat the hell is going on out there at the Institute?" Brandon said. He slid an apologetic glance at Maggie. "Sorry about the language, Miss Lodge."

"It suits the circumstances," Maggie said.

She did not take her eyes off the smoldering wreckage at the foot of the cliffs.

"The answer to your question," Sam said to Brandon, "is we don't know what's happening. All I can tell you is that the Institute is a slick con selling a program that claims to be able to teach psychic dreaming techniques and that someone at the conference is blackmailing one or more of the attendees. But it gets complicated, because it's entirely possible the blackmailer is dead."

Brandon narrowed his eyes. "Beverly Nevins?"

"Maybe," Sam said. "If so, the extortionist is no longer a threat, but we're left with other problems. Someone went to a lot of trouble to murder the woman in that car at the bottom of the cliffs. Valerie Warren was running. She said the Nevins death had frightened her—but there may have been other reasons."

"Think she was the blackmailer?"

"That's also a possibility," Sam said. "She worked inside the Guilfoyle operation for quite a while. She knew some secrets. On top of everything else, we can confirm there are drugs involved."

"After Nevins, I figured as much. Not good."

"In addition to the con job the Guilfoyles are pulling, there's a doctor named Emerson Oxlade in the mix. He's got a hallucinogenic drug he thinks enhances the lucid dream experience. That may have been what Nevins injected."

That got Maggie's attention. "I don't think so. Oxlade's enhancer is administered orally. It's odorless and tasteless." She paused, thinking. "I suppose he may have come up with an injectable version, but why would he?"

Brandon groaned. "Stop trying to cheer me up."

"Maybe it really was just an accident," Maggie ventured.

Sam glanced at her. "What?"

"Valerie was in a rush to get out of town," Maggie said. "She was very anxious. She had been here for less than two months and she probably hadn't had a lot of experience driving Cliff Road, at least not at night."

Both men watched her in silence. She crossed her arms and blew out a breath.

"All right," she said. "It probably wasn't an accident."

The three of them were not alone at the top of the scenic overlook. There were a couple of police vehicles and a fire truck crowded into the small space at the side of the road. Several people were standing around but no one was doing much of anything because there was nothing to be done. The vehicle was still hot, and the location was too dangerous to risk a rescue team at night when it was obvious no one could have survived the crash.

"I don't see a body," Maggie said. "Maybe she got out."

"No," Brandon said. He spoke with the world-weary authority of a man who had seen enough bad car crashes to know what he was talking about. "The windshield was shattered. If the body isn't in the car it's because it was flung into the ocean. It will wash ashore in a day or two."

Maggie nodded and fell silent again. The fire had burned out by the time she and Sam had returned from the task of locating a pay phone to report the tragedy. All they could do at this point was contemplate the disaster and try to make sense of it.

"Give us a little more time," Sam said to Brandon. "I have that feeling you get when you're closing in on the answers. I could use some help, though."

Brandon slanted him a speculative glance. "Yeah?"

"There are some phone calls that have to be made. You know how it goes. It takes time to track down people and get them to talk. I don't want to risk making the calls from the hotel. Guilfoyle's people run the place. But I'd rather not waste a few hours shoving coins into a pay phone."

"If you've got a list of names and some questions and your client is willing to pay for the long-distance calls, I can spare one of my men tomorrow," Brandon said.

"I think it would be better to handle this quietly," Sam said. "You know what police stations are like."

Brandon snorted. "Rumor mills."

"Know a local private investigator who can be trusted to handle this kind of thing?"

"I do, as a matter of fact," Brandon said. "Kirk Investigations."

"Can you arrange for me to meet Kirk privately? I don't want to be seen going into the office of a private detective here in town. Can't meet at the hotel, either."

"I think I can arrange it," Brandon said.

"When?" Sam asked.

"How about tonight?"

"That would be very helpful," Sam said. "But it's almost midnight. Think the detective will be willing to meet this late?"

"Not a problem," Brandon said. "You'll have to go back to the hotel and get that classy evening jacket you wore last night."

"I'm going to need an evening jacket to meet the investigator?"

"Can't get into the Paradise Club without one," Brandon said.

Chapter 25

I t's an interesting case," Raina Kirk said. "Tell me what you know, Mr. Sage."

"It goes back to the death of a young woman named Virginia Jennaway," Sam said.

He gave Raina a concise summary of the case. Maggie listened somewhat absently, not just because she had heard it all but because she was fascinated by the proprietor of Kirk Investigations. Raina spoke with a hint of an upper-class East Coast accent. She wore a fashionable evening gown of cognac-colored silk that fell in tiny pleats to her ankles. Her hair was caught up in a sophisticated chignon. Dainty diamond earrings danced below her ears.

She was not at all what one expected in a private investigator, Maggie thought. Sam would be annoyed if she whipped out her notebook and jotted down a few details, so she told herself she would wait until she got back to the hotel.

She and Sam had arrived at the Paradise a short time ago. They had been met by a maître d' and discreetly escorted to a small intimate booth deep in the shadows at the back of the nightclub. A few minutes later the owner of the club, Luther Pell, had arrived at the table to greet them.

Apparently satisfied with whatever he saw, he had invited them up a concealed staircase to his office in his private quarters above the club. That was where the four of them were gathered now, drinking coffee from delicate porcelain cups served on a silver tray.

She and Raina were seated in large padded leather chairs. Sam was on his feet near the French doors that looked out into a garden and the moonlit ocean beyond.

Luther was behind a polished wooden desk. Maggie had concluded that, unlike Raina Kirk, he looked exactly like what he was—a successful nightclub owner who probably had shady business acquaintances. But the fierce, dark landscapes on the paneled walls of the office cast invisible shadows across the room, telling her there was a lot more to Pell than what he allowed the world to see.

She was certain he was profoundly connected to the art. Her intuition told her he was the artist.

"I appreciate the help," Sam said, when he finished outlining the case. "The first priority is to find out more about the Guilfoyles and how they acquired the Carson Flint estate."

Raina inclined her head. "I agree. It's always smart to follow the money. Anything else?"

"This started out looking like a straightforward case of blackmail," Sam said. "But I'm starting to wonder if there's something more personal involved."

Luther studied him. "What do you mean by *personal?*"

"Blackmail is about money, pure and simple. But we've got three deaths—Jennaway, Nevins, and now Valerie Warren. It feels like something else is going on."

Startled, Maggie turned toward him. "Such as?"

"I don't know. Revenge, maybe."

"For Virginia Jennaway's death?" Luther suggested.

"A possibility," Sam said.

Luther nodded. "An old lover, perhaps."

"That would explain a revenge angle," Sam said.

Maggie cleared her throat. "A lover out to exact revenge is an interesting notion. But it's hard to believe anyone would still care deeply enough about a past relationship after four years to take the risk of committing murder."

"No," Luther said. He looked at Raina. "It's not at all hard to believe."

Raina smiled a misty smile. A sheen of moisture lit her eyes. She blinked away the telltale hint of tears.

Maggie did not need a lucid dream to know the bond between Raina Kirk and Luther Pell was strong. They were not just lovers; they were soul mates. If anything happened to Raina, Pell would stop at nothing to avenge her, regardless of how much time passed.

What would it be like to share such a powerful connection with a lover? she wondered. She squelched the wistful question immediately. A year and a half ago she had fooled herself into thinking she had found a man who understood and accepted her as she was. She had been heartbreakingly wrong. She would not make that mistake again.

Raina turned to Sam. "I understand you want to keep our association confidential."

"Yes," Sam said.

"That's normal. How shall I contact you?"

"Call the hotel and leave a message from my aunt," Sam said. "I'll check the front desk during the lunch break tomorrow and again around five when the seminars are over for the day. If I hear from you, I'll call you back from a pay phone."

"All right," Raina said.

"Do you need anything else?" Luther asked.

"No," Sam said. "Not tonight. Thanks for seeing us on such short notice."

"Brandon mentioned you used to work homicide in L.A.," Luther said. "He told me you handled the Bloody Scarf Murders. Said you were the detective who arrested Chichester."

"That's right," Sam said.

"I followed that case," Luther said. "You arrested the right man. Not always a good career move."

"The Chichester family convinced a judge and my boss that Chichester the Third was an innocent man," Sam said.

"There was talk that the innocent man tried to murder someone else while he was out on bail," Luther said. "Got caught in the act. After it became clear the press was on the story, the family had Chichester the Third committed to a private asylum. Coincidentally, the Bloody Scarf Murders stopped."

"They say coincidences do happen," Sam said. He looked at Maggie. "It's getting late. We should go. Busy day tomorrow."

"Yes," she said. She stood.

Luther got to his feet. "One more thing, Sage. I got the impression Brandon is using you as his eyes and ears out there at the Institute."

"He needs someone inside, and I'm available," Sam said. "It's good to know he's paying attention."

"So am I," Luther said. "Call me if it looks like you're going to need some backup. The people working security for me know how to keep out of sight when necessary."

"Thanks," Sam said. "I appreciate the offer. I may take you up on it."

"Carl is waiting outside the door," Luther said. "He'll escort you downstairs and out through the private entrance."

It was obviously not the first time Luther Pell had held a clandestine late-night meeting, Maggie thought. She smiled at Raina. "Thank you for assisting us, Miss Kirk."

"A pleasure to meet you, Miss Lodge," Raina said. "As you apparently have a long-standing interest in dream analysis, do you mind if I ask you a question?"

"Not at all," Maggie said.

"Do you think there's anything to the Guilfoyle Method? I understand Mr. Sage has concluded it's a con, but I would like your opinion."

The shadows in Raina's eyes made it clear she was not merely indulging her curiosity. This was personal.

"To be honest, I'm not sure yet," Maggie said. "At this point it's difficult to be certain how much of Guilfoyle's act is just that—an act—and how much might be a useful approach to gaining control of one's dreams."

"I see," Raina said. Her disappointment was reflected in her eyes, but she managed a gracious smile. "I was just curious."

Maggie turned to walk out of the office with Sam. She tried not to look at any of the paintings on the walls, but her gaze snagged on one. She stilled. So much darkness. So much pain. She was suddenly very certain the energy came from deep inside Luther Pell and that it flowed from his past.

He was old enough to have served as a young man in the Great War. One of her uncles had also served. She had met some of his friends who had endured things overseas they refused to discuss. Her uncle said that was because no one wanted to hear the truth about war. But she knew the effects of the violence haunted their dreams.

Keep quiet, she thought. Pell wouldn't thank her for her advice. He wouldn't even admit to having nightmares, at least not to her. But perhaps he talked to Raina. Or maybe Raina simply sensed the darkness because of the bond she shared with the man who loved her.

Whatever the case, Raina needed an answer.

Maggie changed course and walked to stand in front of the stormy landscape. Sam stopped. He did not ask any questions. He simply waited. Luther Pell did not move. Neither did Raina. They were all watching her now. No one spoke.

"There are a number of techniques for controlling one's dreams," she said, choosing her words with care. "Not all of them work for all dreamers. Most people give up trying to control their dreamscapes because it requires constant effort and because it isn't always successful."

"Very interesting," Raina said.

"Some people experience lucid dreaming more readily than others," Maggie continued. She did not take her eyes off the storm on the canvas. "There are those who have a natural talent for it. I would not be surprised if that is the case with the artist who did these paintings, for example."

"Do you think so?" Raina asked.

"Yes," Maggie said. "The fact that the painter is able to translate the nightmares onto canvas tells me that may be true. But he doesn't know how to control the dream."

"What advice would you give the artist?" Raina said.

"He should paint two more pictures." Maggie took a breath and allowed her intuition to guide her. "One must illustrate a scene that is calm and serene. The subject doesn't matter, but there should be sunlight and a sense of peace."

"What about the second picture?" Raina asked.

"The scene will be a hallway with no beginning and no end. There will be two doors."

"Why two doors?" Raina asked.

"Because you can open doors," Maggie said. "More importantly, you can also close them."

Sam and Luther did not speak, but Maggie knew they were listening.

"What would you advise the artist to do after he completes the paintings?" Raina asked.

"Each night before he goes to bed he should meditate on the painting of the doors and envision an art gallery behind each. One holds scenes from his nightmares. The serene picture hangs in the other gallery. When he finds himself trapped in a nightmare, he will remember that there is a door. He will go through it into the hallway and close the door behind him. He will understand that while the nightmares will always be there, he has the power to walk away from them. He can go down the hall and open the other door."

"And enter the gallery that holds the serene painting," Raina concluded.

Maggie turned around and smiled at her. "Yes. The technique will require practice and time. I must warn you there is no such thing as perfect control."

"Some measure of control is preferable to none," Raina said.

Chapter 26

"Do you want to tell me what happened back there in Luther Pell's office?" Sam asked.

"You're talking about my advice to the artist who painted those landscapes, aren't you?" Maggie said.

"Raina Kirk was very interested in what you had to say. Do you think she painted the pictures?"

"No, I think she was asking for a friend."

"Luther Pell?"

"That would be my guess."

They were standing in the connecting doorway between their hotel rooms. She was on her side. Sam was on his. There was an invisible wall between them. Sam had discarded his evening jacket. His shirt was open at the collar, and the bow tie was undone and draped around his neck.

She was in her robe and slippers. Her notebook was open on the table near the window. She had been jotting down a few observations and plot ideas when Sam had knocked on the connecting door a moment ago.

They had spoken very little on the drive back to the hotel. Both of them had retreated to their own private thoughts. When they unlocked the doors of their rooms, Sam had said a casual good night, as if he had intended to go straight to bed. She had envied him. She was too tense to sleep, and that was fortunate because she knew that when she did there would probably be dreams of a dead woman in a fiery crash and paintings that cast shadows.

She wasn't feeling up to handling that sort of dreamscape tonight. Exhaustion and stress played havoc with her ability to control her dreams.

"I noticed you didn't advise Miss Kirk to throw the paintings into the trash," Sam said.

"That wouldn't have worked," Maggie said. "The energy in them was laid down by the artist. It came from his own dreams. I don't know how to explain it. All I can tell you is that it wouldn't do any good to try to separate the painter from the paintings. It wouldn't change anything. He would just create more art infused with the same bad heat. He wouldn't be able to stop himself."

"Think Pell will take your advice to paint a serene picture and then paint a hallway with a couple of doors?" Sam asked.

"I don't know. People almost never—"

"—take good advice. Given that bit of wisdom, you picked an odd career path."

"Assisting Lillian with the Aunt Cornelia column isn't a career; it's a job. I told you, I can't make a living on confession stories. I need to support myself while I work on my novel."

"I understand."

"There's another reason why I want to become a successful author," she said.

"What's that?"

"I will never be happy working for someone else. I don't take orders well."

Sam's mouth curved in the faint smile she was learning meant he was genuinely amused. "Or good advice."

"Evidently you possess a similar character flaw," she said. "It explains why you made the career-ending mistake of arresting that horrible man in L.A."

"Chichester."

"The reason I hired you instead of one of those other two private detectives in Adelina Beach was because you struck me as a man who could not be bought."

"Not all cops are on the take, Maggie."

"I know." She smiled. "And not all those who are interested in dreams are con artists or the sadly deluded victims of con artists."

"I don't think you're a fraud, and I don't think you're deluded," Sam said.

"Really? What am I, then? Besides a client, I mean."

"You're a mystery."

"You're in the business of solving mysteries."

"I find them interesting."

"I think you need them," she whispered.

"You may be right." He took a step back, retreating into his room. "Get some sleep, Maggie. I'll see you at breakfast."

"Do you want to kiss me?" she asked.

He went still. "What kind of question is that?"

"The yes-or-no kind."

"Yes." He moved forward, crossing the threshold into her room. He brushed the side of her face with his knuckles. "I want to kiss you very much, but it would probably be a mistake."

"I'm a mystery, and you like to solve mysteries."

"That would be my excuse," he said. "What's yours?"

"That's easy." She flattened her palm against his chest. "Research."

His eyes tightened ominously. "For your book."

"There's a romance at the heart of the story, you see," she said.

"I'm sure you've already done some research on the subject. You did mention that you enjoy writing the sinning parts of the sin, suffer, and repent stories you sell to the confession magazines."

"Yes, but thus far the results of my research have been extremely disappointing. Luckily for the sake of my confession-writing business, I have a very good imagination."

"Don't remind me."

He covered her mouth with his own. She sensed his restraint and knew he intended to remain in full control of the kiss. That was fine by her. She was in control, too. This was their first embrace, after all, an experiment for both of them.

She did not see the storm coming until it struck. She possessed a vivid imagination and she knew how to dream, but nothing could have prepared her for the dizzying rush of sensation that swept through her. When she found herself caged, her back to the wall, Sam's hands flattened on either side of her head, she knew she wasn't the only one who had been caught off guard.

She gripped his shoulders and hung on for dear life as she tried to identify and label the fiery rush of sensations. She needed to remember every aspect of the kiss—she needed the words—but it was impossible to keep the emotional distance required to step back and *observe*. The kiss was fierce, hot, demanding. They were fighting each other for the embrace. When you found yourself in intimate hand-to-hand combat there was no choice but to be fully engaged.

Sam wrenched his mouth off hers and kissed the side of her throat.

"So soft," he groaned.

He pried his hands away from the wall, gripped her waist, and pulled her tightly against him. After a moment he lifted her off her feet and out of her slippers.

She clenched his shoulders to steady herself. The laughter bubbled out of her.

"I'm not frigid," she announced.

He stilled. "What the hell are you talking about?"

"Long story. Some other time."

"Right. Some other time."

His mouth came down on hers again. He carried her into the other room—his room—stood her on her feet beside the bed, and undid the sash of her robe. He eased the garment off her shoulders as if he were unveiling a priceless work of art.

She struggled with the front of his shirt. When she finally succeeded in getting it undone, she flattened her hands against his hard chest and threaded her fingers through the crisp hair she found there. His scent was a heady mix of shaving soap, sweat, and the raw essence of Sam Sage. It acted like a tonic on her senses.

He undid the small buttons that closed the front of her nightgown and pushed the silky fabric down over her hips. It pooled on the floor around her bare feet.

He paused long enough to yank the covers down to the foot of the bed, and then he picked her up and settled her on the sheets.

"Don't go away," he said.

He turned off the bedside lamp and disappeared into the bathroom. She heard him open a case of some kind—his shaving kit, she decided. When he returned he was nude except for his briefs. She watched him step out of those and sheathe his rigid erection in a prophylactic.

In the next moment he was on the bed beside her, gathering her into his arms. He slid one leg between hers and closed his hand gently over her breast.

"You smell so good," he said, his voice low and husky. "I can't get enough of you."

"I'm glad"—she stroked her palm down his chest, exploring him—"because I want more of you, too."

"Good. Perfect."

The edge of his tongue dampened the peak of her breast, and his hand eased down her body, over the curve of her hip, and into the wet heat between her thighs.

She took a sharp, startled breath when he began to stroke her. Again he stilled. He raised his head and looked down at her. His eyes burned in the shadows.

"Did I hurt you?" he asked.

"No." She moved against his hand. "I just wasn't expecting you to touch me there."

"Where do you want me to touch you?"

"There." She grabbed his hand and held it in place. "Right there."

His laugh was hoarse and quickly changed into a groan. The pressure of his hand became more insistent, more demanding. She could feel an exciting tension deep inside. Anticipation gave way to desperation.

"More," she said.

"Come for me first." His voice was a soft rasp that set all her senses on fire. "I want you to come harder than you've ever come before. Then I'm going to find out what it feels like to be inside you."

In the end she did not know whether it was the thrilling pressure of his hand or the sensual demand in his voice that sent her over the edge. The orgasm was upon her before she realized what was happening, at once surprising and satisfying.

"Yes," he said against her throat. "Just like that."

She was still savoring the unfamiliar but delightful sensation when he moved on top of her and thrust heavily into her soaking-wet, highly sensitized body. She flinched, but the shock of his entry was unexpectedly satisfying, too. It felt right.

When his own climax pounded through him a short time later, she held him close. He collapsed on top of her, his face in the pillow. She lay quietly for a moment, marveling at the strange and astonishingly intimate energy that whispered in the atmosphere. It was as if the act of sex had opened up a new connection between them. It was probably her imagination; nevertheless, she needed to get the feeling down while it was still fresh.

Words. She needed words. Her notebook was in the other room.

She started to edge out from under Sam's weight.

"Don't even think about it," he said.

Chapter 27

Sam reluctantly rolled away from Maggie's warm, damp body and retreated briefly into the bathroom. When he returned he collapsed onto the bed and gathered her close against his side. She felt good. Soft, warm, damp with perspiration and the heat of sex. Everything about her felt right. But the mysteries of Maggie Lodge remained. He needed answers.

"What the hell made you think you were frigid?" he asked.

She levered herself up on her elbow and looked down at him. "It was one of two theories that the doctors and therapists came up with to explain my reluctance to get married. I preferred frigidity to the other one."

"Which was?"

"Female hysteria. They don't put you in an asylum because you're frigid. That's just a sexual problem. But hysteria can get you locked up."

"I see. Well, given what you've been through recently—two suspicious deaths, an encounter with the obsessed doctor who once tried to poison you, and a midnight meeting with a nightclub owner who probably has mob connections—I think it's safe to say you are not suffering from hysteria."

She smiled. "That is, of course, a great relief, especially coming from a professional such as yourself."

"Trust me, I've seen people of every gender get hysterical. You're not the type. Also, I'm not a doctor, but I could have told you before we did what we just did that you aren't frigid, either."

"You knew that all along?"

"From the moment you walked into my office."

She folded her arms on top of his chest and rested her chin on her hands. "That's very interesting. What made you so sure?"

He smiled a little. "Intuition."

"To be perfectly honest, I wasn't so sure that I didn't have a problem in that department. I've never had conclusive proof that I wasn't frigid, you see. Not until tonight, that is."

It took him a beat to realize what she was saying.

"You've never had a climax?" he asked.

"Nope. Not until a few minutes ago."

He thought about that. "You said you came dangerously close to getting married."

"I did. And when I called off the wedding, my ex-fiancé informed everyone it was because I was both frigid and inclined toward hysteria."

"Damn. No wonder you aren't interested in marriage."

Maggie smiled a slow, seductive smile. "Luckily it turns out I'm good at the sinning thing."

He wanted to ask more questions, but something told him this was not the time. He wrapped a palm around the back of her head.

"Yes, you are. You are very, very good at it," he said. "I'm starting to think I might have a talent for it, too."

"More than a talent. I do believe you've got a psychic gift for this kind of sinning."

Chapter 28

found some interesting background information about the legend of the Traveler," Pru said. "Got paper and a pencil?"

There was the usual crackling on the line and Pru's voice sounded somewhat tinny and far away, but otherwise the long-distance connection was good.

"Yes, I'm ready." Maggie pushed the stack of coins to one side of the small shelf beneath the pay phone and made room for her notebook. "Talk fast. I'm calling from a gas station."

Pru had left word at the hotel saying she had some "news from home." She had left a number and instructions to call at twelve fifteen, when she would be on her lunch break and stationed at a pay phone.

Maggie could see Sam through the open door of the phone booth. He was leaning against the front fender of the Packard, fedora angled over his eyes, arms folded across his chest.

Every time she looked at him she thought about what had happened during the night and got a little thrill. She thought about it when she wasn't looking at him, too, and got the same frisson of awareness. She had not, however, been able to tell if Sam was also thinking about last night. It was frustrating. Irritating.

At breakfast she had been optimistic that the passionate encounter had meant something to him. She was almost certain she had caught a glint of sensual heat in his eyes. But now she could no longer be sure. He was back in control mode. Ever the professional private detective. *Just doing my job, ma'am.*

"I can't talk long," Pru said. "I'm using the pay phone at the coffee shop across the street from the college. About the Traveler. There have been various versions of the legend circulating for centuries. The one thing the stories all have in common is the notion of an assassin who possesses the ability to travel on the astral plane. He murders people in their dreams."

"I knew that much. Anything else?"

"Maybe. The Traveler manipulates the individual's dreams, encouraging desperate or dangerous actions that result in deaths that look like accidents or natural causes."

"Or an overdose?"

"Right," Pru said. "The Traveler began as a human avenger who could be summoned by a dreamer for the purpose of securing justice when there was no other recourse. But somewhere along the line the assassin's spirit became unmoored from its body. It's been trapped on the astral plane ever since. The closest it can get to human form is when it's summoned by a powerful lucid dreamer."

The operator came on the line requesting more money.

"Hang on," Maggie said. She shoved coins into the slot. "Okay, Pru. Keep talking."

"I saved the most interesting bit for last," Pru said. "I found a paper in the *Journal of Psychic Dream Discoveries* that discusses the legend. It was published in the quarterly issue that appeared a couple of months after Virginia Jennaway's death. The author claims to have investigated the rumors that a spirit named the Traveler was responsible for the murder of a young woman from Keeley Point who drowned."

Maggie caught her breath. "Jennaway."

"The woman was not named in the article, but given the date of the journal and the other details, yes, the victim must have been Jennaway. The author went to a great deal of effort to debunk the legend and the possibility that the spirit caused the woman's death."

"I get the feeling you've got a surprise ending to this story."

"How's this? The authority who adamantly denied the possibility of astral projection and the existence of the Traveler was none other than Dr. Emerson Oxlade."

"Well, well, well," Maggie said. "Small world."

"It is when it comes to lucid dreaming and legends."

"Thanks, Pru, I appreciate the information."

"Anytime. But I'm worried about you. It sounds like things are getting complicated and dangerous there in Burning Cove."

"They are certainly getting weird."

"Do you feel comfortable with your private detective?"

Maggie looked at Sam, who was still propped against the car. "I told you, he's not my private detective, and *comfortable* may not be the appropriate word, but he is very . . . competent. Listen to this, Pru. Last night I met the owner of the hottest nightclub in town and his lover, who just happens to be a private investigator herself."

"How thrilling. I knew you were going off on an adventure. I just wish I was there with you."

"When this is over we will both find a way to spend some time here in Burning Cove."

"Absolutely. Meanwhile, please be careful."

"I will. Thanks for the information."

The operator interrupted to request more money.

"Goodbye," Pru said quickly and hung up.

Maggie replaced the receiver and scooped up the leftover coins and the notepad. She stepped out of the booth.

Sam unfolded his arms and straightened away from the fender. "Anything new from your friend?"

"Maybe."

Maggie adjusted the strap of her handbag and walked around the hood of the Packard, heading for the passenger side. Sam followed her and opened the door. She had decided to give up trying to persuade him to let her drive. She would have plenty of time to zip around in the Packard once they were back in Adelina Beach.

All the time in the world. It was a depressing thought.

She did not want to contemplate the very distinct possibility that once Sam's work was done she might never see him again, except perhaps on the streets of Adelina Beach. Or in a restaurant. At the grocery store. In a theater. The gas station.

Adelina Beach was a small community. She might have to move.

Apparently oblivious to her mood, Sam closed her door, got behind the wheel, and drove back toward the hotel. He was a very good driver, she decided. Not an exciting driver, but a calm, careful driver. There was something to be said for calm and careful.

Last night she had witnessed a very different side to Sam Sage. He was not calm when he made love. He had been very, very careful, however—careful to make sure she was completely satisfied.

"Well?" he prompted.

"Pru filled me in on the legend of the Traveler, most of which we already knew, but she came across what looks like a reference to Virginia Jennaway's death in a journal dedicated to dream research. The article was written by a distinguished authority who was apparently extremely anxious to squelch the rumors of the Traveler's involvement in Jennaway's death. Dr. Emerson Oxlade."

"Interesting."

"Oxlade is very keen to make sure his professional reputation remains unsullied. He doesn't want the other experts in the field concluding he's a quack."

"Yet he's now affiliated with the Guilfoyles, who are walking a very fine line when it comes to respectability."

Maggie considered that for a moment. "Dolores Guilfoyle is certainly skilled when it comes to selling dreams. She obviously has a talent for promoting the business. Arthur is a good actor."

"It's safe to say both of them are in it for the money, but Oxlade has a different agenda," Sam said. "His research and his reputation are more important to him than making a profit, and he holds all the cards because he controls the drug."

When they returned to the hotel, the front desk clerk handed Sam a message from Raina Kirk. Sam read it quickly and handed it to Maggie.

Expect to have news of your aunt tomorrow.

Chapter 29

Maggie braced herself for the disturbing shadow inside the theater and allowed the handsome dream guide named Larry to escort her into the room. For one very unnerving moment she thought he was going to show her to the seat at the far end of the last row, the one where Beverly Nevins's body had been found. She definitely could not sit there. But to her relief he settled her closer to the stage.

"Mr. Guilfoyle was very specific about the location of your seat," Larry confided. "He wanted to make sure you had a good view."

So Guilfoyle had ordered Larry to seat her on the side of the theater that was farthest away from the door? Interesting. There were no bad seats in the small space. Each one had a clear view of the stage. The only thing that had been accomplished by positioning her at the far end of an aisle was making sure she would be one of the last people out the door when the demonstration was over.

"Thank you," she said.

Larry smiled. "Enjoy the dream reading."

She caught a whiff of marijuana smoke clinging to his clothes and remembered what Valerie had said about the dream guides. *They all smoked some of Larry's reefers.*

The dream generator had been removed from the elevated stage. In its place was a gilded crimson velvet couch and a single chair. There were only twelve people in the audience, as Dolores Guilfoyle had promised.

Maggie felt underdressed. She had chosen a crisp business suit for the demonstration, but everyone else looked as if they had been invited to a formal reception. The men were in evening jackets and the women wore cocktail gowns. Maybe they were planning to go out on the town after the event.

The other eleven observers—four couples, a single man, and two women—varied in age, but they all had one thing in common: They were clearly affluent. These were the people who were expected to buy their way up to the highest, most expensive levels of the Guilfoyle program. Aside from a few polite murmurs, the attendees ignored each other. They were here for one reason only—to witness an exhibition of psychic lucid dreaming.

There was no sign of either the Guilfoyles or Emerson Oxlade. Maggie assumed they were all backstage.

When the lights were lowered, Maggie took one last look at her watch before the room darkened. It was a little after eight. Sam would be making his way through the gardens to the guest villa Oxlade was using. The thought sent another unsettling frisson down her spine.

There was no more time to think about the risks that Sam was planning to take because Dolores Guilfoyle, dressed in a long, heavily beaded beige gown, walked out onto the stage. Her dramatic makeup and the deep waves of her hair enhanced her aura of glamour. Elbow-length gloves and sparkling earrings finished the look.

"Welcome to this exclusive demonstration of the power of the Guilfoyle Method," she said. "Each of you was selected for this opportunity because Mr. Guilfoyle sensed you possess the special spark of latent psychic talent that enables certain individuals to advance to the highest level of the Method. Very few individuals have the ability, let alone the determination, to make it to the top."

In other words, not everyone has the cash required to climb the Guilfoyle Method ladder, Maggie thought.

"Dr. Oxlade will be assisting in tonight's demonstration," Dolores continued. "He will act as Mr. Guilfoyle's guide and interpreter. Please understand that a dream reading requires an enormous amount of focus and mental power. When tonight's exhibition is over, Mr. Guilfoyle will be exhausted. He will not be able to take questions. Each of you will have an opportunity to meet privately with him tomorrow to discuss how you can personally benefit from the Guilfoyle Method."

Dolores walked gracefully off the stage and vanished behind the heavy curtain. There was a hushed silence. Emerson Oxlade appeared from the wings. He fiddled with his spectacles, cleared his throat, and addressed the audience.

"Please understand that what you are about to witness is an example of a form of lucid dreaming that very few individuals possess. Everyone dreams, but the vast majority of people do not have the ability to use their dreams to access their latent psychic senses. When Mr. Guilfoyle is in a trance he will attempt to communicate, but his remarks may sound cryptic at times. Keep in mind he will be speaking to you from a dream."

Oxlade paused, trying to see the faces of the people in the audience. Maggie knew he was looking for her. She wished she could sink deeper into the shadows. Being fancied by an obsessive scientist was not thrilling.

Sure enough, when he spotted her, a dark glitter of unwholesome excitement lit his eyes. For a horrible moment she thought he might have the nerve to summon her to the stage.

But he turned away, walked to the chair, sat down, and opened his notebook. He adjusted his glasses one more time and cleared his throat again.

"We are ready for you, Mr. Guilfoyle," he said.

Arthur Guilfoyle, dressed in his dramatic high-collared black coat, strode out from behind the curtain. His oiled hair gleamed in the light. He wore eye makeup, just as he had for the opening lecture.

Showtime, Maggie thought.

Arthur inclined his head in a dramatic gesture, acknowledging his audience with aloof dignity. He did not speak. He sat down on the gilded couch and braced a hand on each knee. He gazed at the audience for a long moment, as though fortifying himself for what lay ahead.

Abruptly he closed his eyes. The theater lights went lower still. Maggie wondered who was handling the switches in the wings. Dolores or one of the dream guides, perhaps.

Oxlade, seated at the outer edge of the glare of the spotlight, spoke to the audience.

"Silence, please," he said. "Mr. Guilfoyle will now prepare to enter the lucid dreamstate. This requires intense concentration and mental discipline."

Guilfoyle continued to stare at the audience, unblinking, for a long moment. The crowd waited expectantly.

Without warning he shut his eyes.

"Are you in the lucid dreamstate, Mr. Guilfoyle?" Oxlade asked.

"Yes," Guilfoyle intoned.

"Describe what you see, sir."

"I am in the center of a clear crystal sphere. When I look up I see the majesty of the cosmos. When I look out to the horizon I see no limits or barriers. I am gazing into infinity."

"What do you see when you look down?" Oxlade asked.

"This theater. I see myself and you, Dr. Oxlade. I see the aspiring dreamers in the audience. There is latent power in each of them. They all have the potential to discover the secrets of extreme lucid dreaming, the potential to open the pathway to their psychic senses."

The audience responded with a murmur of excitement.

"You have accessed all of your senses," Oxlade continued. "You are now able to perceive what the rest of us cannot. Are you prepared to respond to questions from the audience?"

"Yes."

Oxlade turned to the crowd. "Who wishes to ask Mr. Guilfoyle a question?"

A man in the second row raised his hand. Oxlade nodded to him.

"I am considering a large investment in a certain mining company," the man said. "Do you advise me to go forward with the purchase of the stock?"

Arthur was silent for a moment, radiating intense concentration.

"The company will do well," he said finally. "You will profit from the investment."

"Next question," Oxlade said to the audience.

Hands shot up around the room.

Maggie stifled a sigh. It was going to be a long night.

Chapter 30

Sam stood in the darkened kitchen of the guest villa, giving himself some time to absorb the atmosphere. It was the house Oxlade was staying in and it was supposed to be empty because the doctor was in the main building of the Institute assisting in Guilfoyle's reading.

The villa did feel empty. The curtains and shades were closed but moonlight filtered in through the transom windows above the doors.

After a moment he switched on the flashlight and looked around. The kitchen was neat and tidy—probably the work of a daily house-keeper provided by the Institute. On the other hand, Oxlade appeared to be a fussy man by nature, and he was in the drug business, so maybe he did his own housekeeping.

Sam crossed the linoleum floor, went into a hallway, and set about exploring the villa. He did not know what he was looking for—he just hoped he would recognize it when he saw it.

He had left the Packard in the parking lot of the hotel and made his way onto the grounds of the Institute on foot via a service gate. Night and the elaborate gardens and the various garages, toolsheds, and boarded-up buildings provided ample cover. He was reasonably satisfied no one had seen him, but there was no way to be certain.

The hall led to two bedrooms, one of which had been transformed into a temporary office. A large well-worn briefcase was positioned next to a table.

The simple lock on the briefcase was easily overcome with a paper clip. Sam reached inside and removed a leather-bound journal.

He opened the journal, took a pencil and a notepad out of the pocket of his trench coat, and started making notes. The pages were filled with excited speculations about the potential of the dream-enhancing drug but nothing that looked like a formula or a list of ingredients.

The first entry was dated some seven months earlier, which meant the journal covered the time during which Maggie had booked appointments with Oxlade. Sure enough, there was a great deal of elated detail about a female patient named Smith.

A uniquely powerful lucid dreamer . . . Requires firm guidance . . . Refuses to accept the reality of her talent . . . Suffered a fit of hysteria . . . Attempt at sedation failed . . . Unable to locate . . . Great loss to science . . .

From an entry dated the night before:

. . . Smith is here. Note: Name changed to Lodge. I have found her at last. The Guilfoyles assure me she will cooperate. The first step is to remove her from the influence of her research assistant as soon as possible . . .

The last entry:

The dream guides are spreading rumors about the death of the Nevins woman. The legend of the Traveler has been referenced. This nonsense must be halted immediately . . .

Sam checked his watch with the flashlight. There wasn't time to read the journal cover to cover. The dream reading was scheduled to run for an hour and a half, and he had used up the first twenty minutes working his way through the garden and breaking into the villa. He had to get back to the hotel, get the car, and drive to the Institute to pick up Maggie when the demonstration concluded.

Reluctantly he dropped the journal into the briefcase and swept the flashlight around the room. Nothing seemed out of place—just the opposite. There was an air of precision and order in the space. He opened the closet door. The few clothes hanging inside were positioned precisely the same distance apart.

There was no sign of a lockbox or a safe. Where would a man hide a drug in a house that did not belong to him? There were more options than in a hotel room, but a man like Oxlade—a man who was not in a familiar environment—would probably keep his valuables close.

After a moment Sam went into the bathroom. A handsome travel Dopp kit sat on the counter. There was nothing unusual about the items inside—shaving brush, soap, hairbrush, tweezers, shoehorn, and a bottle of cologne.

Sam opened the bottle of cologne. There was no scent.

He left the grounds of the Institute and made his way back to the hotel. Emerging from a narrow break in the long row of leafy oleanders that bordered the Sea Dream parking lot, he walked across the dimly lit pavement, heading for the Packard. The demonstration would be over soon. It was almost time to drive to the Institute to pick up Maggie. It was one thing for a woman to walk the short distance during the day when she was wearing the right shoes. Night, high heels, and a tight skirt complicated things.

The roar of an accelerating car engine and the shriek of tires sounded in the night. The vehicle was behind him and closing in fast.

There was no time to turn around to see what was happening, no need to confirm the obvious. He dove for the narrow space between two parked cars and went down hard on the pavement.

The sedan flashed past and kept going, its headlights off.

Sam got to his feet, wincing. He found his fedora on the ground near the rear tire of one of the cars that had protected him. In the dim glare of the lights at the entrance of the hotel he could make out a smudge mark. He tried to brush it off, but he only succeeded in smearing the stain. There were a couple of oily streaks on his trench coat, too.

It occurred to him that he ought to go to his room and clean up before he drove to the Institute. He glanced at his watch. No time.

Chapter 31

Maggie tried again to make out the time, but the theater lights were still turned down. Earlier she had been bored with the dream reading, but a few minutes ago an unnerving frisson of anxiety had iced the back of her neck. The sensation had come and gone quickly, but it had left her on edge. She could not explain it, but intuitively she knew the small shock was somehow connected to Sam.

She wished she could slip out the door unnoticed, but given the intimate setting, there was no way to do so. She was stuck until the show ended. And it was just that—a show.

A woman spoke up from the front row. "My sister died and left me a large house on the East Coast. Should I move back there or sell it?"

"Sell it," Arthur said, evidently speaking from the depths of his trance. "Your future is here on the West Coast."

Maggie suppressed a sigh. Guilfoyle's answers to the questions from the audience were no better than one might expect from a carnival fortune-teller. The only thing that made his responses stand out was his acting talent. He really was an extraordinary performer. But a con was a con no matter how polished the performance.

The most interesting information she had acquired this evening pertained to Emerson Oxlade, and it had come as a surprise until she gave it some serious thought. She had known from the outset that although Oxlade was obsessive, he was not a con artist. He truly believed in lucid dreaming and in his own theories. What had come as a revelation was that he was clearly convinced Guilfoyle was using his dream talent to access his paranormal senses.

Oxlade had fallen for Guilfoyle's con just like most of the audience.

Another hand shot up. A man rose to his feet.

"Shortly before my brother died he told me that he left all of his money to me. We buried him last week but we can't find the will. Where should we look?"

"I see a house darkened by recent death," Arthur said. "There is a road. A garden. There is water nearby."

"A pond?" the man asked eagerly. "My brother had a fishpond behind his house."

"Yes, a pond," Arthur said. "There is a hidden safe somewhere inside the dark house."

"Huh." The man dropped back into his seat, unsatisfied. "We searched the damn house."

"You must search it again," Arthur said. "I can do no more tonight. I must rest. No. Not yet. Something is wrong." A visible shudder arced through him. He rose to his feet, eyes brilliant and hypnotic. "I see a figure cloaked in shadows."

Oxlade frowned, glanced at the notebook on his lap, and looked up quickly, apparently confused.

"Calm yourself, Mr. Guilfoyle," he urged. "Remember, you are in control of your dream trance."

"I must know what this spirit seeks. I sense that it is malevolent. Dangerous. It is hunting."

Maggie heard the audience take a sharp collective breath.

Oxlade appeared torn now. Maggie knew that part of him wanted to believe Guilfoyle was experiencing a true psychic vision, but another part was skeptical and decidedly worried.

"You must control yourself, Mr. Guilfoyle," he said firmly. "Describe what you see."

"The hunter moves through the shadows," Guilfoyle declared in a resonant voice. "He stalks a woman. I must warn her."

"Who is this woman?" Oxlade asked, clearly alarmed and bewildered.

"She is close," Guilfoyle said. "Very close. Perhaps here in this room."

There was another shocked gasp from the audience.

Oxlade tried to take control. "Wake up, Mr. Guilfoyle."

"I fear the hunter is the spirit known as the Traveler. I must stop him. Only I can protect the woman he stalks. I cannot leave the astral plane until I have sent him away. I will not let him hurt her."

"The Traveler." Oxlade stood abruptly, breaking the spell Arthur had cast over the audience. "This is ridiculous. There is no such being as the Traveler. You are hallucinating, Mr. Guilfoyle. I insist you snap out of the trance immediately."

"I've had enough," a man in the front row bellowed. He rose from his seat. "This is an act. Guilfoyle is trying to scare us into signing up for his program. My wife and I are leaving."

"But, Henry," the woman in the seat next to his said. "We can't leave now. I haven't had a chance to ask my question."

"Come along, Martha." Henry gripped his wife's arm and propelled her up out of the seat. "I agreed to let you watch this idiotic performance because I thought it would make you realize Guilfoyle is a fraud."

"Henry, please, you're making a scene," Martha hissed.

Her husband ignored her. He steered Martha up the aisle and opened the door. Light from the hallway slanted across the theater. People got to their feet, mumbling uneasily, and headed for the exit.

Stuck on the far side of the room, Maggie stood and waited for the theater to empty.

Onstage, Guilfoyle and Oxlade were both on their feet. Oxlade clutched his notebook in one hand.

"I understand you are an actor," he said, his voice tight with anger. "I realize you are trying to put on a show. But I will not allow you to make a mockery of my theories. Is that clear? If there is one more incident like the one that just took place, I will terminate our arrangement."

He stomped offstage, not waiting for an answer, and disappeared into the wings. Arthur smiled at Maggie, a slow, knowing smile that she knew was intended to be intimate and seductive. Ice touched the back of her neck and trickled down her spine.

"A moment, if you please, Miss Lodge," Arthur said.

He descended the steps at the side of the stage and walked up the aisle toward the entrance of the theater. He closed the door and turned to confront her from the opposite end of the last row of seats.

"I have something of great importance to say to you. In spite of what Oxlade just said, I was not acting tonight. While I was in the trance I sensed an ominous presence on the grounds of the Institute. Whatever it is—whoever it is—it is hunting you."

Chapter 32

Another flicker of glacially cold electricity sparked across Maggie's senses. She was alone with Guilfoyle in the theater, and he had positioned himself between her and the door.

"I don't believe for a minute that anyone is hunting me," she said. She gripped the strap of her handbag very tightly. "I am going to leave now. Mr. Sage will be waiting for me at the lobby entrance."

"Sage is your chauffeur as well as your research assistant?" Arthur asked.

"He is very useful."

"Evidently." Arthur chuckled. "How long have you known him?"

"Not long," she said, aiming for a breezy, who-cares tone.

"How does one go about hiring a research assistant?" Arthur asked, seemingly intrigued.

"The same way one finds everything else—the phone book."

"Does he claim to be a lucid dreamer, too?"

"No," Maggie said. "His interest is purely professional."

"In other words, he can never truly understand you," Arthur said, "not the way I do."

"I have no idea what you mean. You must excuse me."

"I will only take a moment of your time. You are a special woman, Miss Lodge. The first time I saw you I realized I had been searching for you for a very long time. I just hadn't realized it. There is a connection between us. I can sense it."

Maggie considered her options. She did not feel genuinely threatened—not yet. Guilfoyle was making no attempt to close the distance between them. She could still hear voices out in the hall. If she screamed, people would hear her. And then there was Sam. If she did not show up outside the lobby soon, he would come looking for her.

There was no need to panic. This was, in fact, a golden opportunity to acquire information. She might be able to take advantage of the situation.

"You gave a very interesting performance, Mr. Guilfoyle," she said.

He regarded her as if she were the most beautiful woman he had ever met.

"I apologize if I frightened you," he said.

"Not at all."

"I was afraid the reference to the Traveler might have upset you."

"Why? I don't believe in that legend, just as I don't believe that it is possible to travel on the astral plane. Credit where it's due, Mr. Guilfoyle; you are an excellent actor. You had the audience riveted until you overplayed your hand with that nonsense about the Traveler. But we both know your dream readings tonight were no better than those of a storefront fortune-teller."

Arthur sighed. "I do my best. Very well, you didn't buy my psychic readings, but you do believe there is such a thing as lucid dreaming."

"Yes, of course. That's why I'm writing a book on the subject and why I bought a ticket for this conference."

AMANDA QUICK

"Oxlade told me you were a patient of his at one time."

"You are misinformed. I was never a patient of Oxlade's. I booked couple of professional consultations with him, but I was not at all impressed with his theories and techniques. I realize he has a certain reputation in the field, so I understand why you want to use him to promote the Guilfoyle Method."

Arthur's eyelids lowered very slightly. She knew he was recalculating.

"Oxlade's reputation is impressive and helpful when it comes to promotion," he said. "But I will admit I have lost confidence in him."

"Really? Why?"

Arthur snorted. "Because he was so easily taken in by my psychic dreaming act. He claims to be a brilliant dream analyst, but he is extraordinarily credulous. Like the vast majority of people in the world, he can easily be convinced to believe what he desperately wants to believe."

"And as it happens, he really wants to believe that lucid dreaming can open the door to latent psychic talents."

Arthur shrugged. "All serious dream research runs into the problem of independent verification. In the end, one is entirely dependent on the report of the dreamer. There is no way to confirm it."

"You went too far tonight. Oxlade believes there is a link between lucid dreaming and latent psychic senses, but he does not believe in astral projection or legends like the Traveler."

"I brought Oxlade in as a lecturer for one reason and one reason only—marketing. If he doesn't work out, he can be replaced."

"At least you're honest about it," Maggie said.

"I am also being honest when I tell you I have been a strong lucid dreamer since my teens. I've spent years learning how to gain control over my dreams and put them to good use."

"Good use?"

"People like you and me have been given a rare talent, Miss Lodge. I think we were meant to discover a purpose for our lucid dreaming ability. I admit I've been willing to try any number of experiments, analysis, and therapies in the hope of finding out how I can employ my gift to help others. I realize now that I need you to fulfill my vision. We share a destiny, Miss Lodge. We can fulfill it together here at the Institute."

"This has gone far enough," Maggie said. "I have no interest in assisting you in the promotion of the Guilfoyle Method. It is obviously a con. You are in the dream business for the money. Admit it."

"That's not true—"

Footsteps sounded on the stage. Oxlade appeared from the wings, clipboard in one fist. His face was tight and twisted in rage.

"It is true," he roared. "Every word of it. You have deceived me, you lying bastard. I was a fool to put my professional reputation at risk for the sake of a fraud. Our association is finished."

Oxlade stomped down the side steps, marched up the aisle, and stormed out of the entrance of the theater. He slammed the door.

A tense silence fell.

Arthur groaned. "Shit. Dolores is not going to be happy about this."

"You must excuse me," Maggie said. She started toward him. "Please get out of my way. Mr. Sage will be waiting."

"I will see you to your car."

"That won't be necessary. If you don't get out of my way I will scream."

"Calm down," Arthur said soothingly. "You are allowing yourself to become hysterical. Oxlade mentioned your delicate nerves."

"That is the dumbest thing you could have said to me." She flashed her coldest smile. "Take my advice and stop talking."

For the first time he looked uncertain. She got ready to scream. He must have realized she was going to go through with her threat, because at the last second he stepped out of her way.

She yanked open the door and went out into the hall. Guilfoyle hurried after her. She ignored him.

"Miss Lodge, please wait," he said. "There's been a terrible misunderstanding."

She hurried down the hall. The lobby was nearly empty. Dolores Guilfoyle was chatting with a couple that was waiting for their car to be brought around. When she saw Maggie and Arthur her face tightened. Maggie remembered the words from her dream: *Stay away from my husband.*

The dream guide named Jake opened the front door for Maggie.

"Can I get your car, ma'am?" he asked.

"No, thank you," she said. "Someone is picking me up."

Jake looked out at the driveway. "The Packard?"

"Yes," she said.

"Nice car."

"It is." She smiled. "I just wish I got to drive it more often. My research assistant insists on being behind the wheel."

Jake chuckled. "Can't blame a man for wanting to drive that speedster."

"Can't blame a woman for wanting to drive it, either," Maggie said.

She went briskly outside, aware that Arthur was right behind her.

"Miss Lodge," he said. "Let me explain."

Sam was waiting in the shadows, the fedora angled a little lower than usual over one side of his face. The result was that he looked a little more dangerous than usual. Relief splashed through her. He was all right. The disturbing sensation she had experienced a short time ago in the theater must have been a trick of her imagination, generated by the shadows from the seat in which Nevins had died.

Sam saw her and started forward, but his attention shifted immediately to Arthur. A hard, cold light appeared in his eyes.

"Ready to leave?" he asked. He took her arm but he did not take his eyes off Guilfoyle.

"Yes." She gave Arthur a cool smile. "It's been an insightful evening."

"Tomorrow is the last day of the conference," Arthur said. "I hope you will attend the seminars."

He inclined his head in a courtly gesture and strode back into the lobby.

Sam watched him leave. "An insightful evening?"

"I'll explain later," she said. "What about you?"

"An insightful evening."

He eased her into the front seat and closed the door. Rounding the hood, he got behind the wheel, turned the key in the ignition, and put the car in gear. A prickly sensation made her glance back at the lobby.

Distance and darkness made it impossible to make out Dolores Guilfoyle's expression, but there was no need for a closer look. Her stiff posture and rigid shoulders told the story. She was furious.

Sam drove out through the main gates of the Institute and headed toward the lights of the Sea Dream Hotel.

Maggie settled back into the seat. The memory of the earlier flash of anxiety returned. This time she did not dismiss it. She turned to study Sam's hard-edged profile.

"Were you hurt?" she asked. "Did someone see you go into Oxlade's villa? I know something bad happened. Tell me."

Chapter 33

Her concern made no sense, Sam thought. She could not know he had been very nearly run down in the hotel parking lot, so how had she guessed there had been a problem? Another Maggie mystery.

"I'm fine," he said. "No one saw me search Oxlade's villa. At least, I don't think I was seen."

"That does not reassure me. I know something bad happened. Tell me. I'm the client, remember?"

"Trust me, I'm not going to forget that." He pulled into the hotel parking lot and shut down the engine. "All right, I'll give you the facts, but try not to leap to conclusions, okay?"

"Too late. I've already made the leap and I don't like where I landed."

"I can tell."

He studied the other vehicles in the lot. There were a couple of Ford sedans, but he knew it was highly unlikely the one that had almost struck him was there—not unless the near miss really had been an accident. The parking area was poorly lit. Maybe the driver hadn't seen him.

Right. Now he was the one with the overactive imagination.

"Sam?"

He rested one hand on the wheel. "The search took me longer than I had planned, so on my way back from the gardens I didn't go into the hotel. I went straight toward the car. As I was crossing the parking lot, a vehicle came out of nowhere. Well, no, that's not right. It came from the far side of the lot. The driver gunned the engine on the way to the exit. No headlights. I would have been hit if I hadn't managed to get out of the way."

"Someone tried to murder you," she said.

She sounded shocked. Horrified.

"Could have been an accident," he said, automatically trying to reassure her. "The driver might have been drinking in the hotel bar. Forgot to turn on the headlights, so he never saw me."

"And you have the nerve to accuse me of having a vivid imagination. Someone tries to run you down in a parking lot while you are in the middle of what is very likely a murder investigation and you're trying to call it an *accident*?"

He should have known better than to try to lie to her. He exhaled and cracked open the door. "Let's go inside. I'd rather have this conversation somewhere other than this damn parking lot."

He got out from behind the wheel. Maggie did not wait for him to reach her side of the Packard. She extracted herself from the passenger seat and hurried to join him.

"What did the car look like?" she asked, scanning the parking lot.

"Like every other late-model Ford sedan on the road."

"Did you see the driver?"

"No. The car came from behind. By the time I picked myself up off the ground, the Ford was out of the parking lot. It disappeared around the curve, heading toward Cliff Road."

"Or the Institute," Maggie said.

"Or the Institute," he agreed. "I did a quick check of the parking lot there while I waited for you."

"Great idea."

"I certainly thought so. There were two Fords in the lot. Both engines were cold."

"Oh." She hesitated, clearly disappointed. But true to form, her spirits quickly revived. "When you think about it, there are a number of places where you could conceal a vehicle on the grounds of the Institute. The old caretaker's garage. Behind the gardener's toolshed or one of the buildings that is still boarded up. For that matter, you could hide a car off the grounds as well and walk back through the gardens."

"Unfortunately, I didn't have time to check all the possibilities," he said.

"And you didn't get a look at the driver."

"No. Just a short glimpse of the silhouette from the back. Whoever it was wore a man's hat, but that's all I could see."

"So it was a man at the wheel?"

"Maybe."

Maggie shot him a quick glance. "Maybe?"

"A man's hat set at the right angle makes a very good disguise for a woman, especially if you only catch a glimpse of her silhouette from the back."

"I hate to tell you this, but you make a lousy eyewitness, considering you used to be a cop."

"I know."

Chapter 34

What have you done, Arthur?" Dolores Guilfoyle used the silver lighter on the coffee table to ignite a cigarette. She inhaled deeply and was shocked to see that her hand was shaking. "What did you say to the Lodge woman that made Oxlade think he had been deceived?"

Arthur grimaced and went to the drinks cart. "He was upset because I used the Traveler in the dream reading."

"The *Traveler*?" Dolores snapped the cigarette out of her mouth. "What were you thinking? You know Oxlade is paranoid about that legend. He doesn't want to be associated with it."

"I know, but I was in danger of losing my audience." Arthur poured himself a scotch and soda. "The questions were the usual: Where is the missing will? Should I invest in this company? I needed a dramatic touch. I'm trying to sell the Method, not tickets to a two-bit traveling psychic reading show."

"But why the Traveler? You know how Oxlade feels about that subject."

"All right, I went overboard, but I did it for Oxlade's sake."

"What do you mean?"

"I was trying to set the hook with Lodge. Oxlade told me she had fragile nerves because of her talent. He said she was prone to hysteria. I assumed she was the type to buy the Traveler story and become anxious. I would then be able to step in and gallantly offer to rescue her with my talent."

Dolores shook her head, disgusted. "You acted on impulse, and your plan backfired."

Arthur gulped some of his scotch and soda. "I managed to persuade Lodge to stay behind in the theater for a few minutes after the performance. We . . . talked. Unfortunately, she doesn't believe in astral projection or the idea of a psychic assassin who murders people in their dreams. She accused me of running a con."

"So you backpedaled, didn't you? Tried to convince her you don't really believe in astral projection or the Traveler?"

"I went a little beyond that," Arthur admitted. "I explained I had fooled Oxlade into thinking I had tapped into my psychic senses because I needed him and his reputation to make the Institute look good. Oxlade was backstage. He overheard me."

"Damn it to hell," Dolores whispered. "He's going to cut off his association with us, isn't he?"

"He was annoyed, Dolores. I think we're going to lose him, and if we do, we'll lose the drug. You have to do something."

"Such as?" She went to the window and looked out into the night. "I've cleaned up a lot of your messes but I don't know if I can deal with this one."

"Don't say that. Look, I agree with you. We can get by without Oxlade, but we need the drug. That's what will set the Guilfoyle Method apart from all the other lucid dreaming programs. The drug makes people *believe*."

She looked back at him. "You mean you need the drug, Arthur.

You've fallen for your own con. You really think the enhancer has opened the pathway to your psychic senses."

"It's the truth. I know you don't believe me. That's because you're not a lucid dreamer. You don't know what happens when someone like me takes the drug."

"Is that right?"

"Even if you don't understand how it affects me, you must realize we need the enhancer to take the Guilfoyle Institute to the top." Arthur started to pace the room. "I've been thinking."

"That doesn't usually end well."

"I'm serious," Arthur said. "We don't need the actual formula for the drug. I'll bet a sample of it would be enough."

"What do you mean?"

"We could take some of it to a laboratory and have it analyzed," Arthur said. "Once we know the ingredients, we could pay a chemist to make up the enhancer for us."

She inhaled smoke while she considered his words. For once he had a glimmer of an idea.

"Maybe," she said. "But there's the problem of getting a sample of the drug."

"We know Oxlade brought some with him, enough to run several experiments on me and a few of the conference guests."

"I agree it would be useful to have the enhancer," Dolores said. "What about Lodge? Do you need her, too, Arthur?"

"She's not important. I told you, the only reason I talked to her after the performance was to get her to stick around. I was afraid that if we lost her we would lose Oxlade and the drug."

He was lying, just as he always did when it came to his women.

"Sounds like you managed to lose Oxlade all by yourself," she said.

Arthur gave her an anguished, pleading look. "Darling, you have to understand. Everything I did was for us."

"Everything you did—everything you ever do—is for you."

"That's not true. You know you're the only woman I've ever loved."

"Go away, Arthur. I don't want to talk to you anymore tonight. I need to think."

"Sure, right, I understand." Relief flashed across Arthur's face. He gulped the remainder of his drink and set the glass on the cart. "You'll come up with a solution. You always do. I'm going to take a walk in the gardens. You know how it is after a performance. I need to work off the energy."

"You do that," Dolores said.

You stupid, self-centered bastard.

She opened the French doors and went out onto the terrace. She had to get control of the situation. Arthur had put all of her goals at risk with his impulsive nature. If they lost the Institute, she would lose her inheritance.

It dawned on her that she had succeeded in marrying a man who was just like her father—a self-centered womanizer who cared only about himself. How had that happened?

She could not afford to waste time dwelling on the past. She had to save the Institute, and that meant saving Arthur from his own worst impulses. As they said in Hollywood, he was the box-office draw. She had always done what she had to do to protect him and their shared future. That probably made her the Institute's version of a studio fixer.

She certainly knew what it felt like to be forced to extricate her moneymaking star from a situation that could take them both down, a situation he had created.

But this time was different.

Why was he obsessed with Margaret Lodge? She did not fit into the category of rich, glamorous, and beautiful. She was not connected to Hollywood. Yes, Arthur was impulsive, but even for him this was an unusual—make that *unique*—distraction.

His first priority was himself. The more she thought about it, the more it seemed unlike him to risk his own dream by having a fling with a woman who did not offer him any of the things he wanted.

There was only one possible explanation. After all these years Arthur had concluded he no longer needed a partner with a sharp mind for business and marketing. He was convinced he required one who was a powerful lucid dreamer, a woman who could help him transform the Guilfoyle Method from a flashy con job into a genuine therapy—a dazzling operation that delivered real results and would draw the attention of Hollywood celebrities. He wanted a woman who could help him fulfill his vision of his own future. A woman who could make him a star.

Emerson Oxlade had apparently convinced Arthur that Maggie Lodge was the real deal—a lucid dreamer who could use her talent to open a pathway to her psychic senses.

That was the reason Arthur was obsessed with Lodge. It explained everything.

Dolores dropped the cigarette onto the tiles of the terrace and ground it out with the toe of her high-heeled shoe.

You're not going to replace me that easily, you stupid bastard.

It was time to clean up Arthur's latest mess.

Chapter 35

The doorman touched his cap and opened the door of the hotel lobby. Sam nodded at him and then steered Maggie to the front desk. They picked up their keys and headed for the stairs.

Inside his room, Sam checked the fedora for damage and grimaced when he saw the oily smudge on the brim. It was worse than he had thought. You couldn't get that kind of stain out. He wondered if it was legitimate to put the cost of a new hat on the final bill.

He shrugged out of the trench coat and examined it briefly. There were some dark streaks on it, but they blended in with the other evidence of hard use. When he hung it on the brass wall hook he got an unpleasant jolt in his right shoulder. There would be a few bruises in the morning. He was not getting any younger.

He peeled off his jacket, opened his collar, and loosened his tie. He collected the bottle of whiskey and two glasses and rapped twice, softly, on the connecting door. He could get used to having Maggie on the other side of the door. He could get used to having her in his bed.

Maggie opened the door so quickly he knew she must have been preparing to knock. She had unfastened the snug jacket of her tailored suit, but that was as far as she had gotten with undressing. Her hair was still clipped back behind her ears.

He pushed aside the memory of the previous night when she had opened the door dressed in a robe and slippers, her hair loose around her shoulders. The sex had been amazing. He reminded himself that last night had broken a long dry spell. His judgment was probably somewhat cloudy. Still.

"What did you find inside Oxlade's villa?" she asked.

Obviously she was not thinking about the scorching-hot sex.

He set the bottle on the table, poured some whiskey, and handed her one of the glasses. He picked up his own glass and began to prowl the room. He needed to put a little distance between the two of them.

He gave her a concise summary of the search.

Maggie set aside her unfinished whiskey.

"The Guilfoyles are professional liars," she said. "It would be pointless to confront them, at least not without evidence. But Oxlade is different. His weakness is his fear of losing his reputation as an esteemed expert. I think he might talk if he is approached in the right way."

"I agree," Sam said.

"Now," Maggie said. "Tonight."

Sam looked at her. "Why tonight?"

"Because I think he'll be leaving first thing in the morning," Maggie said. "I haven't had a chance to tell you about my conversation with Arthur Guilfoyle after the psychic reading demonstration. Guilfoyle and Oxlade quarreled. Well, to be precise, Oxlade quarreled. He was furious because he overheard Guilfoyle admit to me that he had conned Oxlade. Oxlade stomped out of the theater. I'm sure he's planning to leave town as soon as possible."

Sam considered that. "Guilfoyle actually fooled Oxlade?"

"To be fair, I think Guilfoyle probably is a lucid dreamer. There's no way to know for sure. But he's definitely a skilled actor and a practiced con artist."

"And Oxlade desperately wants to believe in his own theories and the drug," Sam said. "He was an easy mark for Guilfoyle."

"Until tonight," Maggie said. "Guilfoyle took things a step too far at the dream reading. He told the audience he could see the Traveler hunting for a victim—a woman—who might be in the room."

Sam went still. "You?"

"He was trying to scare me, yes."

"Bastard."

"It did not go well for him," Maggie said. She went to the closet and took out a pair of trousers. "I could see that Oxlade was upset onstage. Later, when he overheard Guilfoyle admit to the con, he was furious. I'll tell you all about it on the way back to the Institute. But first I have to change my clothes. This suit isn't practical for sneaking into the gardens."

"I agree, but before you get too excited about a confrontation with Oxlade, I think we should make a plan."

"Certainly. What did you have in mind?"

"Are your acting skills as good as your imagination?"

"I am an excellent actress," she said. "I admit I have a limited repertoire, but what I do, I do very, very well. I'm especially good at playing normal."

"What makes you so sure of that?"

"The fact that I am not currently residing in an asylum."

Sam watched her unfasten her skirt.

"Yet another Maggie Lodge mystery," he said. "As it happens, normal is not what we're going for tonight. Can you play the opposite?"

"Sure, but I'll need your word of honor that you won't let anyone put me away because of a really good acting job."

She was trying to make light of it, but the wariness in her eyes was only a half step from fear.

He walked to stand in front of her and caught her chin on the edge of his hand.

"I promise you that if anyone ever locks you up I will tear down the walls of your prison and take you out of it," he vowed.

A sheen of tears glittered in her eyes. She blinked them away and managed a shaky smile.

"Deal," she said.

Chapter 36

The rain started shortly before midnight. Emerson Oxlade almost changed his mind about leaving. He did not like the thought of driving back to L.A. in such weather, especially at night. But the urge to escape the looming disaster that threatened his reputation and his career was too powerful to ignore.

He had to get away from the Institute and Burning Cove as soon as possible. If he stayed to give his lecture in the morning he would be swamped with silly questions about the Traveler and Guilfoyle's ridiculous statements onstage earlier in the evening. The press would no doubt pick up the story. He could not face any of it. He had to leave.

The woman carrying the dark umbrella emerged from the rain-drenched gardens just as he was about to stow the first suitcase in the trunk of his car. In the weak light of the lamp over the door she was little more than a shadowy silhouette.

"Going somewhere, Dr. Oxlade?" she said. "You mustn't leave before I have a chance to thank you for the great gift you gave me."

There was something odd about her tone, an eerie, dreamy quality that was unnatural, but he recognized her voice.

"Miss Smith, I mean, Miss Lodge." He was so shocked he almost dropped the suitcase and his umbrella. "What are you doing here?"

"I owe you a debt of gratitude. I had a psychic vision in which I saw you leaving tonight. I simply had to tell you that you changed my life."

He went still. "You had a vision I was leaving?"

"I saw it in a dream. I sense all sorts of things these days, thanks to your drug. You were right. The enhancer opened the door to my psychic talents. What's more, the door is still open. I don't need the enhancer every time I dream."

Something was very wrong. Oxlade edged back toward the front steps of the villa.

"What are you talking about?" he said.

"I'm telling you that your drug works, Dr. Oxlade." Maggie chuckled, a light, giddy little laugh. "I thought you had poisoned me when you put the enhancer in my tea. For days afterward I was convinced I was going mad. For weeks I fought the effects because I didn't understand what was happening. But eventually I realized your drug not only gave me access to my psychic senses but allowed me to journey on the astral plane, just like the Traveler."

"No, that's not possible," Oxlade yelped.

"It's true, and it's an astounding experience."

He retreated a couple more steps toward the safety of the villa. For a moment he had dared to hope the enhancer was even more powerful than he had realized. But now it was clear that Maggie Lodge was unhinged.

The drug had caused her to lose her grip on reality. It was the only explanation. He knew she was prone to hysteria, but he had hoped her lucid dreaming ability would allow her to control the effects of the enhancer. Now he was forced to consider the possibility that the drug had pushed her over the edge. He was dealing with a woman who was dangerously unbalanced. He was alone with her. In the dark.

He could feel the rip current of panic tugging at him. He reminded himself she had once been a patient. He knew how to handle patients.

"I don't understand, Miss Lodge," he said, trying to sound both reassuring and authoritative, trying to sound like a doctor. The expert who knew best. "Please explain."

"You heard Arthur Guilfoyle tonight," she said. "He's a fraud, but I'm not. The Traveler is abroad on the astral plane and he is stalking a victim, just like he stalked Virginia Jennaway and Beverly Nevins."

Another frisson of panic lanced Oxlade's nerves. "That's nonsense. You don't know what you're talking about."

"I have dreams all the time now, not just when I sleep but when I'm wide awake." Maggie giggled. "I don't mind telling you it can be a little disconcerting to have a vision just pop up while you're eating breakfast or chatting with a friend."

"Calm down, Miss Lodge," he said. "You are allowing yourself to become hysterical."

"You really should not say that to me, Dr. Oxlade. I don't like it when people say that."

Something in her voice sent a jolt of raw panic through him.

"I agree that Guilfoyle is a fraud," he said quickly. "I don't know where he got that ridiculous story about the Traveler. I suppose he couldn't resist the opportunity to shock his audience. He finds it impossible to resist the spotlight. He craves it."

"I know, but the fascinating thing is that he was right about the Traveler. The spirit of the psychic assassin really was hunting me."

"You?"

"Yes, but thanks to your drug I am strong enough to control it. The Traveler does my bidding now. Imagine how it feels to command such power. Then again, there is no need for you to use your imagination, is there? You have already witnessed the work of the Traveler."

Oxlade risked a glance over his shoulder. Just a few more steps. If he could get into the villa he would be able to lock the door and phone the police.

"The Traveler is nothing more than a legend," he said.

"You're wrong, Dr. Oxlade. The Traveler is mine to command."

"You're delusional, Miss Lodge."

"You don't really believe that, do you? Just think, you have devoted your life to finding a way to access the power of the latent psychic senses. I am the living proof of your success."

"You are imagining things. Hallucinating. Obviously the drug was too much for your delicate nerves."

She giggled again. "If you're right it means your enhancer is deeply flawed. It drives people mad. You don't want to believe that, do you?"

Rage arced through him. "It's not the drug that is at fault, you stupid woman. You are too weak to handle the effects. You should be in an asylum."

"I don't want to be locked up, Dr. Oxlade. That's why I summoned the Traveler. He will protect me."

"You are mad."

"Is that what happened to Virginia Jennaway? Did you drive her insane with your drug? Is that why she walked into the ocean and drowned?"

The tide of horror was rising so quickly now he could no longer catch his breath. His heart pounded. Sweat trickled down his forehead into his eyes. He tried to blink away the moisture, but the effort blurred the scene, combining with the rain to turn the gardens into an ominous dreamscape.

A terrifying thought struck him. What if he was the one imagining things? Over the years he had been forced to run some experiments with the drug on himself. Perhaps he had gone too far.

"I don't understand any of this," he whispered. "Can't you see I'm packing my car? I'm leaving tonight."

"Tell me the truth about Jennaway's death and I will send the Traveler back to the astral plane. He will not come for you."

"Are you threatening me?"

"Why did you murder Virginia Jennaway?"

He was beyond panic now. "I had nothing to do with what happened to Jennaway. It was an accident." So much for the strong, authoritative voice. He knew he sounded shrill and frantic. "Why are you accusing me?"

"There are rumors that she died because of your drug."

"That's not true."

"Convince me. What happened to Virginia Jennaway, Dr. Oxlade?"

"She was a fast, frivolous socialite who happened to have a little lucid dreaming talent. She loved the drug. Treated it like a cocktail. She wanted more of it. I warned her it was only in the experimental stage. I was still fine-tuning the formula, you see. She begged for it. When I wouldn't give it to her, she stole some and apparently overdosed on it."

"She stole a supply of the drug?"

"The day after she died I discovered that a vial of the enhancer was missing. She stole it and overdosed on it. She drowned because she was too weak to handle such a powerful drug. Evidently you are also too weak to control it. I have begun to think only a man can use it for the purpose of accessing the paranormal senses."

He was almost at the door now. A few more steps and he would be inside. He would be safe.

"What about the rumors of the Traveler?"

"Ridiculous stories," Oxlade yelped. "This has gone far enough. The only reason I agreed to attend the conference here at the Institute was because I was assured it would take a serious, scientific approach to dream research. I believed Guilfoyle when he went into his psychic dreaming act. But I realized tonight that he is a fraud. I am going to leave before my reputation is tarnished. Stay away from me."

He fled up the steps and into the villa. Inside he dropped the suitcase and the umbrella, whirled around, slammed the door, and set the lock.

He slumped against the wall and tried to think. The Lodge woman was delusional and dangerous. The side effects of the drug had overwhelmed her frail nerves. She should be in an institution.

But what if the enhancer really had opened the door to her paranormal senses? Yes, Lodge was obviously too weak to control the enhancer, but in a way that only went to prove that it worked.

It was a thrilling thought. It was also another reason for leaving the Institute tonight, regardless of the rain. If the visibility got too bad, he would turn off onto a farm road and spend the night in his car. The important thing was to get away from the Institute.

He put his ear to the door and listened closely. When he didn't hear anyone coming up the steps, he went to the window and peeked through the curtains.

The Lodge woman was gone. She had vanished into the rain-shrouded gardens. He shuddered. Now that he had some time to think, one thing was very clear: Margaret Lodge knew too much about everything, including the past. Calling the police would not only be pointless, it would be a terrible risk. Having her arrested might lead to questions he did not want to answer.

He collected himself and went down the hall to finish packing the second suitcase. He saved the journal and the Dopp kit for last.

Chapter 37

"T hat didn't go well," Maggie said. "So much for my acting talent.
I was sure I would be able to trick Oxlade into a confession."

The rain was still falling. The path through the Institute gardens was muddy and difficult to make out. Sam had switched on the flashlight as soon as they were safely away from the villa. He kept it aimed low and shielded the glow.

"You did a great job of acting not normal," Sam said.

"Thanks. I think."

"I disagree with you about the result of your performance." Sam stopped to open the service gate. "We picked up some valuable information."

He was even more difficult to read than usual, but she could feel his sense of certainty. She went past him into the lane that ran behind the estate and held the umbrella for him while he relocked the gate. When he was finished they started back toward the hotel.

"Why do you say we got some information?" she asked. "Oxlade denied having anything to do with Jennaway's death."

"Not exactly. He told you a different story."

"Do you believe his version of events?"

"He said Jennaway pleaded with him to give her the drug but he refused. The next thing he knew, a vial went missing. He assumed she stole it, overdosed, and drowned. That sounds like a reasonable conclusion. The good news is that if Oxlade was telling the truth, we can eliminate him as a suspect in Jennaway's death."

"I never got the chance to ask him about Beverly Nevins."

"Only because he managed to escape into the villa," Sam said.

"I frightened him, didn't I?"

"Yep. You're a born actress."

"No, I had to *learn* how to act."

"Either way, it worked."

He wasn't going to push her on the subject. She relaxed a little and shoved her hands deeper into the pockets of her coat.

"Okay, so maybe Oxlade didn't murder Jennaway," she said. "Do you think he killed Nevins because she was blackmailing him over his connection to the Jennaway death?"

"If she was threatening his professional reputation, he definitely had motive—and probably means. He's a doctor, after all. He knows a lot about drugs, and he knows how to obtain them."

"If he didn't murder Jennaway, we're back to square one," Maggie said, frustrated.

"No. The pot has been stirred and Oxlade is about to piss in it."

"By leaving in the middle of the night?"

"It will be interesting to see how the Guilfoyles react tomorrow when they discover he's gone."

"They won't be happy," Maggie said. "But you and I are going to have another problem. Tomorrow is the last day of the conference. There's a farewell cocktail party in the evening, and that's the end. We won't have any excuse for staying on to investigate."

"I don't think we're going to need an excuse," Sam said.

She shot him a quick, searching look. She still couldn't make out his expression, but once again there was no mistaking the conviction in his words.

"What makes you so sure?" she asked.

"The Guilfoyles are trying to build an impressive business, but there are major cracks in the foundation. Lies. Murder. Blackmail. Drugs. Sooner or later it's all going to fall apart. I'm betting on sooner."

"Is that your intuition talking?"

"It is."

Chapter 38

Oxlade checked the cap on the cologne bottle, making sure it was tightly fastened before he positioned it securely in the leather Dopp kit.

In a few more minutes he would be in the car and heading for L.A. Safe. That was all that mattered now, getting away from the Institute. The panic that Margaret Lodge had triggered was getting worse. His heart was racing and his hands were trembling so badly he could barely get the Dopp kit closed.

From the start he had been worried about the arrangement with the two con artists who called themselves Guilfoyles these days, but he had been desperate to continue his experiments. They had offered him what he needed to complete his research: an unlimited pool of test subjects. When he discovered Margaret Lodge on the opening night of the reception and realized he might be able to resume his experiments on her, he was certain the risks were worthwhile. It had all seemed too good to be true—and, of course, it was.

Like a gullible fool he had fallen for the Guilfoyles' lures. He, of all people, should have known better than to get involved with them again.

He sensed a presence in the bathroom doorway behind him and stopped breathing. He looked up from the shaving kit. His shocked gaze locked with that of the figure reflected in the mirror over the sink.

"What are you doing here?" he squeaked.

The hammer slammed into the back of his skull. The pain exploded through him and then there was nothing. He never felt the next three entirely unnecessary blows.

*

The killer stared at the body on the floor, fascinated. So much blood. It was everywhere—the tiles, the sink, the mirror. The mess was . . . unexpected.

The killer stopped focusing on the bloody scene and started searching for the drug. Oxlade had almost finished with the packing. He would have made certain the enhancer was secured, most likely in one of the suitcases.

A few minutes later panic set in. Both suitcases had been dragged out of the car and were now open on the living room floor. There was no sign of the enhancer.

The killer returned to the bathroom and tried to think logically. Oxlade had been about to pack the Dopp kit. He had saved it for last. But the suitcases had already been closed and latched. That indicated Oxlade hadn't planned to put the shaving kit in one of them. Why pack it separately?

The killer stepped over the body, opened the shaving kit, and examined the contents for a moment.

The cologne bottle.

The killer unscrewed the cap, sniffed cautiously, and smiled. No scent.

Cologne bottle safely tucked into a coat pocket, the killer turned to

224 . . .

leave—and stopped. The partial imprint of a shoe was clearly etched into one crimson blob on the floor.

A towel took care of the problem. The last of the rain would muddy any prints left on the ground outside the villa.

The killer turned off all the lights on the way out. Oxlade would not be found until mid-morning, when someone at the Institute finally noticed he had not arrived to give the farewell lecture.

Chapter 39

I've been thinking about what almost happened to you tonight," Maggie said.

They were in her room. Sam lounged in a chair, legs outstretched, and watched her pace. They had been discussing how the Guilfoyles might deal with the bad publicity that would strike the Institute when they and everyone else discovered that Oxlade had vanished.

Without warning Maggie had abruptly reverted to the topic of the near miss in the parking lot. Sam reminded himself she had a tendency to take unpredictable turns at a high rate of speed.

"Look on the bright side," he said. "If it wasn't an accident—if someone really did try to take me out of the picture—we can eliminate several suspects."

Maggie stopped and turned to face him. "You mean Dr. Oxlade and Guilfoyle?"

"Yes. You're their alibi. You saw them onstage during the performance and again immediately afterward. Neither of them would have had time to jump into a car and race over to the hotel parking lot to wait for an opportunity to run me down."

Maggie's expressive face tightened. "What about Dolores Guilfoyle?"

"Wasn't she at the demonstration?"

"She introduced the dream reading, but I didn't see her again until Guilfoyle and I walked into the lobby. After she greeted the audience she could have driven over to the hotel parking lot and waited for you to come out to get the car."

He thought about that. "She was in the lobby of the Institute after the demonstration."

"Yes, but when did she show up there?"

"I don't know," he admitted. "I wasted several minutes in the parking lot of the Institute trying to find a Ford with a hot engine."

"And I was stuck in the theater with Arthur Guilfoyle."

"The timing would have been tight, but it could have worked for her," Sam agreed. "She would know where to conceal the car on the grounds of the Institute, and she would know all the back-door and side entrances of the main building."

"What about the three dream guides?" Maggie asked. "One of them might be mixed up in this."

"Did you see them during the demonstration?"

"I saw all three at the beginning when they seated us. I didn't see any of them again until Guilfoyle and I returned to the lobby."

"Larry and Jake were acting as valets for the guests when I arrived to pick you up, but they were coming and going very quickly," Sam said. "One of them could have returned from the hotel parking lot and made it look as if he was fetching a car for a guest. But again, the timing would have been tight—a matter of planning and a bit of luck."

Maggie squared her shoulders and got what he now recognized as her fiercely determined expression. *Stubborn* was another word for it. She was about to take another sharp turn.

"We need to talk," she said.

"We are talking. I keep coming back to the fact that two of the people involved in this thing disappeared right at the beginning—even before the beginning in one case—and haven't been seen since."

That succeeded in distracting Maggie for a moment. "You mean Lillian Dewhurst and that actress who was playing the part of Aunt Cornelia?"

"Phyllis Gaines, right."

"I know you've got questions about Lillian, but we saw Miss Gaines leave town the first night of the conference."

"How do we know she left town? She's an actress who wore a wig and some glamorous clothes for her performance. She looked like a very different person when we saw her packing up her Ford."

Maggie's eyes widened. "It was a Ford sedan, wasn't it?"

"A lot of those around," he said. "My point is that no one would recognize her if she drove across town and checked into a hotel or a bed-and-breakfast."

"Hmm. I see what you mean. About the Ford—"

"It's one of the most common cars on the road."

"This may be even worse than I thought," Maggie said. She straightened her shoulders again. "At first I believed it was a simple case of blackmail."

"A *simple* case?"

"The next thing I know we're dealing with an imposter. Then a woman is found dead. Drugs are involved. A homicide detective asks you to become an undercover agent."

"One cop asked another ex-cop for a favor, that's all."

She ignored him and swept out her hands. "The situation keeps deteriorating. Now we know the Guilfoyles are a couple of con artists who want to get their hands on Oxlade's ghastly enhancer."

"Damn it, Maggie, we're getting off track here."

"We're talking about a killer who has targeted you. I never intended to put you in the path of a murderer."

A chill of alarm shot through him. "Maggie, I can do without the drama tonight."

She raised her chin. "You may consider this investigation concluded. You will take the train back to Adelina Beach in the morning. Please send your bill to the Sunset Lane address at your earliest convenience."

For a couple of seconds he thought he had not heard her correctly. Then the full impact of the words hit him.

"Are you trying to fire me?" he said.

"Not *trying*, Mr. Sage. I *am* firing you. If you stay on the case someone may attack you again. If that happens, I will feel personally responsible. I do not want your death or serious injury on my conscience."

"Because it would give you nightmares?"

"Yes, damn it. You don't want drama? I don't want a load of guilt."

"So you're firing me because I might cause you a few bad dreams?"

She shot him an accusing look. "You're twisting my words."

"No." He got to his feet and started toward her. "I'm clarifying them. I want to make sure I understand exactly what you meant."

She watched warily as he closed the space between them, but she did not retreat. "Do you understand, Mr. Sage?"

"Perfectly, Miss Lodge. For your information, you can't fire me."

"Why not?"

"Because I quit."

She thought about that for a beat and then nodded, satisfied. "I suppose it amounts to the same thing. I will, of course, cover the cost of your train ticket back to Adelina Beach."

"I won't be on the train tomorrow. I will be here in Burning Cove, working this screwy case."

She nodded in weary understanding. "You're worried about me. That is very sweet of you."

"*Sweet?*"

"I appreciate your concern, but there's no need for you to feel responsible for me. I'm perfectly capable of taking care of myself. I've been doing that for quite a while."

"What happened to our working relationship? You've got a partner now, like it or not, and partners look out for each other."

She frowned. "There's been no threat against me."

"No threat? Oxlade wanted to run experiments on you."

"He's gone now."

"I'm supposed to find that reassuring?"

"I'm trying to be logical and rational."

"You're not succeeding."

She narrowed her eyes. "Do you think I'm behaving illogically and irrationally?"

"I didn't say that. Now you're the one twisting words."

"Do you think I'm in danger of becoming hysterical?"

"No, Miss Lodge. I'm the one who is on the verge of hysteria, and it's your fault."

"*My* fault?"

"Let's get a few things straight," he said. "I am not going back to Adelina Beach, because I am not going to leave you here alone in Burning Cove. You are in over your head, and I think you know it. You need me. Admit it."

She looked at him, her eyes suddenly brilliant with the wonder of discovery.

"Yes," she said. "Yes, I do need you."

He had been braced for more argument. The surrender, if that's what it was, happened so abruptly he was blindsided. Another curve taken at high speed.

"Okay, that settles it," he said, trying to regain his balance.

"You are offering good advice. I've decided to take it."

"Fine," he said.

"There's something else we should discuss."

"It would be a good idea if you stopped talking now, because you're starting to irritate me again."

She smiled. "Would you rather I kiss you instead?"

"So that you can prove to yourself you aren't frigid?"

"Nope. Because I recently discovered I like being kissed by a man who isn't afraid I might suffer a fit of hysteria at any moment."

The heat in her eyes was real. That was all he needed. She wanted him, and he wanted her—so badly he ached.

"Talk about your amazing coincidences," he said. "I like kissing a lady who has a vivid imagination."

He gripped her shoulders and pulled her close, covering her mouth with his own.

He went into the kiss thinking that this time he was prepared for the bone-deep sense of rightness. He was wrong. The sensation zinged through him again, stronger than the first time. His marriage had started out red-hot. He ought to know how to handle raw physical attraction. He *did* know how to handle it. What's more, he was older now—maybe not wiser, but definitely older. More experienced. He liked to think he had learned a few things along the way.

But kissing Maggie was different. Somehow he knew it would always be different, because Maggie was unlike any other woman.

Last night he had been shaken by the longing that had welled up inside him when he held her in his arms. It was the feeling a man got when he knew that something he desperately wanted was just out of reach. Tonight the longing was shot through with something infinitely more dangerous—the euphoric pleasure that came with knowing Maggie wanted him.

When her mouth softened under his and she started to fumble with the buttons of his shirt, he forgot about all the excellent reasons why going to bed with Maggie was probably a mistake.

He eased the blouse off her shoulders and took the pins out of her hair. When he picked her up and carried her through the doorway to his bed, he was intoxicated with anticipation.

He pulled the covers down and then slowly went about the process of undressing Maggie. She returned the favor. It wasn't long before most of their clothes were scattered across the rug and draped over the chair and the table.

When she was wearing only a pair of silky, wide-legged panties and he was in his briefs, she went up on her toes and sank her teeth gently into his ear.

"Sam," she whispered.

They fell onto the bed together. The feel of her soft, warm body beneath his filled him with pleasure. He tasted her mouth again and then the scented skin of her shoulder, her breast, and lower still.

When she slid one bare foot down his leg he took a sharp breath and rolled off her and onto his feet.

"Back in a minute," he said.

He turned off the lights on his way across the room. In the bathroom he got a pro from the tin in his Dopp kit, sheathed himself, and went back into the bedroom. He stopped when he saw Maggie lying in the light angling through the connecting doorway. Her hair spilled across the pillow. Her eyes were mysterious pools of sensual invitation and desire.

"You are so beautiful," he said.

She smiled. "You make me feel beautiful."

He continued across the room to the bed and lowered himself beside her. When he started to kiss her she stopped him with a finger on his mouth.

"What's wrong?" he asked. "Are you having second thoughts?"

"I was just wondering if most men travel with a tin of condoms."

He groaned. "I have absolutely no idea and zero interest in the answer. I bought mine from the pharmacist on Tyler Avenue in Adelina Beach the day before we left for Burning Cove."

"Really?"

"He keeps them behind the counter. Guarantees they are the best quality."

He started to pull her closer. She moved her hand to his shoulder, stopping him again.

"You planned to seduce me?" she asked.

She sounded curious. Intrigued. Not angry.

"I don't have that much faith in my powers of seduction, and even though I haven't been in the private detective business very long, I'm pretty sure it's a bad idea to sleep with the client. So no, there was no plan." He paused. "But deep down I had hope."

She brightened. "So did I."

He suddenly felt on top of the world. "You did?"

"After I met you I finally understood what was wrong with the hero in my novel. That night I rewrote him, and now he works perfectly. You inspired me."

He stared at her. "You're joking."

"No, I'm very serious. My first version was boring, but after we met I realized I was going about things the wrong way."

"I don't think I want to hear any more of this."

"I understand," she said, earnest now. "You're afraid I'm judging you by an impossible standard—the archetype of the ideal romantic hero. But that's not true."

"It's not?"

"A true hero is never perfect. If he were, he wouldn't be a hero, you see."

"I think I'm losing the thread of this conversation."

"There's nothing heroic about perfection. Also, it's boring, and the last thing one wants in a novel is a boring hero."

"If you will stop talking, I will try very hard not to bore you."

"Okay."

He used the pad of one thumb to gently pry her lower lip downward. When her mouth was open he cupped the back of her head, urged her closer, and kissed her, long and deep. He forgot about the alarming discussion of heroes and let himself fall into the deep waters of the kiss.

He eased her onto her back and prowled her sleek curves with his hand, exploring her secrets. When he found the heat between her thighs he began to experiment. She responded immediately.

"This is how it's supposed to be," she whispered.

"Not yet," he said.

He stroked the small, taut bud at the top of her sex. She pushed against his hand, seeking more pressure.

"Tell me what you want," he said against her throat. "Tell me how you want it."

With a small, sharp gasp she reached down, found his hand, and positioned his fingers.

"There," she said. "Right there."

She guided his hand until he found the cadence and pressure she wanted. He fought the demands of his own body, wanting to savor the thrill of watching her achieve satisfaction and the intoxicating knowledge that she had found that satisfaction with him.

The tension inside her was unmistakable. Her whole body tightened. She clawed at the sheet with her free hand.

He managed to hold himself in check until he sensed the first subtle ripples of her climax shivering through her. She took her guiding hand off his and dug her nails into his back.

He elevated her knees and drove slowly, steadily into her hot, snug core. Her mouth opened on a soundless cry. He moved inside her, sinking himself to the hilt again and again.

"This is so real," Maggie whispered. "So real."

His release pounded through him in endless waves that left him exhausted and at peace. The past could not touch him in this moment. Neither could the future. He was with Maggie and all was right with the world.

After a while he managed to rouse himself long enough to ask the only question that mattered.

"Are you thinking about your novel?" he said into the pillow.

"No."

"Hallelujah."

Chapter 40

S am emerged from the bathroom, settled back into the warm, rumpled bed, and flopped onto his back. He folded one arm beneath his head. The position gave him a good view of the ceiling.

Maggie rolled onto her side to face him and levered herself up on one elbow. She leaned over and kissed his chest. When she raised her head, she was smiling a sensual smile, and he was pretty sure her eyes were actually glowing.

She was warm and soft and damp and inviting. The intimate scent of satisfying sex drifted in the atmosphere. This was as good as it got. A smart man would not shatter the mood with unnecessary conversation. In his experience, after-the-act discussions were a bad idea. The last time he'd had one that had appeared to go well he had found himself driving to Reno with a beautiful woman to start a doomed marriage.

Keep your mouth shut, Sage.

But people rarely take good advice, even when they give it to themselves, he thought then. *Why be the exception to the rule?*

"What did you mean when you said *this is so real*?" he asked. "You hadn't even finished yet."

"I didn't need to finish to know it was real." She threaded her fingertips through the hair of his chest and tugged gently. "It felt real. That was all that mattered."

He thought about that for a moment and then abandoned the effort to decipher what the hell she was saying. He pulled his arm out from under the pillow and turned onto his side to face her.

"What does *real* mean?" he said.

"It felt like real passion. Shared passion."

"As opposed to?"

"Being assaulted by a vampire."

He sat up fast. "I may not be the most exciting man you've ever met, but I hope to hell that going to bed with me was better than being attacked by a vampire."

"Sorry." She lay back against the pillows and looked up at him. "I probably used the wrong visual image."

"Think so?"

"You're getting mad, aren't you?"

"No."

Not mad, he thought. *Hurt*. Probably just his pride. *Okay, mad*.

"Yes," he said.

The sensual warmth faded from her eyes. The serious, watchful expression returned.

"When I refer to a vampire, I'm talking about the kind of man who is attracted to a woman like me because he thinks that if he has sex with her he can somehow control her, and that if he controls her he can use her."

"A woman like you?"

"An extreme lucid dreamer," she explained.

"You're talking about men like Oxlade and Guilfoyle?"

"Oxlade isn't interested in having sex with me. He just wants to run experiments on me. Arthur Guilfoyle would be happy to seduce me if he thought that would get him what he wants, but it would just be business as usual. Make no mistake, both men are extremely annoying, but I wouldn't classify them as vampires."

"You seem to know a lot about men like Oxlade and Guilfoyle."

"I've spent years booking appointments with therapists and doctors and analysts who claim to be experts in dreams. Some tried to be helpful. Others were frauds and cons. Several took a genuinely scientific or medical approach. A few were delusional. But there is another category."

"The vampires?"

She touched his jaw with the tip of a finger. "You are a very smart detective."

"I told you, I keep up with the literature of the profession."

"Yes, you did mention that."

"You're going to tell me about your close brush with marriage, aren't you?"

"Only if you want to hear the gory details," she said.

"I'm not sure I want to hear them, but I need to know what happened to you that left you so gun-shy when it comes to marriage."

"Nearly two years ago I walked into the office of Dr. Brighton Forrester. He was the first man I had ever met who truly understood me when I explained my dreams and why I wanted to get better control of them. He was—is—a lucid dreamer himself."

"He dreams the way you do."

Maggie smiled, but it wasn't the smile that made him catch his breath. This smile made him want to pound Dr. Brighton Forrester into the ground.

"Yes," she said. "It was such a relief to be able to talk to someone who didn't think I was delusional or that I suffered from weak nerves or was prone to hysteria."

"You fell in love with him?" he asked.

Maggie scrunched up her nose. "I told myself that what I felt was love. I was certainly attracted to Brighton, and he was attracted to me, at least at the beginning. We had so much in common."

Unlike, say, you and me, Sam thought. He decided he would not dwell on that unwelcome thought, not now.

"Go on," he said.

"It didn't hurt that he was handsome, well-educated, and intelligent," Maggie said. "He was a doctor with a distinguished reputation. My family loved him."

"What went wrong?"

She winced. "I told you the gossip that circulated after the disaster was not accurate. I did *not* leave Brighton standing alone at the altar on the day of the wedding."

"Noted."

"Yes, Brighton and I were engaged, and yes, all the arrangements had been made, and yes, I suppose everyone had bought the gifts, and yes, I'd had the final fitting for the dress, but I called off the wedding seventeen whole days before the ceremony—not at the last minute."

In spite of himself, Sam could not suppress a quick grin. "Sounds like a good idea to me. Keep talking."

"It was generally assumed I had suffered a severe attack of bridal nerves. The stress of the wedding preparation had induced a fit of hysteria. There was talk of sending me back to Sweet Creek for a rest cure. I decided it was past time I left home. So I did. In the middle of the night. Turns out it's a lot harder to have someone committed when the adult in question is not living under the same roof as those who believe she ought to be committed, especially if that individual can't be found."

"Wow. You went into hiding?"

"For several months," Maggie said. "That's how I ended up in Adelina Beach. Everyone assumed I would come home when I ran out of money, but I managed to survive writing for the confession magazines.

Finally I landed the job as Lillian's assistant. Somewhere along the line Brighton got engaged to someone else and my family concluded that if I was strong enough to get by in the world without their help or their money, then maybe my nerves were okay after all."

"You have nerves of steel, lady. What went wrong at the last minute that made you call off the wedding?"

"Seventeen days before the last minute," Maggie corrected.

"Right. Seventeen days before the big day."

"I decided to surprise Brighton by showing up at his office for lunch. When I walked into the reception room, his secretary was away from her desk. There was a file open on the blotter and a sheet of paper in the typewriter. It looked like she was in the process of typing up some of Brighton's notes." Maggie paused. "I saw my name."

"Were you still Forrester's patient at the time?"

"I had never been his patient."

"You consulted with him?"

"Yes. I ended the consultations before our first date. After that we became colleagues. At least that was how I viewed the relationship. But the notes in the file were recent and they indicated Brighton thought there *was* something very wrong with me."

"You read them?"

"They were about me," Maggie said. "Of course I read them."

"And?"

"That's when I discovered that I apparently suffered from *female sexual dysfunction*. I was frigid. But that was not the most infuriating thing in the file."

"This story gets worse?"

"Oh, yes," Maggie said. "Brighton speculated that my inability to achieve an orgasm with him might be linked to my failure to exercise proper control over my lucid dreams. I admit there was an unfortunate incident one afternoon when we went to the beach."

"How unfortunate?"

"It was a lovely day. I dozed off while reading a book under the umbrella. Dreamed. Woke up in the middle of a terrible anxiety attack. Brighton was quite alarmed, to say the least. Between you and me, I think he had a panic attack himself."

"What did you dream about?"

Maggie sighed. "Brighton. In my dream he was transformed into a vampire. I realized later it was my intuition warning me that he was not good husband material."

"I'd say a dream like that warrants an anxiety attack."

"Apparently it was too much for Brighton. His notes made it clear he was convinced that the combination of female sexual dysfunction and the stress of my extreme lucid dreaming was too much for my delicate nerves. It was obvious he was preparing a medical case history that would enable him to have me committed after we were married."

"He wanted to marry you and then get you out of the way? Why?"

"The oldest reason in the world," Maggie said. "Money. My family has a lot of it. Brighton's family lost almost everything in the years right after the crash. He makes a very good living as a doctor, but he grew up in a family that once possessed a great fortune. He wanted to move back into that world."

"So he planned to get rich the old-fashioned way—he was going to marry money."

"Yes, but that wasn't the reason I did what I did when I ended our engagement."

"Are we getting to the psychic vampire part?" Sam said.

"I realized later he really was very attracted to me at the beginning. I hadn't been completely fooled. But I failed to understand that the reason he wanted me was because I am a more powerful lucid dreamer than he is. He believed he could use me to learn how to control his own lucid dreaming talent. According to the notes, in the beginning he was convinced an intimate relationship with me was a way to open the door to his latent psychic abilities."

"Well, damn. I get the vampire reference now," Sam said. "He was not only an opportunist who was out to take advantage of you; he was delusional."

"No, not in the least," Maggie said. "A bit obsessive, perhaps, but not delusional."

"Are you sure of that?"

"Brighton really is quite sane and intelligent. His theories about a connection between sex, dreams, and the paranormal might be valid. Who knows? The problem as far as he was concerned was my failure to achieve orgasm. After all, if I was frigid, his approach to achieving a higher level of dreaming probably wouldn't work. Not with me, at any rate."

"But he didn't want to give up the opportunity to marry into money," Sam said.

"That was the plan, but things didn't go well for him."

Sam looked down at her for a long moment. Maggie was in a somber, serious mood. Obviously she had suffered a traumatic experience. He ought to respect that.

But he couldn't help himself. He let the laughter roll through him.

Maggie watched him, curious but evidently not offended. She smiled. "What's so funny?"

"You scared the living hell out of Dr. Brighton Forrester, didn't you? That's why he was plotting to have you put away right after the wedding."

She gave that a moment's reflection. "In the end he was definitely afraid of me."

"Is this where the fire comes in?"

"I was reading the file when I heard certain suggestive noises emanating from the inner office."

"You opened the door?"

"Naturally," Maggie said.

"Forrester was inside. So was the missing secretary."

"You really are good at this detecting business," Maggie said. "Yes, she was sitting on his desk. He was standing between her legs. His pants were down around his ankles. That was fortunate."

"Why? Because it gave you the proof you needed to know he was cheating?"

"No, because Brighton got tangled up in his pants when he turned to see who had walked into the room. He tripped and went down on his hands and knees. That gave me time to dump the papers from the file into the trash can and use the cigarette lighter on his desk to start the fire."

"You do know how to go for the dramatic touch. Probably the writer in you."

She smiled, and this time it was the smile that kicked up his pulse.

"Probably," she said.

She reached down, curled her fingers around him, leaned over, and brushed her lips across his.

And just like that he was fully, fiercely erect.

He wrapped one hand around the back of her head. "It occurs to me that there is a lot to be said for a vivid imagination."

"I don't scare you, do I?" Maggie said.

"Lady, you're welcome to walk into my dreams anytime."

Chapter 41

It took a few long-distance calls," Raina said, "but we managed to dig up some information about the Guilfoyles and their financial situation."

"Someone else helped you with those phone calls?" Sam asked.

Startled by the sharp edge on the question, Maggie turned to look at him. It was eight thirty in the morning. Raina had called the hotel and left a message from Sam's "aunt" a short time ago. He had returned the call from a pay phone. Raina had suggested the three of them meet in a secluded location to discuss her findings. They had gathered in a quiet corner of a small park.

"I have another investigator in my firm, Lyra Brazier," Raina said. "Please don't worry. She's very good. I realize you are concerned with keeping this business confidential, but I assure you Lyra is trustworthy, and she has certain skills that are useful when it comes to getting information. I swear, it's a psychic talent. People talk to her before they realize what's going on."

Sam nodded, satisfied.

"Don't worry about the cost of the long-distance calls," Maggie said. "Just add them to your bill."

Raina looked amused. "I'll do that. You said your employer is covering my fees and those of Mr. Sage?"

"That's right," Maggie said. "But I'm the one who will be writing the checks."

"I see."

Raina took out a notebook, opened it, and flipped through a few pages. Maggie caught a glimpse of the odd handwriting and was briefly sidetracked.

"Shorthand?" she asked, curious.

"I used to be a secretary," Raina said. "Shorthand is not only efficient for taking notes in my current line of work, it guarantees a certain level of confidentiality."

Sam raised his brows. "It's almost a private code, isn't it?"

"Exactly." Raina found the page she was looking for and paused. "Here we go. Before she married Arthur Guilfoyle, Dolores was Dolores Johnson. She was the illegitimate daughter of Carson Flint and a failed starlet named Elizabeth Johnson."

"Carson Flint the Hollywood producer?" Sam asked. "The man who built the estate that is now the Institute?"

"One and the same," Raina said. "Flint died eighteen months ago. He ignored Dolores her whole life. He always maintained he was not her father. Dolores's mother couldn't prove otherwise, of course. She was fired by the studio as soon as word got out that she was pregnant."

"What happened to her?" Maggie asked.

"She worked at lunch counters until her death a few years ago. Dolores got her mother's looks and tried to become an actress. She landed a few small parts, but in the end she failed. She found work as a receptionist in the office of a doctor who specialized in dream analysis."

"Is that how she met Arthur Guilfoyle?" Sam asked.

"Yes, but at the time he was a struggling actor named Arthur Ellis. Apparently he had dream issues."

"I think he really is a lucid dreamer," Maggie said. "It explains why he booked an appointment with that doctor."

"True," Raina said. "At any rate, it wasn't long before Dolores and Arthur apparently realized there was money to be made in the dream business. They decided to go out on their own as a team."

"How did they end up here in Burning Cove?" Sam asked.

"Dolores's financial situation underwent a dramatic transformation when Carson Flint died," Raina said. She turned a page in the notebook. "He had a change of heart after his son was killed in a motorcycle accident. Flint redid his will and left everything to Dolores. Mostly that meant the Summer House estate here in Burning Cove. There was some money, but not a lot, because Flint was hit hard by the crash and lost more when the Depression got underway. The Guilfoyles must have used every last penny to renovate and refurbish Summer House in order to convert it into the Institute."

"When did Dolores Johnson and Arthur Ellis become the Guilfoyles?" Sam asked.

"They did not become Mr. and Mrs. Guilfoyle until Dolores discovered she had inherited the Flint estate," Raina said.

"Hah," Maggie said. "Arthur married her because she inherited Summer House."

"The timing is somewhat questionable," Raina said.

"But why the name change?" Sam asked.

"That," Raina said, "is a very good question. I suspect it has something to do with the fact that four years ago, Dolores Johnson and Arthur Ellis were living in Keeley Point."

Sam smiled slowly. "Well, damn."

"According to the librarian at the Keeley Point Library, they were running ads in the local paper promoting the Ellis Dream Program.

Arthur Ellis billed himself as the Dream Master. They both disappeared shortly after Virginia Jennaway was found dead on the beach."

Maggie looked at Sam. "The Dream Master signature on the bracelet. That's Arthur Guilfoyle."

"That's it." Sam snapped his fingers. He went to stand at the edge of the small pond. "The blackmailer found out the couple now known as the Guilfoyles could be linked to the Jennaway death."

"At this late date it won't be possible to prove that either of the Guilfoyles drugged Jennaway on the night she drowned."

"That's the thing about blackmail, isn't it?" Sam said. "The extortionist doesn't have to prove that a crime was committed. All that is necessary is to threaten the target with public exposure. The fear of scandal and tarnished reputations does the rest."

"Very true," Raina said.

"But why blackmail Lillian Dewhurst?" Maggie said.

Sam turned away from the pond. "I've got a feeling Dewhurst was a target of opportunity. The blackmailer must have discovered that she was a member of the Astral Travelers Society for a while. Dewhurst has a big secret to protect—her identity. A scandal involving drugs and a dead woman could ruin her career."

"How did the blackmailer know Aunt Cornelia would attend the conference?" Raina asked.

"There was no way to know," Sam said. "That's why the instructions in the note told her to purchase a ticket and attend the opening event."

Raina nodded. "A target of opportunity, but not one of the primary targets. Things got confused because the imposter showed up claiming to be Cornelia."

"I'm almost positive now that Nevins was the blackmailer," Sam said.

"Who was murdered by one of her intended victims that first night," Raina said. "That fits."

"Where does all this leave us?" Maggie asked.

"It leaves Detective Brandon with a probable murder on his hands," Sam said. "But I doubt he'll be able to pursue the Nevins investigation. There isn't any hard evidence, and no one seems to be applying pressure."

"One thing is clear," Raina said. She closed the notebook. "The Guilfoyles have to make the Institute pay off. If it doesn't start making money soon, they will be destroyed financially."

"Dreams and drugs," Sam said. "You really can't go wrong selling either one, can you?"

"Wrap up both in one package, tie it with a pretty ribbon, sell it to a few stars, and you've got the foundation of a financial empire," Raina said. "Do you need anything else from me?"

"Not right now." Sam took out a business card and gave it to her. "I appreciate the help. I owe you, and I'm happy to repay the favor. I'm in Adelina Beach. Call if there is anything I can do for you there. I've still got a few good connections in L.A., as well."

Raina smiled. "I'll keep that in mind. Our business runs on connections. I am always happy to find a new one."

"Don't forget the bill," Maggie said.

"I won't." Raina looked at her. "One more thing before I leave."

"Yes?"

"About the advice you suggested I give to the artist who painted the landscapes in Luther's office."

Maggie braced herself. "I'm sorry; I should have kept my mouth shut. I realize I had no business offering that advice."

"I want to thank you," Raina said.

"You do?"

"This morning when I stopped by Luther's office to tell him I was on my way to meet you, I found him in his studio. Painting."

"Another stormy landscape?" Maggie asked, her heart sinking.

Raina smiled. "No. Looked like a couple of doors in an endless hallway."

Chapter 42

"Evidently Oxlade decided not to leave after all," Sam said.

He stopped on the garden path and looked at the sedan sitting in front of the guest villa. His cop intuition wasn't just whispering—it was shrieking a warning.

It was ten thirty. After the early-morning meeting with Raina, he and Maggie had returned to the hotel for a late breakfast and then opted to walk to the Institute for what was supposed to have been Oxlade's lecture. He wanted to see the reactions of everyone involved when it became evident Oxlade wasn't going to show up. The path took them through the lush grounds and close to the villa.

"I definitely rattled his nerves last night with my dazzling performance as an unhinged woman," Maggie said. "He must have been too upset to drive back to L.A."

"He was shaken last night," Sam said. "But I think that would have made him even more determined to get away from Burning Cove as fast as possible. Let's talk to him."

Maggie glanced at her watch. "It's almost time for his lecture.

Maybe he decided that as long as he's still here, he might as well present it. After all, it's a great opportunity to attract new patients."

"Given Oxlade's mood last night, I can't see him lending any more of his professional credibility to the Guilfoyle Method. He won't be giving a lecture this morning."

"You're right," Maggie said. "So why is he still here?"

They walked to the villa. Sam checked the trunk of Oxlade's car. It was unlocked and empty. He went up the steps and rapped sharply on the front door. Maggie stood to one side.

There was no response.

"He's probably not feeling very friendly toward me at the moment," Maggie volunteered. "If he sees me out here, he won't open the door."

Sam tried the knob. "Unlocked." He eased the door open and looked down the length of the gloom-filled front hall. "The curtains are closed and the lights are off. Stay here."

"Why?"

"Because I don't think I'm going to find anything good inside."

"Maybe he's still asleep," Maggie offered. She did not sound optimistic.

"Just promise me you'll wait out here."

"I promise."

He reached under the edge of his jacket and slipped the pistol out of the shoulder holster. Maggie gave the weapon an uneasy look but she did not comment.

He left the door open and went into the gloom.

He wasn't surprised when he found the body, and he wasn't startled to discover that the cologne bottle was missing.

It was the blood-spattered bathroom and the hammer that came as a shock. They changed everything.

Chapter 43

"W hy?" Maggie asked. "What difference does it make that Oxlade was murdered with a hammer?"

"It indicates there's a second killer involved," Sam said. "The first prefers to use drugs. They make for a neat, clean kill and leave very little evidence. The other killer doesn't give a damn about being tidy. He may have been in a rage or maybe he got too excited. Maybe he's simply insane. Hard to say. Whatever the case, he was after the enhancer. He took the cologne bottle."

"He?" Maggie asked sharply. "Are you sure the killer is a man?"

They were standing outside the entrance to the guest villa. The driveway was packed with police cars, an ambulance, and a handful of uniformed officers. There was also a crowd of curious onlookers, including the three dream guides, various members of the Institute staff, and several conference attendees.

Dolores and Arthur Guilfoyle were on the front steps of the villa, talking to Detective Brandon. Maggie couldn't hear what was being said, but it was obvious that Arthur was agitated. He seemed to be pleading with Brandon. Dolores stood quietly, her posture rigid, her face grim. She did not look shocked so much as outraged.

Another publicity problem for the Institute, Maggie thought.

A short time ago a reporter and a photographer had arrived in a speedster convertible. The woman behind the wheel had jumped out, notebook and pencil in hand, and announced that she was Irene Ward, the crime beat reporter for the *Burning Cove Herald*.

She had headed directly toward the open door of the villa, photographer in tow. Brandon had ordered both to stay out of the house. Irritated, Ward had directed the man with the camera to grab as many photos of the scene outside the villa as possible, and then she had started moving through the crowd, talking to anyone and everyone.

"I can't be absolutely certain the killer is a man," Sam said. "But the fact that whoever it was used a hammer and didn't have a problem creating that scene in the bathroom makes me think it's the most likely possibility. Women usually prefer not to get covered in blood and . . . other stuff if they can avoid it."

"What other stuff?" Maggie asked.

"You don't want to know," Sam said. "My point is, whoever murdered Oxlade would have left the villa with a lot of gore on his clothes."

Maggie realized he was studying the crowd, not the Guilfoyles.

"Who are you looking at?" she asked

"The two male dream guides, Larry and Jake."

Maggie followed his gaze and saw the young men. They appeared to be trying to get Irene Ward's attention.

"They want to get their names in the papers," Maggie said. She paused, thinking. "I see what you mean about the unlikelihood of a woman using a hammer. I would certainly grab one in self-defense if that was all that was available, but if I planned to murder someone, I would want to keep some distance between myself and the other person, especially if I was attempting to murder a man. It isn't just the notion of getting covered in blood. It's common sense. I wouldn't want to get too close and take the risk of being overpowered."

"You're taking notes for your book again, aren't you?"

"Just making an observation."

"Liar. But your observation is interesting."

"Because it confirms your theory?" Maggie asked.

"No, because it makes me think the killer didn't have time to do a lot of planning. A pistol would make too much noise, especially in the middle of the night. It would have awakened the three dream guides in their quarters. The hammer was probably convenient, and it was guaranteed to be a lot more quiet than a gun."

"There must be a lot of tools stored here on the grounds of the Institute," Maggie said. "A place this big and this old is in need of constant minor repairs."

"There's a toolshed behind the hotel, too," Sam said. "Tools are expensive. Both sheds are probably locked at night. If the hammer that was used on Oxlade came from either of them—"

"It would indicate that whoever murdered Oxlade knows his way around the Institute and the hotel," Maggie said.

"Right. Brandon will figure that out, just as we did." Sam stopped talking because the detective was coming toward them. "Listen to me, Maggie. You will not volunteer your personal connection to Oxlade, and above all you will not tell Brandon you think the doctor once tried to poison you."

"But—"

"If you breathe a word about how much you loathed Oxlade and why, you will go straight to the top of Brandon's list of suspects."

Startled, Maggie stared at him. "But I thought we agreed he'll be looking for a male suspect."

"Oxlade was a well-known figure in the world of dream research. His death is going to be big news, especially given the violence involved and the fact that it happened here at the Institute. That means

Brandon will be under a lot of pressure to make an arrest. We don't want to give him an excuse to put you in jail."

"Okay, I get it," Maggie said.

"Also, it wouldn't look good for Sage Investigations if the firm's first client gets arrested for murder. I'd be lucky to even get divorce work after that kind of press."

Maggie sniffed. "Nice to know you're putting your client's interests first."

"Don't mention the Jennaway case, either. I'll handle that."

Brandon stopped in front of them. He nodded at Maggie and touched the brim of his beat-up fedora. "Miss Lodge."

"Detective," she said. "Sam told me the scene inside the villa is ghastly. I'm so sorry both of you had to see the body."

Brandon went blank for a beat, evidently at a loss to figure out what to do with her sympathy.

He grunted. "Part of the job."

"I understand," she said gently. "But it must make for some terrible dreams."

"Uh." Brandon pulled himself together. "Everyone has bad dreams sometimes."

"Yes," Maggie said. "But there are ways—"

Sam shot her a stern look. She got the message and stopped talking. He turned to Brandon.

"Find anything useful besides the hammer?" he said.

"Nothing yet." Brandon shoved his hat back on his head. "No decent prints in the blood. The killer used a towel to wipe down the floor."

"There will be plenty of blood on the clothes of whoever used that hammer," Sam said.

"Yeah, hard to get rid of a lot of bloodstained clothes," Brandon agreed. He glanced at the Guilfoyles. "Theoretically I should eliminate those two as suspects. If you're right about the drug connection, it looks like they just lost the goose that was supposed to lay the golden eggs for them here at the Institute."

"I wouldn't be too quick to cross them off the list," Sam said. "Maggie witnessed a quarrel between Oxlade and Guilfoyle last night right after Guilfoyle gave a dream reading. Oxlade announced he was ending their business arrangement and stormed out."

"Interesting," Brandon said. He looked at Maggie. "You saw the two argue?"

"Yes," she said. "Mr. Guilfoyle and I chatted for a few minutes after the reading. I more or less accused him of being a fraud, and he admitted it. Oxlade was backstage at the time and overheard the conversation. He was furious."

"That explains the suitcases in the living room," Brandon said. "So Oxlade was trying to leave town, and someone made sure he didn't. Gotta say, that's a relief."

"Why?" Maggie asked.

Brandon exhaled a deep, weary sigh. "Points to a motive, which means I'm looking for a human suspect."

Sam raised his brows. "Was there ever any doubt?"

"No, but my men tell me someone is spreading rumors about a psychic assassin who murders people in their dreams."

"It should be obvious Oxlade was not murdered by supernatural forces," Sam said.

"Sure," Brandon said. "A ghost or a spirit wouldn't need a hammer. But we both know that little fact won't stop the rumors or the headlines."

"True," Maggie said.

"My men are checking to see if the hammer came from the toolshed here at the Institute or the one at the hotel," Brandon said. "If that's the case it would be a useful lead. The officers are looking for the bloody clothes, too."

"Has there been any progress on the Nevins case?" Maggie asked.

"No," Brandon said. "Unless something new turns up, it will go down as natural causes. Nevins's next of kin is an elderly aunt back East. She said she couldn't afford to come out West to claim the body."

"No one is going to bury Beverly Nevins?" Maggie asked.

"When I struck out with the aunt, I managed to track down Nevins's roommate. Pamela Springs is driving from L.A. today to pack up Miss Nevins's things. She said she can't afford to pay for a funeral. Looks like the county will have to handle it."

"How did Pamela Springs react when you told her Nevins was dead?" Sam asked.

"Seemed sad but not exactly shocked to hear Nevins may have overdosed. Apparently there was a history of heavy drinking and sleeping pills." Brandon checked his watch. "I've got to be on my way. If anything comes up, give me a call."

"Sure," Sam said.

Brandon started to leave, but he paused. "A word of warning, Sage. The Guilfoyles suggested I put you at the top of the suspect list."

"Figures," Sam said.

"What?" Outrage slammed through Maggie. "How dare they suggest such a thing? What possible motive could Sam have?"

Brandon snorted. "Back in detective school they made a point of telling us that the first suspect is the one who discovered the body."

"That's ridiculous," Maggie said.

"You'd be surprised how often it proves true," Brandon said.

He turned and headed toward a group of officers gathered around the front of the guest villa.

"This is unbelievable," Maggie fumed.

"No, it was predictable," Sam said. "Brace yourself. The Guilfoyles just spotted us. They're headed our way and they look annoyed. This kind of publicity probably isn't what they had in mind when they asked Oxlade to lend his name to the conference."

Maggie started to respond, but she stopped because Dolores and Arthur were suddenly right in front of them. Sam was right. They were furious.

Dolores glared at Sam. "Do you have any idea what you've done, Mr. Sage?"

"Found the body?" he offered.

"You've ruined us," Arthur said, his voice tight with rage. "You've destroyed the Institute." He swept out a hand in a gesture meant to encompass the entire estate. "We got through Nevins's death, but there's no keeping this one out of the headlines."

"Even though you did predict it?" Maggie asked softly.

Sam glanced at her, frowning, but he didn't try to shush her.

"What are you talking about?" Dolores demanded. She sounded uncertain. Wary.

"At the end of the reading last night Mr. Guilfoyle announced the Traveler was abroad on the grounds of the Institute," Maggie said. "Hunting."

Arthur stared at her, dumbfounded.

"Yes," he said. "I did say something like that, didn't I?"

"I believe you suggested that the Traveler's target was a woman, but that's just a detail, isn't it?" Maggie said.

Arthur turned to Dolores, silently pleading for help. But her attention was focused on Maggie.

"Come with me, Arthur," Dolores said. She ripped her gaze away from Maggie and took Arthur's arm in a firm grip. "We must talk to the reporter from the *Herald*. We may have a chance to get on top of this story after all."

Sam watched the couple hurry through the crowd. Then he looked at Maggie.

"It's going to be rather ironic if it turns out you just saved the Institute a second time," he said.

"Yes, it will be," Maggie said. "I did it so that you could judge their reaction to the notion of saving the Institute."

"I know."

"Well? Did you learn anything?"

"Their reaction confirmed what we already knew. They'll do anything to salvage the Institute and the business."

Chapter 44

"Beverly was a desperate, unhappy woman," Pamela Springs said. "She grew up with money, you see. She was accustomed to good clothes and jewelry. She liked to party with her rich friends. But her father lost everything during the worst of the hard times. Took his own life with booze and pills. Earlier this year her sister did the same thing."

"Detective Brandon wasn't able to track down any close family members," Sam said. "Apparently there is just an elderly aunt back East."

Pamela had been reluctant to talk about Beverly Nevins, but Maggie had assured her she would be paid for her time. Pamela said she needed gas money for the drive back to L.A. and enough cash to cover Nevins's portion of the rent that month. Maggie told her that was not a problem.

The three of them were drinking coffee at a sidewalk café in the heart of Burning Cove's fashionable shopping district. Well-dressed tourists and locals strolled the palm-shaded sidewalks and studied the

AMANDA QUICK

expensive offerings in the windows of the boutiques and galleries. Viewed from this perspective, Maggie thought, you'd never know the country was still hauling itself out of a terrible depression.

"I told you Bev had a sister," Pamela said. "Eleanor. She and Bev roomed together in a boardinghouse. Eleanor was a very troubled woman. After she took her own life, Bev moved in with me. For a while she seemed to be doing okay. She got a job working at Bullocks on Wilshire. It was a good position, and she had the polish and the background to sell luxury goods to wealthy people, but she hated it."

"That explains the fashionable clothes in her hotel room," Sam said. "Did she steal them so that she could look good for the conference?"

Pamela grimaced. "She said she was borrowing the clothes. She planned to return them to the stockroom when she went back to L.A. Now it looks like I'll be the one who has to take them back to the store. I just hope I don't get accused of theft."

"If there is any problem, give me a call," Sam said. "I'll contact Brandon and get things cleared up."

Pamela relaxed a little. "Thanks."

"Did Beverly attend the conference at the Institute because she was interested in lucid dreaming?" Maggie asked.

"She wasn't the least bit interested in dreams," Pamela said. "Not until she read her sister's diary."

Sam didn't move, but Maggie realized he was suddenly even more focused and intent than he had been a moment ago.

"The sister left a diary?" he said very softly.

Pamela nodded and selected a small sandwich off the tray. "Bev was curious, so she read it. She told me that four years ago Eleanor ran with a fast crowd of society people who were excited by the theories of psychic dream analysis. They joined a group formed by a man who called himself the Dream Master. Silly stuff, Bev said. But apparently the Dream Master was very good-looking. Eleanor fell hard for him. Bev found a photo of the two of them tucked into the diary."

"Did Beverly come across any other secrets in the diary that might make blackmail material?" Sam asked.

"Apparently one of the members of the group died under mysterious circumstances. There were rumors of drugs. The only other interesting thing was that, according to the diary, the woman who later became Aunt Cornelia was a member of the dream group for a brief time. I think her last name was Dunstan or Danvers or something."

"Dewhurst," Maggie said quietly.

"Maybe," Pamela said. "I don't remember. I know Bev tried to find her in the Keeley Point phone book and also tried the L.A. phone book, but she didn't come up with anyone who was female, the right age, and the right social class, so she gave up."

Lillian was not in the phone book, and she lived in Adelina Beach, not L.A. or Keeley Point, Maggie thought. It would have been very difficult to find her unless you knew more about her than just her name.

"Go on," Sam said to Pamela.

"That was it, at least at the time," she said. "Bev boxed up the diary and seemed to forget about it until a month ago. That's when she saw the photos of the Guilfoyles in the newspapers."

"She recognized Arthur Guilfoyle as the Dream Master from the picture she found in the diary," Sam said.

"Yes." Pamela drank some coffee and lowered the cup. "She got very excited. All she could talk about was the money the Guilfoyles would pay to keep the stories of the Dream Master and the Jennaway death out of the papers. Something about drugs being involved. She said the rumors could ruin them."

"She set out to blackmail the Guilfoyles," Sam said. "What about Aunt Cornelia?"

Pamela grimaced. "She got the notion to try to get Aunt Cornelia to pay for silence, too. She said she could connect her to the Astral Travelers Society and therefore to the mysterious death of Jennaway. She didn't know how to reach the woman who wrote the column, so she sent a letter via the newspaper editor. She said it was a long shot because Cornelia might not get the letter in time. She wasn't particularly concerned."

"Because the Guilfoyles were her primary targets," Sam said.

Pamela nodded. "She figured they had the most to lose."

"Did she mention Dr. Oxlade?" Sam asked.

"No, not that I recall." Pamela sighed. "I warned her that extortion is a very dangerous business."

"You were right," Sam said quietly.

Pamela looked at him. "Bev was murdered, wasn't she?"

"Looks like it," Sam said. "But the police probably won't be able to prove it."

"Poor Beverly," Pamela whispered. "She was so unhappy."

Maggie lowered her cup. "Did Beverly find a photograph of Aunt Cornelia in her sister's things?"

"No," Pamela said. "The only picture she had to go by was the one of Aunt Cornelia at the nightclub in Burning Cove. But that woman turned out to be an imposter. Bev didn't know what she was doing. The Guilfoyles are selling dreams. They stand to make a lot of money. People in that position will do whatever they think is necessary to protect themselves. Killing a small-time blackmailer wouldn't bother them at all."

"You're right," Maggie said gently. "The problem was that Beverly Nevins sold herself a dream. She thought she was going to make a lot of money in a hurry and reclaim the life she had known before her father lost the family fortune."

"Yes," Pamela said.

"I know the type," Maggie said. "My ex-fiancé chased the same dream."

"It's just so sad," Pamela said. "If only she had focused on the future. Instead, she obsessed over the past."

"Any chance you brought that diary with you today?" Sam asked.

"No," Pamela said. "Beverly took it with her when she packed for Burning Cove. She said it held the proof she needed to convince the Guilfoyles and Aunt Cornelia that she could ruin them if they didn't pay her."

"Just to confirm," Sam said, "as far as you know, Beverly Nevins intended to blackmail three people? The Guilfoyles and Aunt Cornelia?"

"Those are the only people she talked about," Pamela said. "Look, I need to go. It's a long drive back to L.A. I'd rather not be on that road alone after dark."

"I don't blame you," Maggie said. "You've been very helpful." She opened her handbag, took out several bills, and handed them to Pamela. "Thank you."

Pamela looked at the cash, uncertain. "That's too much. I just need gas money and the rent."

"We appreciate your time," Maggie said. "You answered some questions for us."

"Well, okay," Pamela said. She put the money into her handbag and got to her feet. "Thank you."

"One more question," Sam said. "You said Nevins took the diary and the photo with her when she left for Burning Cove."

"That's right," Pamela said.

"Did she take anything else that she thought would be useful for her blackmail scheme?" Sam asked.

"A bracelet," Pamela said. "It belonged to her sister. She was convinced she could sell it and the diary and the photo to the Guilfoyles."

She turned and walked away to the Hudson parked at the curb. Sam watched her drive off down the street. Maggie watched him.

"What are you thinking?" she asked.

"I'm thinking the person who searched Beverly Nevins's hotel room was looking for the diary, the photo, and the bracelet. Whoever it was found the diary and the photo but not the bracelet."

"I suppose this means we can eliminate Oxlade as a suspect in Beverly Nevins's death," Maggie said. "Apparently he wasn't on her list of blackmail targets. Sounds like she was just after the Guilfoyles and Aunt Cornelia."

"It's possible Eleanor Nevins never knew the name of the doctor who was supplying the enhancer drug to the Guilfoyles back in their Keeley Point days," Sam said. "Either that or she simply didn't care enough to mention him in her diary."

"What do we do now?" Maggie asked.

Sam studied her across the small table. "Viewed from a strictly professional perspective, this case is closed. In fact, it was closed the first night of the dream conference."

"The blackmailer was murdered, and the fake Aunt Cornelia was unmasked and sent packing that night."

"Yes," Sam said. He drank some coffee. "Case closed."

She watched him, aware of the energy in the atmosphere around him.

"The thing is," she said, "there are so many questions left unanswered."

"None of which relates to your case."

She frowned. "You're wrong. One question is very much our business. Who tried to murder you in the parking lot at the hotel?"

"Could have been an accident."

"It wasn't an accident," Maggie said.

Sam waved that off with a slight motion of one hand. "It's a hazard of the investigation business. I was in someone's way. If we leave town I will no longer be in that person's way."

"So many questions," Maggie said.

"Yes."

"We need answers."

Sam gave her a knowing look. "You mean I need answers. I appreciate that, but—"

"You're wrong," Maggie said. "I need them, too. Curiosity is yet another character flaw that is common in writers, just like it is in investigators."

He looked at her for a long moment and then got to his feet, took out his wallet, and put some cash on the table. "I think we'll get at least one answer in the evening edition of the local paper. Let's go back to the hotel and see which of the two male dream guides gets arrested for the murder of Dr. Emerson Oxlade."

Maggie shivered. "Do you really think one of them was responsible?"

"No, but one of them will make headlines in the late edition of the *Burning Cove Herald*."

"That sounds a lot like a psychic prediction."

"Intuition."

Chapter 45

ARREST IN SHOCKING
MURDER OF DREAM DOCTOR

Did Psychic Dream Reader at Guilfoyle Institute
Predict Death and Provide Clues to the Killer?

Late this afternoon local police arrested Lawrence W. Porter for the grisly murder of Dr. Emerson Oxlade, noted dream analyst. Mr. Porter is employed as a dream guide at the recently opened Guilfoyle Institute. Bloodstained clothing and shoes were discovered in the trunk of his Ford sedan.

Detective Brandon of the Burning Cove Police Department said that Mr. Porter has maintained his innocence, but authorities say he has no explanation for the bloody garments found in his possession.

Detective Brandon declined to comment on rumors that Arthur Guilfoyle, the head of the Guilfoyle Institute, predicted the murder during a private psychic reading last night. Several of those who attended the event confirmed that Mr. Guilfoyle made a prediction of death by supernatural means.

Earlier today Mr. Guilfoyle spoke with Detective Brandon. Several onlookers suggested he may have provided the detective with a psychic reading that enabled the prompt arrest.

"You were right," Maggie said. "The police arrested one of the dream guides. Larry. I can't believe it."

She tossed the evening edition of the *Herald* onto the table and went to stand at the window of her hotel room. It was a little after six. In the distance she could see the lights of the Institute. The staff was preparing for the farewell cocktail party.

"That's not a surprise," Sam said. He sat down on the side of the bed and leaned forward to tie the laces of his freshly polished shoes. "He was the obvious choice because of the rumors of drugs. The interesting bit is that not only is Guilfoyle getting credit for predicting the murder, there's a rumor that he may have done a psychic reading for the police. Talk about great publicity."

Maggie turned around. The sight of Sam sitting on her bed, casually going about the process of getting dressed for the evening, was both disconcerting and satisfying. It was as if he belonged here in the same bedroom with her.

This is what love feels like, she thought. The realization shook her, momentarily stealing her breath.

She pulled herself together with a fierce effort of will.

"Do you think Brandon believes Larry is guilty?" she asked.

"Not for a minute." Sam finished tying his shoes, stood, and went to the dressing table to work on his bow tie. "He knows as well as I do that the kid was framed. The problem now is proving it."

She met his eyes in the mirror. "You've got another plan, haven't you?"

"I need to get inside the Guilfoyles' private villa. There will be a big crowd at the cocktail party tonight. No one will notice if I slip away."

"Famous last words. What if someone does notice?"

Sam winked. "Your job is to provide me with a cover story."

"Such as?"

"You're the creative one. You'll think of something."

Chapter 46

S am had been right about one thing, Maggie thought. The farewell gala at the Institute was a triumphant success. Beneath the massive wrought iron chandeliers, elegantly dressed guests consumed the seemingly unlimited supply of cocktails served by the catering staff and the two remaining dream guides.

Nothing like the thrill of murder laced with a suggestion of psychic powers to energize a room. Everyone was talking about the news and speculating that it proved the power of the Guilfoyle Method. Arthur Guilfoyle was basking in the glow of admiration and excitement. Dolores was stationed near the buffet table, clipboard in hand. She was jotting down the names and addresses of the holdouts who had decided they wanted to learn the secrets of the Method after all.

Maggie stood with a small cluster of conference attendees. There was a glass in everyone's hand, including hers, but she was in no mood to enjoy her drink. Sam had slipped away a short time ago. No one appeared to have noticed, which was a relief, but her nerves were on edge. She would not be able to relax until he returned.

"They say the crime scene was horrifying," the woman standing next to Maggie said. "The dream guide used a hammer. Can you imagine? He seemed like such a nice young man. The drugs must have driven him mad."

"I heard the police found cocaine, pills, and marijuana in his room," a portly middle-aged man announced. He downed half his martini in a single gulp and shook his head. "Evidently he wasn't just an addict; he was buying and selling the drugs. What is the younger generation coming to?"

"I'll tell you one thing," the first woman said. "If I needed any more reason to learn the Guilfoyle Method, today provided it. I spoke with one of the guests who was invited to the private psychic reading last night. She said Mr. Guilfoyle did predict murder."

"Astonishing," another woman declared.

Maggie told herself she ought to keep her mouth shut, but as usual, she was unable to resist a comment.

"I was at that private psychic reading," she said. "Mr. Guilfoyle predicted a woman was in danger, not a man."

"When it comes to the paranormal, you can't expect precise details," the portly man said.

There were murmurs of agreement. Maggie vowed not to make any more attempts to correct the rapidly growing legend of the Guilfoyle Method. There was no point. People were going to believe what they wanted to believe.

"Champagne, Miss Lodge?"

Maggie turned to see the dream guide named Gloria standing right behind her. There was a single glass of champagne and a small slip of folded notepaper on the tray she held out.

"Thank you," Maggie said. "But I haven't had a chance to finish my first drink."

She hadn't touched it, in fact.

"Yours will be warm now," Gloria said. There was an urgency in her tone and a pleading expression in her eyes. The tray trembled a little. "Why don't you take the fresh, chilled glass. Please."

The message was clear. Gloria was frightened and desperate.

"That is an excellent idea," Maggie said. She put the untouched glass on the tray and picked up the fresh champagne with one gloved hand. She managed to palm the folded note at the same time.

Gloria was visibly relieved.

"Thank you," she whispered.

She turned and hurried off into the crowd.

Maggie drifted away from the portly man and the others and found a quiet alcove. She set her glass down on a small table and unfolded the note.

Larry is innocent. I can prove it. Please help me. The ladies' lounge. Ten minutes.

Smart choice of a rendezvous location, Maggie thought. Gloria must have guessed she would hesitate to meet a woman she barely knew in the night-shrouded gardens or in one of the Institute's empty seminar rooms. But the ladies' lounge was safe. There would be women walking in and out at unpredictable times. Given the size of the crowd tonight and the amount of liquor flowing, the restroom was bound to be doing a steady business.

The location had one other singular asset—no man, including Arthur Guilfoyle, would dream of stepping foot inside.

She glanced at the tall, old-fashioned clock standing near the alcove and decided to start making her way toward the hall that led to the women's room. It was going to take a few minutes to move through the crowd at a discreet pace that would not draw attention.

When she reached the entrance to the corridor she paused to check on the whereabouts of the Guilfoyles. They were both chatting with enthusiastic guests.

Satisfied, she moved into the hallway and went briskly toward the ladies' lounge. When she was a few steps away from the door, a fortyish woman in a mauve evening gown emerged. She was in a hurry. When she saw Maggie, she paused.

"I'd advise you not to go in there," she said in confidential tones. "A woman is in one of the stalls. She is quite ill. Food poisoning, apparently. She told me there was a smaller facility available in the north wing."

"I see," Maggie said.

Gloria had apparently found a way to ensure some privacy for their conversation.

She waited until the helpful woman in mauve had disappeared back into the lobby and then pushed open the door of the women's room. She walked into a luxuriously appointed lounge. A row of dressing table stools covered in pink satin sat in front of a long lacquer table and a bank of mirrors. Beyond was the entrance to a tiled room and a row of stalls.

The lounge was empty. That was no doubt due to the sounds of violent retching that emanated from behind the door of the one occupied stall.

"Gloria?"

The retching stopped immediately. The stall opened and Gloria rushed out. Her face was flushed from the effort of pretending to be ill. She had a sign in one hand—*Closed for Cleaning*.

"Thank you so much for coming, Miss Lodge," she said. "Just a minute."

She shot past Maggie, opened the door of the women's room long enough to hang the sign outside, and then ducked back into the lounge and locked the door.

She slumped against the door for a few seconds, catching her breath.

"I've never been so scared in my life," she whispered. "You've got to help me save Larry. He didn't kill Dr. Oxlade, I swear it."

"You're sure of that?"

"Look, Larry smokes reefers now and again to relax. Who doesn't? But he's not a dope fiend. The marijuana the cops found in his room is probably his, but not the cocaine and those pills."

"What about the clothes in the trunk of his car?"

"Isn't it obvious? The killer put them there to frame Larry."

"You said you could prove Larry was innocent. How do you plan to do that?"

"He was with me last night—the whole night. But no one will believe me on account of the drugs. They'll say I was lying to protect him."

Maggie heard a door open behind her. She whirled around in time to watch Dolores Guilfoyle walk out of a supply closet, a black-beaded evening bag clutched in one gloved hand. There was a pistol in her other hand.

"Gloria can't prove anything," Dolores said. "You have caused more than enough trouble, Miss Lodge. This ends tonight."

Chapter 47

The pistol Dolores gripped was a small one, to be sure, but Sam's words shivered through Maggie. *A small pistol can be just as scary as a big one at close quarters.*

"I'm sorry, Miss Lodge," Gloria whispered.

"What did she promise you in exchange for your help getting me alone tonight?" Maggie asked. She did not take her eyes off Dolores.

"She said she would hire the best lawyer in town to help Larry," Gloria said. Her thin, sad voice indicated she now knew that wasn't going to happen.

"I promised her I would make sure Larry walked free if she did as I asked," Dolores said.

The gun did not waver in her hand. She appeared to be cool and in control. It was obviously not the first time she had done this sort of thing. But there was an air of hot, frantic excitement about her that indicated she was close to some inner edge.

"You're not going to get Larry out of jail, are you?" Maggie said. "You need him to take the fall for Oxlade's murder."

"I'm afraid so," Dolores said.

Gloria whimpered.

"Shut up," Dolores said. "You are only useful to me as long as you do what I tell you."

Gloria's mouth opened and closed. She stared at Maggie with the same desperate look in her eyes that had been there earlier when she had offered the note on a tray and silently pleaded for help.

"What's this all about?" Maggie said to Dolores.

"I don't have time to stand around chatting," Dolores said. She motioned with the pistol. "Into the supply closet, both of you. There's a door inside. It leads to a hallway. Hurry. We've got to make this fast. I have to get back to the lobby before I'm missed. Move."

Maggie went reluctantly to the open door of the supply closet. Gloria, seemingly numb with panic, trailed after her. There was another door on the inside of the closet. It stood open, revealing a narrow corridor illuminated by a wall sconce. An old servant's hallway, Maggie thought. It had not been remodeled.

Maggie moved into the corridor. Gloria followed. Dolores was right behind them. She paused long enough to close the outer door of the supply closet.

"Keep walking," she ordered.

Maggie obeyed. Gloria followed her along the shadowy passage. Dolores stayed very close behind them. In the narrow hall there was no way she could miss if she pulled the trigger.

"Mr. Sage will be looking for me," Maggie warned.

Dolores chuckled. "I saw him slip away earlier. I suspect he's searching our villa, looking for something that will prove Arthur and I are a couple of con artists. That's why you attended the conference, isn't it? You want to expose the Guilfoyle Method as a fraud. You're wasting your time."

"You were the one who tried to murder Sam last night," Maggie said.

"That was the plan. I took Larry's Ford and waited for Sage to come out of the hotel lobby to pick you up after the dream reading. But he came from a different direction. I wasn't expecting that."

"Obviously," Maggie said. "That leaves you with a real problem, doesn't it?"

"I'll worry about Sage later. You are the real problem, Miss Lodge. I realized that when I saw the effect you had first on Oxlade and then on Arthur. That's far enough. Stop."

Maggie halted in front of a door.

"Open it," Dolores said. "It's unlocked."

Maggie turned the knob and moved through the opening into a windowless room lit by a dim overhead fixture. Ahead was a partial wall flanked by a corridor on each side.

"This is the back of the theater," she said.

"Atmosphere is everything when it comes to setting the scene," Dolores said. She gave Gloria a shove. "The stage. Both of you."

Once again Maggie led the way. She stopped at the entrance of the stage. The curtains were open. The rows of seats lay in dense shadow, but there was just enough light coming from the wings to reveal the shapes of the chair and the gilded couch that had been used in the psychic reading the previous night.

She glanced over her shoulder. "If you think you can get away with a repeat of the same scene you used for Beverly Nevins's murder, you're not nearly as smart as I thought you were, Dolores."

"Don't worry," Dolores said. "The press will buy it, and that means the cops will, too."

Gloria started to turn. "You murdered that woman? The one who died in here the first night of the conference?"

"I told you to shut up," Dolores said.

Her voice rose a little. Her control was slipping. Maggie heard a soft thud and turned to see that Dolores had dropped the evening bag. An object gleamed in her fingers. A syringe.

"No," Maggie gasped.

Dolores stabbed the syringe into the curve of Gloria's shoulder.

Gloria managed a shocked yelp, staggered a couple of steps, and turned to stare at Dolores in stunned horror. She grabbed the edge of a nearby curtain in an attempt to steady herself, but she lacked the strength to maintain her grip. Her eyes glazed over. She crumpled to the floor.

Maggie stumbled back a step. She braced one hand on the bank of light switches to keep her balance and looked at Dolores.

"What have you done?" she whispered.

"She's not dead," Dolores said, her voice once again calm. "I used a strong sedative. You learn a lot about drugs and medications when you work for a doctor. Gloria will wake up next to your body. The pistol will be in her hand. It will have her fingerprints on it."

"She'll remember what happened," Maggie said. "She'll tell the police."

"I doubt it. The sedative creates some amnesia. But even if she does remember, no one will believe I was here. Arthur will testify that I was in the lobby with him the whole time. Given the size of the crowd tonight, no one will be able to dispute him."

"You're losing control, aren't you, Dolores? You used to be able to make your kills look like natural causes, or even supernatural causes. I'll bet you're the one who fired up the rumors of the Traveler after you murdered Virginia Jennaway. You resurrected the story after you killed Beverly Nevins."

"I had to kill them," Dolores said. "They gave me no choice."

"Did you murder Jennaway because she slept with your husband?"

"If I got rid of every woman Arthur fucks I wouldn't have time to run the business. I had to take care of Jennaway because she became a problem."

"How?"

"The stupid woman was convinced Arthur loved her and wanted to marry her. When he tried to walk away, she had the nerve to threaten to go to the press and claim that he got her pregnant. She planned to tell the world the Dream Master was fucking his acolytes. The scandal would have destroyed us."

"You were the one who stole the vial of the enhancer drug from Oxlade four years ago. You used it on Virginia Jennaway."

"Jennaway and Arthur went to a nightclub that night," Dolores said. "Neither of them saw me. You know how it is in the clubs. So dark. When they left the booth for a dance, I dropped some of the drug into Jennaway's drink. It took a while for the effects to kick in, but when they did, Arthur was terrified. As usual he panicked. He got Jennaway as far as the parking lot. I was waiting. I told him I would take care of everything."

"That's your job, isn't it? Cleaning up after Arthur."

Dolores shrugged. "I'm the fixer. I do whatever is necessary to protect the star. I sent him home in a cab that night and then I drove Jennaway back to her beach house. I got her out of the car. She was so disoriented and so woozy she never realized I was walking her into the sea. She struggled a bit at the end, but it wasn't difficult to push her head underwater and hold it there. She was hallucinating. Thought I was the Traveler."

"You've made yourself into the human version of the Traveler," Maggie said. "You've caused a lot of death. Virginia Jennaway, Beverly Nevins, Valerie Warren. Did I leave out anyone?"

"They were all distractions and problems," Dolores shrieked. She took a breath and got her voice back under control. "Instead of going away quietly, they tried to make trouble. Jennaway wanted marriage. Nevins and Warren tried to blackmail us."

"Killing me is going to cause you a lot of trouble, trust me."

"In the beginning I didn't think you would be a problem," Dolores said. "You were just another conference attendee. Yes, you were supposedly writing a book about lucid dreaming, but I wasn't worried.

Then you and Sage discovered Nevins's body. I told myself that wouldn't be a problem, either. The situation was under control. Then I realized Oxlade was obsessed with you."

"He wanted to run experiments on me," Maggie said.

"That would have been manageable, too. The real complication was that Oxlade convinced Arthur that you are a truly unique dreamer, that you possess some genuine psychic talent. Now he is obsessed with you. He thinks you are the woman of his dreams, literally. The fool believes he needs you to fulfill his vision of the Guilfoyle Method. He thinks you can make him a star. He has concluded he no longer needs me."

Maggie groped for the master light switch behind her. "If what you're saying is true, he's unhinged."

"Quite possibly. I've been wondering about that. Oxlade did several sessions with him using the drug. I'm afraid Arthur actually believes he can use the enhancer to open the path to his psychic senses. He's an actor who has gone too deeply into his role."

"He's deluded."

"Yes, but I can handle that," Dolores said. "As I said, you are the problem."

"Aren't you worried about the bracelet?" Maggie asked.

Dolores froze. "What do you know about the bracelet?"

"I know Arthur gave it to Eleanor Nevins. You found Eleanor's diary and the photo when you searched the hotel room, but you didn't find the bracelet, did you? In case you're interested, it was taped under the toilet tank lid. There's a lovely inscription on it. *To EN, the woman of my dreams.* It's signed *Dream Master.*"

"Where is it?" Dolores hissed.

"In my evening bag."

"Toss it here. Do it."

"Sure."

Maggie threw the bag straight at Dolores, who tried to catch it with her left hand. She fumbled and missed the small, glittering purse. It fell to the floor at her feet.

Maggie knew it was the only opening she was likely to get. She took advantage of the few seconds of distraction to slam the master light switch downward. The dim overhead fixtures illuminating the stage and the wings went out. Utter darkness, disorienting and claustrophobic, fell with shocking suddenness.

She dropped to the floor.

"Bitch," Dolores shouted.

The pistol roared.

Maggie saw a flash of light. It disappeared immediately but it told her Dolores was still on the other side of Gloria's unconscious body.

"Turn on the lights, you stupid creature," Dolores shrieked.

Another gunshot reverberated through the theater. Maggie realized she could not remain huddled under the light switches. She began to haul herself across the stage on her belly.

Another shot thundered in the darkness. How many bullets were there in a small gun? She would have to remember to ask Sam. Assuming she survived.

Behind her she heard movement, followed by a thump and a shriek of rage. Dolores had stumbled against Gloria, but she was still on her feet.

Maggie kept going, feeling her way over the boards. Her fingers brushed against the leg of the chair. She toppled it onto its side and shoved it across the stage in the general direction of the gunshots.

The pistol blazed again in the darkness, but Dolores was still aiming high. Evidently she hadn't realized her target was on the floor.

Maggie touched the gilded leg of the couch and quickly dragged herself around to the back. With luck it would serve as a barricade until she could get into the wings on the far side of the stage.

There was a solid thud behind her. Dolores had blundered into the chair. She screamed, rage and panic mingling in the unearthly shriek.

There was a flurry of wild footsteps as she struggled to recover her balance.

She failed. There was a quickly silenced scream followed by a jolting thud when she toppled off the stage and landed on the floor in front of the first row of seats.

An ominous silence followed, and then came the sound of muffled sobs.

Maggie hesitated, not certain what to do next. After a moment she started feeling her way back across the stage, hoping to get to the bank of light switches.

The backstage door crashed open.

"Maggie," Sam shouted. "Where are you?"

"Here," she called. "On the stage. She's in here, too, on the floor. She fell. She's got a gun. Don't stumble over Gloria. She's unconscious."

The overhead fixture backstage came on, sending some light into the wings. Footsteps sounded. Sam appeared. He had his pistol in one hand, a flashlight in the other. Jake was right behind him.

Sam saw her and started toward her.

"Are you all right?" he asked.

"Yes, I think so."

Satisfied, Sam walked to the edge of the stage and looked down.

"Get the gun, Jake," he ordered. "It's under the center seat in the front row."

"Yes, sir."

Jake bounded down the side steps.

Arthur appeared, frantic and breathless. "Where is she? Where is my wife? Is she all right?"

"She's alive," Sam said. He leaned down to take the pistol Jake handed up to him.

"Dolores," Arthur whispered. He went down the steps. "Darling, what have you done?"

"Arthur," Dolores said. "Help me. You have to help me."

A man dressed in a catering uniform showed up next. "The lady on the floor back here is unconscious, Mr. Sage, but she's alive. My boss is calling the cops. They'll be here soon."

"Find your boss," Sam said. "Tell him we're going to need an ambulance."

"Right."

The caterer headed up the aisle toward the main entrance of the theater.

Sam slipped the pistol inside his evening jacket and went to Maggie, who was trying to push herself to her feet. She was shivering so badly she didn't trust her balance. Sam wrapped an arm around her and pulled her close.

"Maggie," he said, his voice a hoarse rasp. "Maggie."

"I'm okay," she said. "How did you know where to find me?"

"I knew something was wrong when I returned to the lobby. You were gone and there was no sign of Dolores Guilfoyle. Jake said he'd seen you heading for the ladies' room. He said you hadn't returned."

She looked down at the floor below the stage. Arthur was kneeling beside Dolores, cradling her in his arms.

"Darling, how could you do this?" Arthur murmured.

"I did it to save you," Dolores wailed. "To save our dream. You have to help me."

"I will," Arthur vowed. "I will get you the help you need."

Sam pulled Maggie close and tight against him.

"Don't get me wrong," he said into her hair, "I appreciate the dramatic touch. But you are very hard on the nerves."

She pressed her face into his shoulder. "You were right about one thing. A small pistol can be just as scary as a big one at close quarters."

Chapter 48

Scotch and soda?" Arthur asked.

"Sounds good," Sam said. He crossed the living room of the villa and stopped at the windows. "Great view."

"Dolores loves this house." Arthur went to the drinks cabinet and got busy with the bottles and glassware. "Sadly, I don't think she'll ever see it again. The doctor told me she suffered a total breakdown. She's delusional. The asylum attendants picked her up from the Burning Cove hospital this afternoon. She had to be heavily sedated."

Sam glanced back over his shoulder. "You had her committed?"

"That's what the doctor recommended. I'm assured everything will be handled with great discretion. This way she won't have to stand trial."

Sam turned away from the view. "Did you know she was becoming unstable?"

"I suspected as much." Arthur picked up the two glasses and carried them across the room. He handed one of the glasses to Sam. "I didn't want to believe it. We came so far together. It's hard to imagine the Guilfoyle Institute without her. She was a genius when it came to marketing. But somewhere along the line she became obsessed."

Sam drank some of the scotch and soda and lowered the glass. "She told Maggie that four years ago she murdered a woman named Virginia Jennaway and that she also killed Beverly Nevins and one of the dream guides, Valerie Warren."

"Yes, I know. Detective Brandon said she confessed to all three murders. She accused those women of trying to blackmail us." Arthur swallowed some of his drink and shook his head. "Claimed she had to do it because they were threatening her dream."

"I heard what she said in the theater. As I recall, she indicated it was a dream you both shared."

"In her case it became an obsession. She is paranoid, Mr. Sage. Unstable."

"She intended to kill Maggie last night and frame Gloria for the murder."

"I know." Arthur closed his eyes in sorrow. "I know."

"But she didn't admit to killing Emerson Oxlade."

Arthur's eyes snapped open. "She's insane, Mr. Sage. There is no knowing what is going on in her disordered mind. I'm afraid she can no longer distinguish the difference between dreams and reality."

"So we're told."

"You are showing a great deal of interest in the details of this case. You sound more like a detective than a research assistant."

Sam took another swallow of his drink. "I'm concerned with the details because Miss Lodge was nearly murdered. If you were in my position, I think you would be equally interested."

"I see," Arthur said. "Your relationship with Miss Lodge is personal as well as professional, then?"

"Very personal," Sam said. "I assume that answers your question?"

"My question?"

"You invited me here for drinks and a private conversation today because you want to know how things stand between Maggie and me."

"I am curious, yes."

"Because you're attracted to her?"

"On many levels," Arthur admitted. "Maggie is a very intriguing woman. Has she told you she and I share a talent for lucid dreaming?"

"You think you can use her talent here at the Institute, don't you?"

"I admit I would very much like to have her on my staff."

"Forget it," Sam said. "I accepted your invitation because I've got a question of my own."

Arthur looked at him. "What is that, Mr. Sage?"

"I understand Dolores's motive for murdering those women, but why would she kill Oxlade? I got the impression the two of you needed him and his credentials as a respected dream analyst to enhance the image of the Institute and the Guilfoyle Method."

"You have it backward," Arthur said. "We didn't need him as much as he needed us. Oxlade was difficult, to say the least. All he cared about was proving that his theories of lucid dreaming were valid. I'm sure Miss Lodge told you he lost his temper after the private demonstration."

"Because you went off script and said the Traveler was planning to murder a woman here at the Institute."

"I took a little dramatic license and made the prediction about the Traveler," Arthur said. "I'm an actor at heart, Mr. Sage. I know when I'm not connecting with my audience. I sensed my performance needed a shot of excitement. Energy. Oxlade took offense at what he deemed my nonscientific approach."

"I got the impression that until that night he believed you really were capable of extreme lucid dreaming, that you could take it to a higher plane and access your psychic side."

Arthur chuckled. "I just told you, I'm an actor."

"I get it. Was it hard to fool Oxlade?"

"Not at all. In some ways he was the easiest person to deceive. For a good actor, it's the simplest thing in the world to fool someone like Oxlade. He wanted desperately to believe his drug worked. I gave him reasons to believe that."

"But all the enhancer does is cause a person to hallucinate."

"Yes." Arthur smiled. "But it provides a very interesting experience if it is given under controlled conditions. I've used it a few times, myself. It makes most people extremely suggestible. Takes a strong talent to control it. I can handle the hallucinations and visions. I'm sure Miss Lodge can, as well. But you are not a powerful lucid dreamer, are you?"

Sam frowned, blinked a few times, and pressed his glass against his forehead. "You thought the drug would be useful for promoting the Guilfoyle Method."

Arthur watched him with an air of anticipation. "Extremely useful."

Sam lowered the glass, shook his head, and squinted.

"Which is why you went into a rage when you discovered Oxlade was leaving and taking the drug with him," he said, the words slurred around the edges.

"So you figured that out, did you?" Arthur asked softly.

"That murder just didn't fit with any of the others."

"Because of the blood?"

"That and the fact that it wasn't a very smart murder. There was some planning involved in the others, but killing Oxlade was an act of impulse, anger, and desperation."

"What about the bloody clothes in the trunk of Larry Porter's Ford? Didn't that require some planning?"

"Yes, so Dolores handled that end of the business." Sam turned away from the window and studied the flowers in a nearby vase. "But the murder? Nope. That was just dumb." His words were getting mushier. "The search for the drug afterward was sloppy, too. Clothes hauled out of the suitcase and tossed onto the floor. Not like the search of

Beverly Nevins's hotel room. That was done in a careful way. It was not one hundred percent successful, but it was tidy. Dolores at work again."

"What are you talking about?" Arthur demanded, voice sharpening.

Sam plucked an orchid out of the vase and held it up to the light. "Spectacular, isn't it? Just think. Nature creates incredible beauty with such ease. Over and over again. Amazing."

Arthur took a step toward him and stopped. "What do you know about the search of Nevins's hotel room? Why did you say it was not a hundred percent successful?"

"What?" Sam dropped the orchid on the table and started to turn around. He stumbled a little and grabbed the padded arm of a massive reading chair to catch his balance. "Right. Nevins's room. Whoever searched it found the diary but not the bracelet. Don't worry, I've got it."

Arthur stared at him. "You have the bracelet?"

"Yep. There's a pretty little gold charm with the letters *ATS* on it, but it's the inscription that will ruin you. *To EN, the woman of my dreams.* It's signed *Dream Master.*" Sam winked. "We all know who the Dream Master was, don't we?"

"You can't prove anything," Arthur said.

"Not without the diary. It ties everything together, doesn't it?"

"What, exactly, do you know about the diary?"

Sam chuckled. "Maggie did some lucid dreaming last night. She said whoever searched Beverly Nevins's room at the hotel found the diary and hid it right here in this house. Amazing."

Arthur did not move. "You're hallucinating."

"I know." Sam massaged his temples with his fingertips and tried to sit down on the chair. He ended up falling into it. He leaned his head against the back and closed his eyes.

"Maggie is the real deal," he said. "Not a fake like you." He opened his eyes. "But then you already know that, don't you? It's why you want to seduce her. You want to control her so that you can use her to build your empire here at the Institute. If you get Maggie, you'll have a genuine psychic dream reader. You won't have to rely on a phony like yourself."

"That's ridiculous."

"What's wrong with the ceiling?" Sam said.

Arthur watched him closely. "What do you mean?"

"It's disappearing." Sam squinted. "You're floating in midair."

"About time," Arthur muttered.

"What?"

"Listen to me, Sage. You're hallucinating because I put a double dose of the enhancer in your scotch and soda."

"Is that right?"

"In a few minutes you will be too drugged to make sense. But first we need to talk."

"About Oxlade? You killed him, didn't you? Your wife murdered the others, but you hammered Oxlade to death."

"That's how I got his supply of the drug. Hated to waste two doses of the stuff on you, but I need answers and dosage can be tricky. Consider me your dream guide. I'll ask the questions. You will provide the answers."

Sam smiled and spread his hands. "I'm an open book."

"What else did Maggie tell you about the diary?"

"She said it was hidden in a very dark place. A safe, probably."

Arthur stiffened. "She said it was in a safe?"

"She wasn't positive, but it makes sense, doesn't it? I mean, where else would you hide such a potentially dangerous object?"

Arthur's jaw clenched. "Did she tell Detective Brandon about her dream?"

"Nope. Brandon doesn't believe in psychic dreaming. Something's happening to you, Guilfoyle. You're fading a little. Are you traveling on the astral plane?"

"Where is Miss Lodge right now?"

"At the hotel, packing. We're leaving for Adelina Beach when I get back."

"Good," Arthur said. "There's time."

"Time for what?"

"To make sure she doesn't talk to Brandon. Once you're out of the picture I will deal with Margaret Lodge."

"But I'm in the picture."

"Not for much longer." A fever burned in Arthur's eyes. He took a pistol out from under his coat. "On your feet."

Sam used both hands in an effort to push himself up out of the big chair. When he showed signs of sinking back onto the cushions, Arthur clamped a hand around one of his arms and hauled him to his feet.

"I said get up, you interfering bastard," Arthur muttered.

"Where are we going?" Sam asked.

"We will take a walk through the garden," he said. "We will go out the gate and then you will jump off the cliff into the sea. Who knows where your body will wash ashore? When it does it will look like suicide or an accident."

"The work of the Traveler, huh?"

"It will be interesting to see if those rumors circulate. Unlike Oxlade, I don't think of that old legend as a problem. It adds drama. Gives me a certain mystique."

Sam staggered a little. Arthur tightened his grip.

"Pushing me off a cliff is neat and tidy. Not messy like what you did to Oxlade. You're getting better at this kind of thing."

Arthur's eyes glittered. "Oxlade made me angry."

Sam nodded in solemn understanding. "You lost control. You're as insane as your wife."

Arthur's face twisted. "Shut up."

"Did you enjoy using the hammer on Oxlade?" Sam asked.

"It was very satisfying," Arthur said. "But not nearly as satisfying as watching you go over the cliff will be."

"I don't feel like jumping off a cliff," Sam said.

"You will when the time comes. You'll think you're flying. A real out-of-body experience."

"Because of the enhancer you used to doctor my scotch and soda?"

"Exactly. You must be hallucinating like crazy by now."

"Not really." Sam stopped slurring his words. "I can't say I was impressed with Dashiell Hammett's detective in *The Maltese Falcon*, but I did pick up a couple of pointers. The main one being that it's a bad idea to drink a cocktail the bad guy fixes for you. However, if you do drink it, make sure you know what's in it."

"What are you talking about?" Arthur hissed.

"I found Oxlade's cologne bottle before you did," Sam said. "I emptied the drug down the sink, rinsed out the bottle, and refilled it with tap water. Odorless and colorless. Looks just like the enhancer drug. Found the bottle and the diary when I cracked your safe last night. Left them both there to set you up. Didn't have to put Maggie to the trouble of doing a lucid dream. I lied about that. Got the answers the old-fashioned way—I looked for them."

Arthur released Sam's arm and took a couple of steps back. He raised the pistol. "You're lying."

"Your wife was an expert on sedatives and narcotics because she used to work for a doctor, but the enhancer is the only drug you're familiar with. Also, you were convinced you could use it to get answers. I figured you wouldn't be able to resist giving me a dose of the stuff when you fixed the drinks."

"You think you're so fucking smart?"

"No, but I've got pretty good intuition. Not infallible, but good."

Arthur scrambled back a few more steps. "You're a dead man."

He pulled the trigger. There was a distinct click followed by several more clicks as he jerked the trigger again and again.

Detective Brandon and two uniformed officers appeared on the terrace and walked through the open doors.

"That'll be enough of that nonsense," Brandon said. "Arthur Guilfoyle or Arthur Ellis or whatever the hell your name is, you're under arrest for the murder of Dr. Emerson Oxlade and the attempted murder of Sam Sage. There will be some other charges, too, but we'll talk about that later."

Arthur stared at Sam, stunned. "How?"

"I found the pistol in your desk drawer when I searched your office last night," Sam said. "Seemed like a good idea to remove the cartridges. I was reasonably certain you wouldn't think to check the pistol, because you're sloppy and impulsive. Not good with details."

Arthur roared, a primal scream of rage. He jerked free of the officers' grip, seized the iron poker from the stand on the hearth, and charged Sam.

"Shit," Sam said. "Not again."

He dove for the carpet. The poker punched the air overhead. Arthur was thrown off balance when he missed his target. He tried frantically to recover and swing the poker. Sam grabbed one of his ankles and yanked him off his feet. He landed hard on the tile floor.

The officers seized him and wrestled him into handcuffs.

Brandon looked at Sam. "You said odds were good he'd try to make a run for it when he realized he'd lost control of the situation today. Doesn't look like that's what happened."

"What can I tell you?" Sam brushed off his trousers and straightened his tie. "It's been a screwy case from the start."

"Maybe you should stick with divorce work."

"I've been advised not to take those jobs."

"Yeah?" Brandon eyed him. "Who told you that?"

"Aunt Cornelia."

Brandon nodded. "My wife says you can't go wrong with Aunt Cornelia's advice."

Chapter 49

"What is it with you and household furnishings?" Maggie asked. "First a coatrack and now a poker."

"I'm not sure what's going on," Sam said. He drank some iced tea and settled deeper into the cushions of the lounge chair. "But when we get back to Adelina Beach, I think I'll get rid of any item that could be used to crack my skull. No point taking chances."

They were reclining side by side on the private patio of a guest villa at the legendary Burning Cove Hotel. The secluded suite at the luxury resort had been provided courtesy of Luther Pell, whose connections apparently included not only high-ranking figures in the underworld but also the management of the hotel.

Maggie had made the decision to accept the invitation to spend a couple of extra days in Burning Cove, and Sam was determined to enjoy every minute of it. He had no idea what would happen when they returned to Adelina Beach, but for now he was living a real-life dream with Maggie.

The morning fog had burned off. The scent of citrus trees wafted on the warm breeze. Palms shaded the grounds. He and Maggie had reservations for dinner at the hotel restaurant. Later they would take a taxi to the Paradise Club, where they would join Luther Pell and Raina Kirk for drinks and dancing.

This was the fantasy of Southern California life, the dream the studios and the resorts and the travel agencies sold to the rest of the country and the world. It was, Sam thought, a damn good fantasy—it felt real—but it wouldn't have worked without the woman beside him.

Life was good—for now. But the future was in Adelina Beach, and he wasn't sure what to expect when reality descended. He had to find a way to keep Maggie close. He needed a plan.

Maggie picked up her glass of iced tea. "Call me psychic, but I have a feeling your previous unfortunate encounter with furniture—the coatrack incident—is somehow connected to the reason you decided to open a private investigation agency in Adelina Beach."

"Lucky guess," he said.

"Intuition," she said.

"Okay, maybe intuition."

"I told you how I wound up in Adelina Beach. Feel like telling me how you got there?"

He went silent for a moment, sorting through the bits and pieces of the past that he stored in his personal mental attic.

"It's messy," he warned.

"So was my story, if you will recall."

"I told you I used to be a homicide cop in L.A. I led a small team that rescued a woman who had been kidnapped for ransom. Elizabeth was the daughter of a wealthy industrialist. Afterward she decided I was a hero. I liked being one. It didn't hurt that she was beautiful and glamorous and exciting."

"The two of you fell in love?"

"Or something that felt like love. Her parents objected, of course. Mine were not exactly enthusiastic, either. We ran off to Reno to get married. It was a mistake. Her family was furious. They were sure I was after her money."

"What about your family?"

"My parents have a farm in Washington State, just outside of Walla Walla. They're big on common sense. They knew the marriage was headed for disaster, but after the deed was done they tried to be supportive. Things started falling apart right at the start. It rapidly became apparent I didn't fit in with Elizabeth's high-society crowd and she didn't approve of my job."

"She fell for a hero and then discovered heroes come with a side of reality," Maggie said. "You were enchanted with the beautiful princess you saved and then found out that princesses are real people, too."

"You sound like an advice columnist," he said.

"I do, don't I?"

"Things went from fantasy to reality in a matter of months. Elizabeth wanted me to quit my job and take a position in her father's company. I declined. Couldn't see myself sitting in an office all day long working on budgets, marketing, contracts, and all the rest of the stuff that goes with business. Elizabeth's parents insisted on giving us a very nice, very big house. Elizabeth redid my wardrobe so that I wouldn't embarrass her at social gatherings."

Maggie smiled. "But you managed to do that anyway."

He held up one finger. "Another lucky guess. As I was saying, things continued on a downward trajectory. Then I got saddled with the Chichester case. Still listening? Let me know if I'm boring you."

"I'm riveted," Maggie said.

"Why?"

"I'm always intrigued by drama, real or fictional. Character flaw."

"Because you're a writer?"

"Yep. And don't try to tell me you don't have the same quirk."

He turned his head to look at her. "What makes you say that?"

"Simple. You became a cop, and now you're a private detective. Talk about career paths that are focused on human drama. What makes us different from other people is that we are compelled to find answers and fix the problems that create the drama. We want to somehow make things right. I try to do it in my writing. You do it every time you take a case."

He considered that for a long moment. "Hadn't thought of it that way."

"Go on with your story."

"There's not much more to tell. I was assigned to what became known as the Bloody Scarf Murders. The killer sliced his victims to death with a knife, soaked scarves in their blood, and tied them around the women's throats."

"I remember the headlines," Maggie said.

"There were a lot of them after I arrested Chichester. He was out on bail within hours. The family was furious. He managed to find the address of the house where I had been living with Elizabeth. He planned to murder her. It was his idea of punishing me. But she had moved back into her parents' mansion by then. I was the only one in the house. Chichester came after me instead. He had a knife. There was a struggle. I used the coatrack to defend myself. In the end we fought for control of the damn thing. I won."

"That explains why I couldn't sort out the sources of the shadows on the coatrack," Maggie said, looking satisfied. "You both handled it during the struggle."

He let that go. "Elizabeth went to Reno. I moved out of the house. Six weeks later we were divorced. I picked up my last paycheck and moved to Adelina Beach. Took the wardrobe and the coatrack with me. That's it, the whole story, and if it winds up in a confession magazine or in that novel you're writing—"

"I told you, I always change the names to protect the innocent."

"Somehow that does not reassure me."

She smiled. "But it doesn't scare the daylights out of you."

"Don't be too sure of that."

"I don't frighten you, do I?"

"I seem to recall telling you that you were hard on the nerves."

"But you've got nerves of steel."

"Maybe not steel."

Maggie watched him, her eyes unreadable behind the sunglasses. "For the record, you don't scare me, either."

He put his glass down on the table, sat up on the edge of the lounge chair, reached out, and used both hands to remove her sunglasses. There was no laughter in her eyes. She was intent. Serious. Determined.

"What is that supposed to mean?" he said.

"It means I trust you."

"That's good," he said. "That's very nice."

"Nice?"

"As far as it goes. I was hoping for more."

She touched his hand. "How much more?"

He gripped her fingers. "I love you, Maggie. I know it's too early to say that. You need time. But I'm hoping—dreaming—that maybe you might be able to fall in love with me one of these days."

Her eyes glowed. "You're too late."

"Too late?"

"I'm already there," she said. "I started falling in love with you the day I hired you."

"Maggie."

He got to his feet and pulled her up off the lounge chair. He wrapped his arms around her and kissed her there in the warm, golden light of the California sun. When she responded, he knew he was no longer caught in a dream. Maggie was real. Love was real.

After a while he set her gently away from him and willed her to understand what he was about to say.

"Just so you know, I asked Raina Kirk to make some more phone calls," he said.

Maggie watched him, her eyes shadowed with curiosity and concern. "Why?" she said.

He told her.

Chapter 50

M aggie was still floating on a tide of joy later that evening when she and Sam joined Raina Kirk and Luther Pell in Pell's private booth at the Paradise Club. The day had been perfect, and the night was proving to be even better.

The table, located on the mezzanine, overlooked the main floor of the club. The glamorous scene was cloaked in intimate shadows. The mirror ball above the dance floor showered the couples in drops of jeweled light. The orchestra played a torch song.

Maggie was enjoying her pink lady cocktail and listening to Luther Pell discuss the possibility of doing some business with Sage Investigations when Raina delivered her bombshell.

"I made the phone calls you requested, Sam," Raina said. "Your hunch was right. There is no record of Lillian Dewhurst boarding the ocean liner she was supposed to have sailed on or any other ship that sailed the week she left Adelina Beach. I haven't been able to locate her, but I'm quite certain she isn't in the South Pacific."

Maggie stilled, horrified. "Dear heaven. Dolores Guilfoyle murdered her, too."

"I don't think so," Sam said.

Chapter 51

illian opened the door of the beach house, a sad, knowing smile edging her mouth. "I wondered when you two would show up. I've been trying to work up the courage to call you, Maggie. Come in."

Maggie and Sam followed her into the living room. The windows overlooked a wide stretch of sand and the sea beyond. In the distance was the small town of Keeley Point.

"Please sit down," Lillian said. "I'll make tea."

"I'll help you," Maggie said.

They prepared the tea tray in silence. Maggie knew Lillian was composing herself, deciding how she would tell her story. There was no hurry.

By the time they returned to the living room, Lillian seemed ready. She sat down and poured the tea.

"How did you find me?" she asked.

"It was the Astral Travelers Society bracelet that I urged you to throw into the ocean," Maggie said. "You told me it wasn't yours. You said it was a memento of someone you cared about. There was so much dark energy attached to it that I knew something bad had happened to the person who had worn it."

Lillian sighed. "The bracelet linked me to Keeley Point and Virginia's death."

"Sam was sure you were still in the country and probably not far away," Maggie said. "He had a feeling you were the one who hired Phyllis Gaines to play Aunt Cornelia."

"It wasn't what anyone would call a great piece of detective work," Sam said. "It boiled down to the fact that you were the only person who knew you had never sailed to the South Pacific and you were also the only one who had a motive for hiring an out-of-work actress to pose as Cornelia."

"You figured out my motive?" Lillian asked, startled.

"Revenge," Sam said.

"I went through your files and found the tax records relating to this beach house," Maggie said. "It seemed likely that, if you were hiding out, you might come back to Keeley Point, the place where it all started."

Sam sat down and looked at Lillian. "When I made the first phone call to the Keeley Point police, I was told the body of Virginia Jennaway had been found by a relative who was no longer in town. You're the one who discovered her on the beach, aren't you?"

"Virginia was my half sister," Lillian said. "Same mother but different fathers, so yes, our last names were different. Virginia and I were both fascinated with dreams, and we both got involved in the Astral Travelers Society for a time."

"That's how you met the Guilfoyles," Sam said.

"We knew them as Dolores Johnson and Arthur Ellis. They were selling Ellis as the Dream Master in those days. He promised to teach people how to use their dreams to access their psychic senses."

"The same thing he was selling as the Guilfoyle Method," Maggie said.

"I realized early on that he was a con," Lillian continued. "But Virginia fell for him and his promise of psychic powers. He seduced her.

Told her she was the woman of his dreams. She wasn't the only one in the Society who found him irresistible."

"Eleanor Nevins did, too," Maggie said.

"I was in L.A. the night Virginia died," Lillian continued. "I was to join her here at the beach house the next day. I arrived early and found her body."

"You suspected Arthur Ellis had murdered her, but you couldn't prove it," Maggie said.

"Of course I blamed him," Lillian said. "I despised that man. But even then I wasn't sure he was the one who had carried out the murder. He was certainly capable of drugging her. He used Oxlade's enhancer on us while pretending to teach us how to open our psychic pathways. I hated the stuff. That's why I dropped out of the Society. But if he was the one who had killed Virginia, it seemed more likely he would have strangled her or pushed her off a cliff."

"Because he's the impulsive type," Sam said.

"Yes," Lillian said. "The drowning struck me as more . . . complicated, if you know what I mean."

"I know exactly what you mean," Sam said.

"You knew you could never prove Virginia had been murdered," Maggie said. "When did you realize the Guilfoyles were the same people who had set up the Dream Master operation in Keeley Point?"

"When the photo of them appeared in the *Adelina Beach Courier* I recognized them as the same con artists I had known as Dolores Johnson and Arthur Ellis," Lillian said. "It was obvious they were launching an even bigger con with the Guilfoyle Method. And then they announced that Oxlade would be giving a guest lecture during the opening conference at the Institute."

"You realized the three of them were working together again," Sam said. "And for a few days they would be in one place in Burning Cove."

"All I could think of was that I finally had the opportunity to punish all three of them for what they had done to Virginia. I pretended to book the ocean voyage so that Maggie wouldn't find out what I was going to do." Lillian looked at Maggie. "I didn't want you involved in any way. You made it easy for me because you had already decided not to attend the conference."

"Because I found out Emerson Oxlade would be there," Maggie said.

Lillian shut her eyes briefly. When she opened them, there was a sheen of tears. "I didn't have any intention of getting anyone killed. I just wanted to punish those three dreadful people. I wasn't at all sure my plan would work, but I had to try."

"It occurred to you that Aunt Cornelia might have the power to label the Guilfoyle Method a fraud," Sam said.

"If Aunt Cornelia advised her thousands of loyal readers not to allow themselves to be fooled by the Guilfoyles, it would do a lot of damage to the Institute," Maggie said. "If she moved fast and struck at the very beginning, there was a chance the business could be destroyed before it got up and running, before it attracted the attention of celebrities. Oxlade's reputation would have gone down along with that of the Guilfoyles."

"I still don't know if it would have worked," Lillian said. Her mouth twisted in a humorless smile. "They were in the dreams-and-drugs business, and nothing sells better. Nevertheless, I decided to try."

"You had a problem, though, because you knew Oxlade and the Guilfoyles would recognize you if you showed up at the conference in Burning Cove," Maggie said. "So you hired Phyllis Gaines to play the part of Aunt Cornelia."

"That turned out to be a mistake, obviously." Lillian shook her head. "Actors."

"Phyllis really got into her role, and the next thing you knew, the news that the famous Aunt Cornelia was seen partying at the hottest nightclub in Burning Cove was in the papers," Sam said.

"I was stunned," Lillian said. "I underestimated the public's fascination with Aunt Cornelia. When the photo of Phyllis at the Paradise Club went national, all I could do was hope you wouldn't notice, Maggie, or, if you did, trust that you wouldn't try to confront her. After all, you knew you couldn't prove she wasn't Aunt Cornelia without revealing my real identity."

"I couldn't ignore the imposter or the blackmail threat," Maggie said. "I had to do something."

Lillian gave her a wry smile. "Because you're Maggie."

"Yep," Sam said. He exchanged a knowing look with Lillian. "Because she's Maggie."

Maggie glared at him. He ignored her.

"I was following the news from Burning Cove as best I could in the Keeley Point paper," Lillian continued. "When I read a woman had died at the conference, I didn't know what to think. It was just a tiny headline, so I told myself it had nothing to do with my plan. Then the news that Aunt Cornelia had been exposed as an imposter and had left town hit. That made the front page here. It was on the radio, too. Phyllis was home by then. I called her and she told me she had been confronted by a private investigator from Adelina Beach. She said there was a woman with him. The description matched you, Maggie."

"You realized I was in Burning Cove and I was not alone," Maggie said. "I had brought a private detective with me."

"I knew I had lost control of the situation," Lillian said.

"Don't feel bad," Sam said. "That happens a lot around Maggie. You get used to it."

Maggie shot him a repressive look. Sam was oblivious.

"The next thing I know, Oxlade is dead and the Guilfoyles have been arrested," Lillian said. "I'm so sorry you were dragged into the mess, Maggie. Please believe me when I say I never intended for you to be put in danger."

"I know that," Maggie said. "The Guilfoyles and Oxlade and the Institute went down in flames and people died, but not because of what you did or didn't do. They destroyed themselves with the help of a blackmailer named Beverly Nevins."

"The murder of Virginia Jennaway lit a long-burning fuse," Sam said. "Took a while for the explosion to occur, but in the end, it did."

Lillian looked at him. "I hadn't thought of it like that. It's almost enough to make one believe in the Traveler. He will kill for you, but there's a price."

"We both know there is no such spirit as the Traveler," Maggie said.

"I've been afraid to return to Adelina Beach," Lillian said. She looked at Maggie. "I couldn't face you. You had freed me from my nightmares, and I had lied to you and very nearly got you killed. I didn't know what to do. But deep down I sensed you would find me and I would have to explain everything."

"And now you have," Maggie said. "So stop fretting. Your readers need you. It's time to come home to Adelina Beach and go back to work. You were born to write the Dear Aunt Cornelia column."

"Sounds like good advice, if you ask me," Sam said.

Lillian's eyes glittered with tears. She smiled a tremulous smile.

"Yes, it does," she said. She got to her feet. "I'll go pack."

Maggie smiled. "Sometimes people really do take good advice."

Lillian paused. "This is probably none of my business, but I think I should tell you that something about the two of you feels very right."

Sam was amused. "Got some advice for us, Aunt Cornelia?"

"I don't think you need it," Lillian said. "I have a feeling you've already figured it out on your own."

Sam looked at Maggie. "Yes, we have."

Maggie stood. "I'll help you pack. It's a long drive to Adelina Beach. We should get on the road."

"What's the rush?" Lillian said.

"For one thing, I want to get back to my novel," Maggie said. "I've been away from it for too long. I have so many new ideas for the characters and the plot."

Sam shuddered. "Words that send chills of dread down the spine."

Maggie laughed, joy and certainty stirring her senses. "There's another reason we have to go home. Sam and I have an appointment at the courthouse in a few days. Lots to do to prepare for the wedding."

Lillian looked at her with understanding and something akin to wonder.

"You're getting married?" she asked. "You, of all people?"

"Of course." Maggie smiled at Sam. "I found my hero—a man who isn't afraid of me or my dreams."

Sam laughed and got to his feet. He walked to where she stood and brushed his mouth lightly, intimately across hers.

"I love you but I am not entirely fearless," he said. "I'll do the driving on the way back to Adelina Beach."

Maggie patted his arm and looked at Lillian. "Poor Sam has a delicate stomach. He gets carsick easily unless he's the one behind the wheel."

Lillian gave Sam a knowing smile. "I see."

"Sam is not the most exciting driver in the world, but you can trust him to get you to your destination," Maggie said.

"That's all that matters, isn't it?" Lillian said. "Trust is everything."

"Absolutely." Maggie smiled at Sam and was warmed by the heat in his eyes. "It's everything."

Discover a breathtaking romantic suspense series by Jayne Ann Krentz ...

Praise for the Cutler, Sutter & Salinas series:

'Jayne Ann Krentz is one of my favourite romantic suspense writers. I love her **feisty heroines, her sharp wit and humour,** family loyalty, and all the unexpected twists and turns. *When All the Girls Have Gone* has all of this and more and **will keep you guessing right until the end**'
—Meg Tilly on *When All The Girls Have Gone*

'**The master of romantic suspense** ... Krentz dives into sociopathic psychology and complex characterization to great effect in this twisty story, whose plot clips along at a **terrific pace**'
—*BookPage* on *Promise Not To Tell*

'A couple to root for, a tiny hint of the supernatural, **a page-burning plot** ... a **sexy, heart-warming romance**'
—*Kirkus Reviews* on *Untouchable*

Do you love historical fiction?

Want the chance to hear news about your favourite
authors (and the chance to win free books)?

Suzanne Allain
Mary Balogh
Lenora Bell
Charlotte Betts
Manda Collins
Joanna Courtney
Grace Burrowes
Evie Dunmore
Lynne Francis
Pamela Hart
Elizabeth Hoyt
Eloisa James
Lisa Kleypas
Jayne Ann Krentz
Sarah MacLean
Terri Nixon
Julia Quinn

Then visit the Piatkus website
www.yourswithlove.co.uk

And follow us on Facebook and Instagram
www.facebook.com/yourswithlovex | @yourswithlovex

PIATKUS